CIRCUS SAVE ME

HER FREAKS BOOK 1

ERIN O'KANE AND K.A. KNIGHT

Circus Save Me (Her Freaks Book One).

Written by K.A. Knight & Erin O'Kane
Edited By Jess from Elemental Editing and Proofreading.
Proofreading by Norma's Nook Proofreading LLC
Formatted by The Nutty Formatter
Cover by Jay Aheer at Simply Defined Art

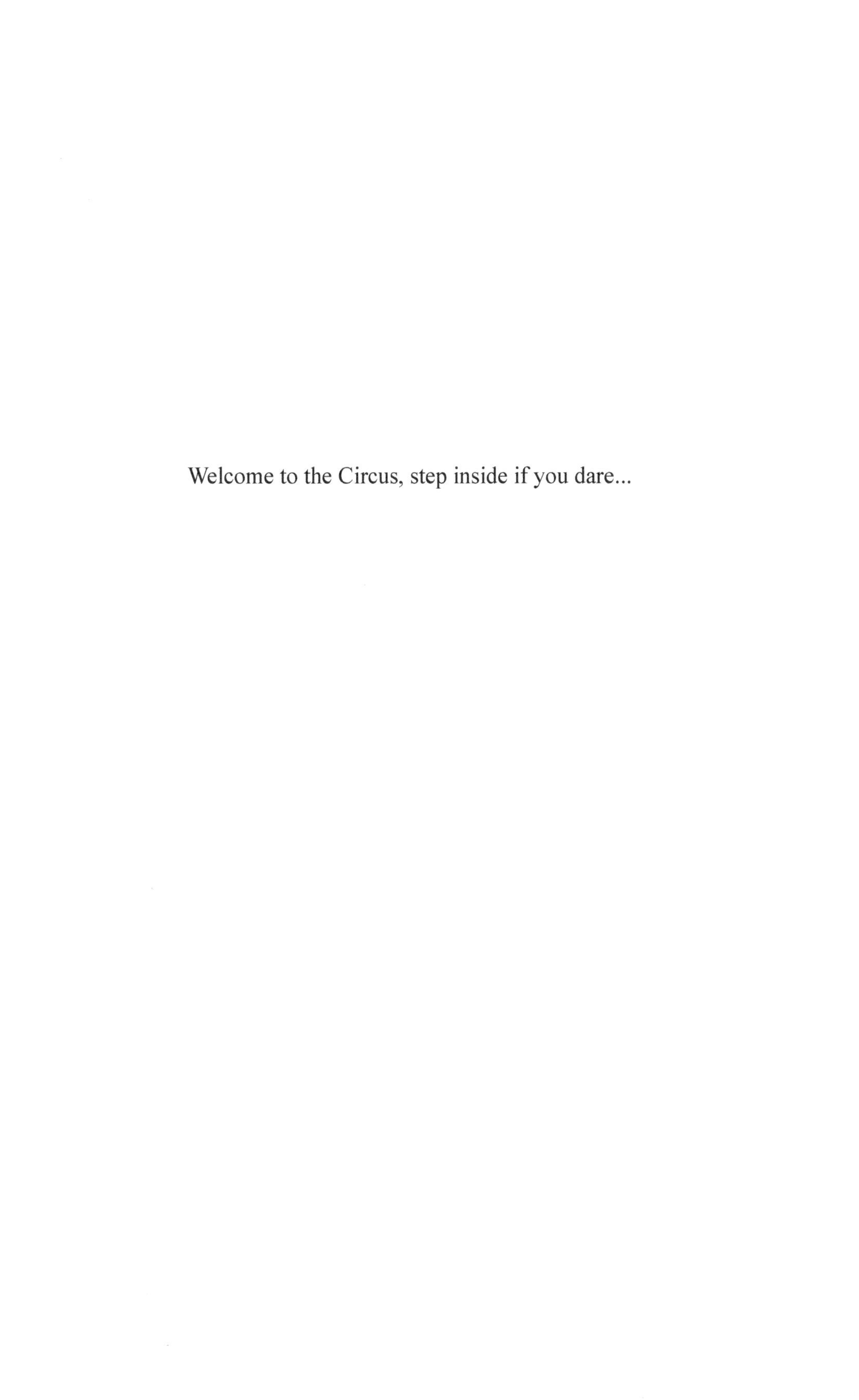

Welcome to the Circus, step inside if you dare...

WORLD DAILY NEWS

World War Three declared, with America and Russia stating that peace is no longer in the cards.

Updated: 1 hour ago

After much debate and political unrest between the two countries, it all came to a climax today with Russian President Vasiliev claiming peace is no longer an option.

America reiterated the message which claimed that Vasiliev is unwilling to accept blame for his part in the bombings which happened only three months ago in Washington D.C.

The bombing was a result of the civil unrest currently prevalent in Russia and America, with Russia claiming America struck first. The attack left the capital in chaos and panic, with the death toll at over 500 civilians. Talks of peace and a truce were rumored until the Russian President went live on air to declare war on the other country.

So, what does this mean for the rest of the world? It looks like World War Three is on the cards, with the two countries possessing the biggest arsenal of weapons and nuclear material, the results could be catastrophic. Japan have already sided with Russia and France with America. Germany among other countries are still deciding. Only time will tell how far they are willing to take this.

The British Prime Minister has warned the public not to panic, advising that the government is in meetings now, discussing how to handle this new information and possible threat. With an emergency Cobra meeting in session, it looks like we are left to wait and see what the future of Britain, and possibly the whole world, will look like.

In other news, scientists claim they have found the future. With new genetic material being grown, human life expectancy is set to be doubled when human trials are given the green light.

**Read more here >
View Comments
Related Topics**

Chapter One

Thirty-five years later...

I brush the tangled locks of hair from my face, trying to get a better view of the unending task before me. My body aches from hours of physical labour as I sit back on my heels and scowl at the dirty footprints that are being tracked onto the freshly cleaned kitchen floor. My hard work erased in a moment. Frederick will have my hide if the floor isn't spotless when he comes in for his dinner. I remember the last time I wasn't quick enough for Frederick, and the newly healed skin on my back throbs in response.

No point in complaining about something that can't be fixed. As I am always reminded, I am lucky to be alive, and if that means working for someone like Frederick, and keeps me off the streets, then so be it. There is always someone less fortunate. At least, that's what I keep telling myself.

With renewed vigor, I start scrubbing at the floor again when some of Frederick's men walk into the room. Keeping my head down, I continue with my work, not wanting to call unwanted attention to myself. I don't think Frederick would ever let one of his lackeys truly hurt me, not out of loyalty to me, but because of what I bring to his business. As one of the few women in this shithole of a settlement, it grants him power that others don't have, and as part of that, I am protected. If I die, he loses that power. That doesn't stop him from getting rough with me when I don't follow his rules, but he has stepped in a few times when a patron wasn't going to take no for an answer.

Two pairs of dirty leather boots appear next to where I am crouched on the floor. I slow my scrubbing, tightly gripping the worn-out brush as if it's my lifeline. Without raising my head, I try to see who has been sent to me today. In my experience there are three types of men left in this world. Most will just leave me alone with a disdainful look or shove out of the way. Others have more violent tendencies, especially towards women, it's best to avoid them. Then there are the friendly ones. Those are the ones to look out for, they are by far the most dangerous. It will start with a smile, or a small gift, and before you know it, you are cornered in a back alley with no one to protect you.

Thankfully for me, both of these men fit in the first category.

"Get up. He wants to see you." Grunt one barks, shoving my shoulder.

With a small gasp I fall forward onto the dirty floor, supporting myself on my hands and knees. I stay in this position, not wanting to antagonize them.

"See? She does know her place after all," the other henchman comments, and I can practically hear the smirk in his voice.

A bolt of anger and disgust fills me at their comments. I should be used to this by now, yet a small part of me kicks and screams to be unleashed on these men that think they own me. Pushing these dangerous thoughts aside, I sit back on my heels and look up at the men. I am playing with fire by looking them in the eyes, but I'm still angry and it makes me bold. The men run their eyes over me and I fight back a shudder. My shapeless tunic covers my body to my ankles, but my hair and delicate facial features do nothing to disguise the fact that I am a woman.

I brace myself for a backhand that never comes, it must be my lucky day. Either that or whatever Frederick has planned for me is worse. I swallow back my fear at the thought and get to my feet, unsteady after hours of being on my knees.

Being ushered out of the meager kitchen, I stumble through the narrow corridors of the tavern Frederick runs his business out of. It's not much to look at, and it's certainly seen better days, but it's the best that we have. People want somewhere they can go to gamble and drown their sorrows, and that's exactly what Frederick gives them. Well, what he gives the richer people; the poorer ones go to the tavern in the middle of the settlement. We can't have them mixing with the rich, can we?

The two men behind me stay quiet, occasionally pushing their makeshift weapons into my lower back, a constant reminder that they are in charge in this situation. As if I needed a reminder that I have no power here.

We arrive outside of Frederick's office and a sense of trepidation fills me. I'm not brought here often, and when I have been it's never for good reasons. His office is for business, and in this world, women have no place unless they are being sold. I have been lucky so far in my twenty-two years on this dead world. Frederick bought me from my last owner years ago, and I have never been at risk to be sold or had to use my 'womanly wiles', but I feel my luck may be coming to an end. Patrons have been offering to 'rent' my services for years now, and so far, Frederick has turned them down, saying they can't afford the fee. One of these days, someone is going to have something that Frederick wants, and he will use me as a bargaining chip.

"Come in," I hear from behind the door and my heart leaps into my mouth.

I shouldn't be surprised that he knows we are outside the door, he always seems to know when we are nearby. I suspect that he was 'altered' by the blast all those years ago. He certainly has the scars to support that theory. Not that anybody would dare accuse him of being 'altered', not if they value their lives.

I walk into the office, aware of Frederick's eyes on me as I take in my surroundings. The room is opulent. Well, as opulent as you can get in a post-apocalyptic wasteland. There are candles everywhere and books lining the walls. Two worn leather sofas fill the room, and there is a large, lacquered desk over by the window. Frederick watches in silence as I enter the room, my head held high and my walk confident. He may own me, but I will not be cowed.

"Girl. Look at me," he orders.

He never calls me Rhea, only Girl, or Slave. There is power in a name, and he knows this. His deep voice sends shivers down my spine. It's a voice that is used to getting what it wants and being obeyed without question. The rumors say he was close to the blast when it went off and that the blast burnt his vocal chords, which is why his voice sounds so deep and raspy now. I tend not to listen to the rumors, they only get you in trouble.

Doing as ordered, I raise my eyes to meet his. For someone who was so badly scarred, he takes great pride in his appearance, and I think this just adds to his reputation. Standing at over six feet tall, he is intimidating at the best of times. His long, greying dark hair and neatly trimmed moustache and beard only add to this. Piercing, steely grey eyes bore into me and I have the distinct impression that I am being tested.

I hold his gaze for four of the longest seconds of my life before I drop my eyes, focusing on my battered shoes. I obviously pass whatever test he intended for me, as I see him nod to himself out of the corner of my eye.

"I need you to go to the market and pick up a package for me."

I glance up at him in shock. All of this to send me to market? Could he not send one of his trusted men to do this? To choose to send a woman to the market, when he had several able bodied men that could do it for him, was an odd decision.

Is he testing me? Sending me out of the house is a risk, one he is apparently willing to take.

"Why?" I ask, the question slipping from my lips before I can stop it.

Pushing up from behind the desk, Frederick slowly walks towards me. I shouldn't have said anything, just been the meek slave that the world expects me to be, but my anger from earlier is still running through my system, making me bold. I keep my eyes down, but clench my fists, the only sign of my rebellion to subservience.

"Do I need to remind you of your place?" His gravelly voice asks as he circles around me, like a predator tracking his prey.

I remain quiet, knowing I will only provoke him if I say anything. Besides, I don't trust myself not to say something that will put me in further trouble.

He remains behind me. He must be standing still as I can't hear him moving. He does this to unnerve me, and it works. I can feel my heart speed up as my mind goes into overdrive thinking of what he might be planning to do.

A sharp crack fills the room as his hand meets my cheek and a white light fills my vision. Falling to my knees, I cradle my face. I must have really pissed him off for him to hit my face. Usually he keeps to areas that are covered. Staying quiet, I press my face to the ground so not to antagonize him further.

With a sigh, he walks back to his desk, wiping his hands on a small towel he keeps there. He acts like I made him punish me; like this is something he would rather not do.

"Go to the market. Thomas knows you are coming, he will give you what I need," his order is a clear dismissal.

I hurry to my feet, my face burning both from the slap and from my wounded pride. Avoiding the eyes of Frederick and the two smirking lackeys waiting outside of the room, I hurry away before I do something that will get me killed.

Leaving the town house through the old slave entrance, I tug my hood up to cover my bright hair. Being spotted and recognized as a woman will only bring me more problems and I don't have the time to deal with them if I want to get back to avoid a punishment. My worn brown cloak offers me little protection from the heat bearing down on me; instead it makes my body sweaty and uncomfortable. The cracked steps leading down to the broken pavement mean I have to tread carefully so not to fall and hurt myself. The fence is rusted and mangled, but the gate still works, even if it does creak worse than the floorboards in my room - if you can call a basement that. I shouldn't complain, Frederick isn't too bad, he doesn't force himself on me even if he is handsy, and I am at least earning a meager wage.

Pulling open the gate, I wince at the noise before gently shutting it behind me. With a glance at the street behind me, showing me the row of undamaged town houses that the rich and powerful occupy, I turn to face the settlement I call home. The road is partly paved, even if holes and cracks run along its surface. I trudge along, reminding myself it could be worse. The large houses slowly turn into smaller houses the closer to the poorer side of town you get, and the pavement ends in a giant crater where one of the pre-war bombs dropped. I carefully pick my way around it, the remaining few trees swaying in the breeze next to me. Crows squawk on their branches, watching me as I walk.

The road eventually splits into four dirt paths, each heading to a different part of the settlement. I quickly cross the section and head down the one that leads to the center of town, the buildings turning into the shacks of the poor. Still, it's better than living outside the protection of the settlement. Although it would be much easier to traverse these roads in the car that Frederick and his lackeys use, instead my feet burn and my calves ache since I've already been up since dawn working.

Men's voices reach me as I turn onto the dirt road. Ducking my head, I let the hood obscure my face. Keeping to the edge of the road, I grip the edge of my cloak carefully, my hands turning sweaty. The temporary boldness I was feeling from being away from Frederick and his guards flees at the thought of being alone with random men. Luckily, they pass by, completely ignoring me, my cape marking me as someone's property offering me the desired protection.

The road stops at the center of Cinders, the shacks here mixed in with old buildings that were not destroyed when the bombs dropped. Stalls populate the main square where the vendors and travelers sell their wares, and traditional shops line the way with the tavern for the poor smack bang in the middle of the square. Men bustle back and forth, busy with their tasks, laughing and joking between themselves. There are no other women present, the only other women who live in Cinders work in the tavern. Anxiety courses through me, as does a sense of elation at being away from Frederick's watchful eyes. It allows me some freedom, and covered as I am, I can dally a little and maybe even spend some of the money I have saved. The breeze rustles my hood, the blonde ends of my hair twirling in it. A smile stretches across my face as a small boy chases a little girl through the man's legs in front of me; the boy with a wooden sword and the girl with a princess tiara. My boldness returns, the meek slave retreating as my shoulders straighten and my inquisitive nature surfaces. I know I shouldn't stare, I should lower my eyes, but something in me screams for once not to give in.

"Daddy, why can't I have a sword, too?" She whines, tugging on the stocky man's pant leg. He looks around before crouching before her.

"Shhh, Angelina, girls like you and your momma don't need a sword, now do they?"

"But why?"

"The men will protect you. Why don't you go look at some dresses?" His face is filled with hope as he watches her. She frowns at him, her bottom lip poking out in a pout as her face twists.

"But I want to fight too, Daddy. I'm stwrong like Peter!" She stomps her foot, her pink dress swaying with the motion.

"You should teach her her place, and soon." The man her father is standing with warns, the disgust evident on his face as he watches the girl. "She should be seen and not heard, remember that next time you come to do business." Her father bows his head in shame and whispers to the girl.

Anger burns through me, but I quickly swallow it. I've been taught my place many times, even if the little girl's thoughts echo my own. It isn't that kind of world anymore. The stories and hushed whispers from the cook where I lived before are the only reason I know anything of the world from before the war. Where women were fighting for equality and could do and love as they wished, where they were free to be what they wanted. Where women fought alongside men, and worked alongside them in what they called politics. It sounds like a dream to me, the wishful thinking of a little girl who only ever wanted to be treated the same as the men. All thoughts of freedom, being able to go where I wish and say whatever I wanted, were soon squashed as I grew up. The rose tinted glasses that only children wear, falling away to reveal the world we live in now. Where the remaining women serve the men. The father stands, turning back to the man he was talking to and engaging him in conversation. The little girl pouting at his feet. As I walk past, I whisper to her.

"One day you will understand, Little Princess. Maybe then you can take the sword instead of the dress."

I hurry away, unwilling to be caught for such words. I slide past the men and hurry to the stall I need.

"Hey!" The shout causes me to stop and turn to watch the commotion on the other side of the stall. At the water well, four large men are pushing a man around. His water spills, splashing all over the floor. He's as tall as them but slimmer, obviously not a worker like these men. His body is trim, but obvious muscle pushes at his shirt and tight pants, the black leather sticking to his legs like glue.

"That ain't for you, freak. Get your water from the other well!" One of the men in a dirty brown shirt and pants spits at his feet as his friends cackle with him. The man's back is to me, but I can see it hunch at the word freak.

"Which well?" The smooth voice asks. The others move restlessly around him as the obvious leader of the group steps into the man's space. To the man's credit, he doesn't back down, instead his spine straightens as his black hair moves with the wind.

"Over there, you stupid freak show," the bigger man shouts, pointing at the contaminated well in the corner. I frown, surely he can't mean to offer this poor soul water which will make him ill? Nibbling on my bottom lip, I debate what to do. My eyes flicker between the scene and the stall I need to visit. My decision is made, however, when the men close the circle, pushing and kicking at the man. I must've missed something, and they have clearly decided to take matters into their own hands. I need to stop this before someone gets hurt! Against my better judgement and all the hard earned lessons about being invisible, I hurry across to stand outside the circle. They ignore me, too busy pushing this poor soul and taunting him. This could go so wrong, the punishment I will receive scaring me even now, but what sort of person would I be if I just watched while someone gets hurt?

"Fucking freak!"

"You see his hair? Fag!"

"Go home, freakshow!"

My anger gets the better of me as I look for a way to help. My eyes land on a rock, I quickly bend over and clutch it. All my insecurities and doubts flying out of the window, my anger getting the better of me, revealing the true self that I hide behind a shy mask.

"Stop!" I shout. They still ignore me, so I throw the rock at the leader's head. It connects with his face, pulling a groan from his lips. Clutching his nose, he spins around to face me. I quickly jump through the spot he made when he stumbles back and stand in front of the man, not even sparing him a look.

"Leave him alone. We all know that water will kill him, why don't you just let him get what he needs and leave each other to it!" I fume, crossing my arms.

"Listen up slave, don't start with me. Walk away before you get hurt, boy," the big man I hit with a rock warns. I swallow quickly, but part my legs in a steadier stance.

"No. I won't stand by and watch as you hurt an innocent man."

"Innocent?!" The man screams, his face turning red with anger as his eyes almost pop out of his head. "He's a fucking freak, he's one of those weirdos."

I freeze as his words finally sink in, that means this man is like me? A soft hand touches my back making me jump before my head swings to the man behind me. He steps up next to me, easing the strain on my neck. My breathing stops as I meet his baby blues, my heart racing as he offers me a soft smile. He's younger than I would have thought, probably close to my age, his face is softer, too. His features almost feminine, pink plump lips, long black eyelashes framing his beautiful eyes. If it wasn't for his body and the cheekbones, he might be womanly. As it is, he's beautiful, like one of the men in the magazines Frederick owns. Models, I think they were called? He doesn't give me a second look, obviously not seeing through the darkness in the hood to the fact I am a woman.

"It's okay. Go on, don't let them hurt you." His voice is smooth and softer than the rough baritones I'm used to. This pushes the leader over the edge as he roars and grabs at me. I squeak as he yanks me, throwing me to the floor. I quickly cover my head as booted feet land on me, the kicks sending pain through my body. A surge of my power rises before I can help it, hardening my skin. The next kick that lands deflects off me, the man screaming as his foot meets my toughened skin.

"Stop it!" The man they were attacking shouts.

The screams finally reach my panicked ears as I lift my head slowly. The hood, forgotten, has fallen to reveal me. The men instantly stop, watching me in horror as they realise that not only am I someone's property - but a woman. My eyes quickly flick over the scene to see the man they branded a freak, fighting the hold of two men, who have one arm each. A man screams close to me, making me scramble to my feet as he hops around holding his obviously injured foot. Pushing my powers back quickly, I let my skin return to normal before they notice. There are people out there that hunt people like me, dangerous people. I learnt at an early age to keep my 'peculiarities' hidden, but as I get older, it only gets harder. The power pushing through me, trying to protect me from punishments and life in general. The beautiful man elbows the man to his left and then spins and punches the man to his right, his movement's fluid, like a dancer I once saw or an animal like the one advertised for the circus passing through. Once free, he rushes to my side, his large hands spanning my waist as he frantically examines me. The heat washing through me causes me to bite my lip. He freezes as his eyes lift to mine in surprise, obviously just now realising I'm not a man. It's like an electric shock when he stares at me, his hands still on me. The world leaves us in this moment as he drinks in my face.

"Well, hello there." His smile is brilliant as he blinds me with its perfection.

CIRCUS
SHOW
CIRCUS
THE GREATEST SHOW

Those three words send heat straight to my cheeks and have my head ducking. He grins as the locals start pushing and shouting at each other behind him. His eyes crinkle as he glances back, before looking at me with a sigh.

"Stay right there a minute." The stranger winks at me before turning and jogging over to the others. In the chaos of the fighting between the locals and the new man, I manage to slip away, pulling up my hood quickly. I hurry through the market to the stall and ask for Frederick's parcel. The brown box is neatly wrapped, and the old pudgy man warns me to be careful with it. My curiosity nearly gets the better of me, but with one look back at where the man I helped is still arguing with locals, I pull my hood tighter and slip out of the market.

Only when I'm on the dirt road again do I breathe deeply and slow my pace, the parcel getting heavier with each step. By the time I get back to Frederick's, my already sore arms are going to be like lead. My stomach chooses that moment to throb from the kick that connected there earlier.

"Stupid, Rhea, really stupid," I grunt at myself as I remember the power rushing through me and hardening my skin.

"Anyone could have been watching!" I kick the dirt as I walk, still muttering to myself. I cross the dirt intersection again and keep my head down as the man's face pops into my head, making me smile. He really was beautiful, my shoulders slump when I realize I probably won't see him again. He must have been a traveler or just passing through.

A noise has me spinning towards the bush next to the road, squinting, as I try to see through the leaves. It comes again, making me frown. What was that? Looking around, I speed up again, unwilling to be caught alone. Turning onto the edge of the dirt road that leads to Frederick's, I frown as a pained roar shakes the ground I'm walking on. Spinning wildly, I spot a man's back retreating behind the tree nearest to me.

Don't do it, Rhea. I frown as I look back at the road before groaning and slipping around the tree to follow him. I freeze in shock as I watch the scene before me. Two men, who I recognize as Frederick's lower lackeys, are pointing guns at an animal that I can only catch glimpses of behind them. Its roar comes again, filled with pain and fear. My heart clenches as I drop Frederick's parcel to the ground, unconcerned about the contents.

Picking my way around the men, I stand to the side and almost cry when I see the poor thing. It's beautiful. Crouching, its long black tail swings behind him, the fur thickening and becoming bushier at the end with the tips varying from orange to red. Strong lean legs move as it crouches lower to the floor, flashing large, sharp fangs at the men. Its bulky, muscular body is the same black with red and orange here and there until a large mane covers its shoulders and head in the same mix of colours. Looking at it, I'm reminded of the predator people used to call a Lion.

It's obviously a mutated animal, but the intelligence shining in its tawny eyes is unlike anything I've ever seen. For a moment, our eyes lock, its tail stops swishing and he stops growling. My eyes fill with tears when I spot the bright red blood seeping from its injured shoulder, bright against his dark fur.

The moment is broken when one of the men shout at it again, making it roar. The lackey raises his gun, aiming at the poor animal. Instinct guides me as I leap in front of it, putting my defenseless back to the predator. I spread my arms wide, the hood falling.

"It's Frederick's little whore. Move, bitch!" The blonde slimy-looking one on the left shouts, waving his gun around threateningly.

The animal stops growling, but I keep my eyes locked on the men in front of me, not letting my fear show. It's the easiest way to become prey.

"Leave it alone!" I yell. The other man with dark brown hair, body all muscle, moves forward pointing the gun right at me. The slimy one looks at him before smacking his shoulder.

"We can't hurt her, idiot, Frederick will kill us."

The bigger guy frowns before lowering the gun. I keep my position and manage to hold in my flinch as warm breath hits my back. It's a good sign it hasn't attacked me yet, but you can never be too careful. I don't have time to soothe it as I wait for the attack I know is coming from the men in front of me.

"Hey, assholes!" Comes a deep shout as loud, booming steps sound to the right of us, further into the barren dead land. Risking it, I glance over as a big man stops just a few feet from us, closer to the men than me. He looks over at me and sees the animal behind me, before anger graces his face as he turns to the men. I only planned a quick look but my eyes stick to him, he's even bigger than the men who work the fields. His trousers mould to thick thighs and his shirt is almost see-through allowing me a glimpse of his wide barrel chest. Blonde, short styled hair, catches the light, as do his emerald eyes as they flash with fury.

His fists clench next to his legs as he faces the men down. He's tall, almost double the height of the slimy one, and over a head bigger than the other lackey.

"Back off, that animal is mine!" His voice echoes between us all, deep and gravelly like the growl of the animal that has started making noises again behind me. Before I know it, the large creature has slipped around me and stands with its paws planted apart, obviously trying to protect me. The slimy man laughs even as the big man steps closer. My eyes swing between them, watching it all unfold.

"Come on Ted, it's not worth it," he mutters to the bigger guy as he watches the newcomer warily.

They both slip their guns away and then turn to me.

"You'll pay for this, cunt," the bigger of the two, Ted, says as he stomps away. The slimy man smiles at me like a snake.

"I can't wait to see what he does to you." He blows me a kiss and scurries after his friend. My shoulders drop as the adrenaline leaves me. The animal whines and I drop to my knees automatically, my hands fluttering over its wound.

"Oh, you poor baby!" I cry as it whines again, plopping itself down at my feet. Its tongue lolls out. I forget about the big man, which is a feat in itself, until he drops to his knees on the other side of the animal. He cups its big head, petting it gently.

"Fluffy, what did they do to you?" He softens his voice, but it's still gravelly and deep. I stare from him to the animal as it head butts him for attention. The thing looks like it eats humans for breakfast and he names it Fluffy? Before I can ask, he rips his shirt off and presses it to the wound, wincing when Fluffy growls.

"Sorry, big guy," he mutters, but my eyes are stuck to his chest. Muscle after muscle makes my mouth water as his tanned chest gleams with sweat. Big broad shoulders tense as he presses harder. I drag my eyes up and watch as he frowns, trying to stop the bleeding. His eyes are filled with sorrow, and I almost smile at the gentle way this huge man is tenderly looking after this deadly creature.

"I think the bullet just grazed him," I offer. His head snaps up as he stares at me, obviously just realising that I'm still here. He turns bright red, the colour adorable on his handsome face.

"So-Sorry, I, erm, forgot you were..., it's just Fluffy and me, erm, I am, shit. Hi, I'm Rex." He bumbles through cringing lips, at the end of the sentence. I smile at him.

"Hi, I'm Rhea."

He goes to stretch his hand out, but frowns down at the blood on his palm and glances at me awkwardly.

"Is he yours?" I ask gently, tenderly reaching out and stroking the creature's head. He purrs deep, shaking Rex's hand as he rubs his head against me. Rex watches in shock, making me drop my hand and blush, my eyes dropping to the creature between us. Fluffy head-butts me, knocking me on my butt as he tries to get me to pet him again.

"No, I mean yes, sorry, I've just never seen him trust anyone apart from me. He snarls at everyone and takes particular pleasure in annoying Blain, he even once-" he snaps his mouth shut and his blush returns. "Sorry, I'm babbling." He rubs his head, messing up his hair. I wonder if it's as soft as it looks. "I'm better with animals, I don't really deal with people," his face is as red as the sun when it first rises and filled with embarrassment.

"I'm that way too. I love animals." I laugh as the big softie nudges me again, making Rex smile. It transforms his face from handsome to downright perfect.

Rex drops his eyes, losing his smile when he sees the blood still flowing.

"Sorry, I need to get him back to tend to his wound before it gets infected."

"Of course, sorry!" I gush, mad at myself for forgetting the poor, hurt cat.

He smiles softly at me before hefting the animal up in his arms. I gape at him as he carries it like a baby. I scramble to my feet.

"Will he be okay?" I ask softly, worrying my bottom lip. His smile is strained.

"I think so, sorry, I really had better go!" Nodding, I step back and watch as he strides away, the giant cat alternating between growling and purring in his arms.

"I know, big guy, it will be okay." The giant coos at him as he walks away. Shaking my head, I trudge to the road and pick up the half smashed parcel. Groaning, I grab it and set off back home. Frederick is going to kill me, but it was worth it to help Fluffy. Giggling at the name, I walk down the road until the townhouse comes into view.

I stare up at the doors of the tavern which I call home. Fear, anger, and emotions that I can't put a name to run through my body. It's quiet out here. Even the crows are silent, like an eerie omen. I have an odd feeling, like this is the last time I will set foot in this house. It may not be much, but it has been a roof over my head and the closest thing to safety and belonging that I have ever known. I swallow back my fear and take a step towards the front door.

If this is to be my last day on this Earth, at least I know I have done something to be proud of. If saving that beautiful animal from further pain and torment means I have to sacrifice my life, then so be it. At least I have made a difference in this pointless world. How else would I spend the rest of my days? Cowering from my 'master' and serving the whim of every man around?

With this decision, I feel a sense of calm and determination run through me. Head held high and back straight for the first time I can remember, I walk into Frederick's tavern to face the consequences of my actions.

The house is just as quiet inside as it was out, and as I enter the main room of the house, I see several of Frederick's lackeys lining the room. They all have a sick, excited gleam in their eyes, their anticipation of what is going to happen clear in their expressions.

"Time to get what you deserve, slut." A weasley excuse of a man spits at me.

I turn to him, steel in my eyes as I slap him as hard as I can. Now that I have accepted my fate, I can't seem to stop myself. A burst of pride hits me. The man I hit tries to grab at me but is held back by one of the other goons in the room. He leans towards the other man and whispers to him in a voice loud enough for me to hear.

"Let Frederick deal with her. Then she is ours," he licks his lips, his eyes not leaving mine for a second as he speaks.

I grimace in disgust, especially as I see him grab at his crotch, adjusting his arousal at whatever sick thoughts are running through his twisted head. I feel sick to my stomach as I wonder if I made the right decision. Closing my eyes briefly, I can still hear the roar of the wounded animal. It fortifies me, allowing my eyes to open as I glare at the creeps.

"I would rather die," I bite out, spitting on them in the process.

The man just grins, not making a move to wipe my spit from his face.

"That can be arranged," he says in a voice that makes my blood run cold.

I stride away, not willing to waste any more of my time on these disgusting men. There is no point delaying any further. Walking up to Frederick's office, I don't hesitate at the doorway; instead, I waltz straight in, not bothering to knock. Frederick is standing behind his desk, staring out the window at the parched, dying land. He turns, raising his eyebrow at what he sees. He nods at someone behind me.

"Take her," he says before turning away to look out the window again.

I startle, but before I can think to do anything to protect myself, a blinding light fills my vision as something connects with my head. I drop to the ground, only able to focus on the pain as darkness fills my vision. I hear shuffling feet around me, and I think I am raised from the ground, but I am helpless to do anything about it as I am pulled into unconsciousness.

My head is pounding and my skin is tight and hot like I have been in the sun for too long. My muscles are screaming at me but it's not until I try to relieve the pain that I realise I can't move. I open my eyes suddenly and quickly close them again against the harsh light, the back of my head throbbing to the frantic beat of my heart. I try to slow my breathing as I search my memory for what is happening.

I hear a distant animalistic roar, and everything comes back to me in a rush. I open my eyes again and try to work out how much shit I am in.

I am in the marketplace, my knees in the dirt with my arms tied to a post in front of me. Biting my lip to stop from crying out, I rest my forehead against the post. *This is not good.* Turning my head, I can see that a crowd has gathered. I see a couple of faces that I recognise, but mostly just the eager faces of strangers gathered to see some bloodshed.

A hush falls on the gathered group as footsteps sound, the person walking closer towards me. My heart rate speeds in anticipation of pain. There is only one reason I am here. Public humiliation. The only question is, how far will they go? Death? In some respects, death would be the kindest option.

The sound of a throat clearing fills the now quiet marketplace. This place is usually a hive of activity, but right now it is silent as the grave.

"We are here today because I have been wronged," Frederick's voice fills the area, making people shift and murmur amongst themselves.

"This girl; my property, thought that she knew better than us. Than me! We need to show her her place. I have been lenient, kind even. Turns out that I have been too lenient. I guess it is my own fault. Women need a strong hand to remind them of their place in this world, and I failed to do that. She needs to be reminded that women only exist to serve us. It is because of that failing that I will spare her life. But mark my words, things will change from today and she will learn her proper value as a woman in a man's world," he finishes, everyone hanging on to every last rasping word.

Dread fills me, and I know that by the end of this, death would have been kinder but still, I do not regret my actions. What makes the rules different for me, a woman, then a man? Why, when we bring new life into this dead world, are we seen as nothing? Just stock, to barter and sell, while they carry on destroying what is left in the ruins of this world.

I gasp as someone roughly rips open the back of my shapeless smock, exposing my bare skin to the watching crowd. Murmurs fill the air, and I notice with dismay that the sounds are of excitement. There would be no help for me here. The sound of a belt being undone has fear filling me once more, pushing back my useless thoughts. I break out in a cold sweat despite the pounding heat of the sun on my skin. Leaning my head against the post in front of me, I grip my hands tightly together. I may be terrified, but I will not give them the satisfaction of seeing me beg.

I barely register a whistle through the air before a crack of what feels like lightning strikes my back. My back arches and my head is thrown back in agony; tears filling my eyes as a silent cry leaves my lips. I start panting, the skin on my back screaming at the harsh movements, my body's natural instincts trying to take over. To protect me, to defend.

It takes every ounce of my strength to stop my body from changing; from revealing to the watching crowd that I am different from them. The power that I have kept hidden since I discovered it when I was just a girl, could make my already difficult life, hell. Those that were 'altered' are not trusted; often hunted and experimented on. For me to be different, and a woman, is bad news.

Every cell in my body fights to protect me, trying to harden to granite to prevent the belt from splitting my delicate skin. My panting increases, I don't even want to contemplate what they would do to me if they discover my power. I pinch my eyes closed, focusing on keeping my skin normal in appearance.

My silent battle ends as the belt hits my skin once more. I cry out, my voice ragged, and I feel my skin ripple across my back as I lose control. What feels like scales run across my back in a wave, before I force it away. In my panic and pain, I turn to granite, becoming a human statue. I hear a gasp run through the crowd, along with angry shouts and heckles.

"Freak!"

"Burn the witch!"

"Kill the slut!"

The noises around me get louder and I'm aware of the sounds of fighting. I guess people are trying to get to me before Frederick is done with me. He will be furious that I have kept this hidden from him for years. The thought is bittersweet.

"I knew it." His raspy voice causes me to open my eyes.

He has a satisfied look on his face, which was not what I had expected from him. My head reels and I take in the scene around me. Men are fighting each other in the crowd as Frederick turns his back on me, his men gathering around him.

"Get in there, you idiots!" He demands. His lackeys throw him a look before jumping into the fray. I lean my head on the pole, exhausted from fighting the change and the welts I can still feel dripping blood down my back. A flash of black at the edge of the crowd has me squinting before it disappears.

"Rhea!" Comes a shout from behind me. Rex drops to his knees next to me as the sounds of fighting and shouting get louder.

"Come on, Wildcat." He gently starts to untie me, his face scrunching in concentration as he tries to hurt me as little as possible.

"Is Fluffy okay?" I croak. He stops for a second and stares at me, blinking incredulously.

"He's fine, I'm more worried about you," he admits before blushing a little, his eyes dropping back to the rope. I stare at him blankly in shock at his comment. I've never had anyone worry about me before. It's strange. I'm brought back to reality at the sounds of a scream behind me, the sound making me flinch.

I hate not being able to see, it makes everything sound closer and more dangerous. My bare back is still exposed to anyone who stumbles close. Rex grunts and rips off the rope, before gently pulling me up. I sway with a small moan as pain rips through my back at moving. He watches me, the worry clear on his face as the man from the market, the beautiful one with the curly hair, comes jogging up next to him, out of breath. Blood is splattered across his cheek and one eye is turning red.

"Come on, we need to get out of here. Oh, I'm Jesse by the way, I didn't get to tell you that before you ran away." he says, winking at me, before turning and watching our backs.

"I don't think I can walk far," I admit in shame. Even now I can feel the blood trickling as the skin pulls tight, my powers choosing now to desert me. The pain is making my head fuzzy, which is not a good sign. Rex looks around before approaching me and gently grabbing the back of my thighs. He lifts me up like I weigh nothing. The sharp movement has me crying out as spots dance in front of my eyes. Fire runs through my body and the darkness closes in on my vision, as the pain overwhelms me. The sounds of fighting, and even Rex's worried voice, fade away as I fall into the awaiting blackness.

Jostling wakes me up, my back throbbing painfully with each sway as someone carries me, each step making me grit my teeth. Before I can try and open my eyes, the darkness reclaims me, the pain too great.

"Why did you do that? We don't even know her. Now we are going to be in so much shit. Fucking morons, the lot of you," the angry voice has me groaning as I come back to myself.

"Shh, Blain, you might wake her. It's best she stays unconscious." The chest I'm held to vibrates as each word comes out soft and quiet. The warmth of his chest and the soft stroking of my hair has me sliding away again, greeting the nothingness like an old friend.

"I can't believe we are still doing this! She's going to have the whole town after us. Just because you two idiots are enchanted by some stupid pussy." The same angry voice from before shouts from somewhere above me. Cracking open my eyes, the light makes them sting as I realise I am laying on something soft. When I can finally focus, I see the edge of a bed in front of me and someone's legs as they stand there.

"Shut up, Blain," Rex complains, his voice closer. He kneels down where I can see him and offers me a small, strained smile.

"Hi-" I start coughing at trying to talk, which only makes me groan in pain at the jarring movements.

"Try not to move, okay? They are treating your back. It's a home-made concoction that should have you as good as new in no time."

Laying my head back down on the soft material, I keep my eyes on him as he smiles at me. Something cold touches my back, making me jump.

"Sorry, but try not to move. This will help," I recognize Jesse's voice as he touches whatever it is to the wound on my exposed back. My skin pebbles as the cold air hits it, making me shiver.

"God damn idiots, that's what you are. When Alcide finds out, he will have you on shit-shoveling duty for the rest of the year!" Comes the yell from the man whose legs I can only see.

"Either help or get out Blain," Rex says, frowning before offering me a shy smile. The room goes quiet before I see the legs moving, Blain leaving wherever we are.

"Thank fuck he's gone, he's such a grumpy bastard," Jesse complains as he smothers my back in something. I crinkle my nose at the feeling, but try to stay as still as possible. My back does seem to hurt less, though, I can barely feel the pain anymore, allowing me to focus on everything else. Like the fact that I'm half naked in a random place with two men I only just met. The thought doesn't scare me as much as it should. I feel oddly comfortable and they are too busy looking after me to notice. My jaw cracks open on a yawn, the day finally catching up to me.

"Sleep Rhea, we will be here when you wake up," Rex offers as he leans forward and moves a stray hair from my face. I try to fight it, but my eyes start to close as he watches me, my body succumbing to sleep.

CIRCUS
SHOW
CIRCUS
THE GREATEST SHOW

Awareness rolls in slowly, my body heavy with sleep. I peel my eyes open, the soft light in the room feeling nice on my tired eyes. I lift my head from where I still lay on my front, I don't even feel a throb in my back. I test it by sitting up and when it doesn't hurt, I stand, having to catch myself on the bed when my body protests.

Letting my eyes wander, I take in the room. The bed is covered in deep red sheets, with black pillows scattered here and there. The walls seem to be made of material, so I would guess we are in a tent. A large mirror is propped up in one corner and a desk in another. Candles are dotted around, the flames flickering and chasing away the darkness. The ground is covered in soft rugs, mismatched ones sewn together to create padding under my feet. Trunks are piled at the end of the bed with an open sketchbook laying on top. Looking around again, I slowly walk to it when I don't spot anyone lurking anywhere. Hesitantly, I graze the page where a detailed drawing of Fluffy sits. It looks like it's drawn with charcoal, but the detail and likeness is incredible. Picking it up, I flip through page after page of amazing drawings, making me smile in awe until I come to the last page.

There staring back at me, is a half-finished drawing of my face. I'm obviously asleep, my head cushioned on the bed and my back bare. Frowning, I glance down at the large shirt I now wear, only now noticing I'm dressed. My eyes drag back to the drawing, my heart beating faster at someone taking the time to draw me, each line lovingly made. The curve of my face, my high, sharp eyebrows; they even managed to get the shades in my hair, although they are black and grey rather than the bright red blending down to blonde. I wonder who drew this?

Nibbling on my lip, I gently put the book down before someone catches me. Hugging my arms to my torso, I debate my options. I could wait here for Rex or Jesse to come back, but from the darkness I can see through the flaps of the tent as they blow in the wind, I'm guessing it's night. Decision made, I trot to the tent flap and stick my head out. When I spot no one, I slowly step through, leaving the safety and warmth of the tent behind. Instantly, the chill has my arms breaking out in goosebumps.

I can't see much in the darkness, the moon's rays only letting me see outlines of shapes spread around the field around me. Noise reaches me, someone's grunts and the clang of metal hitting something. A big top tent sits close to the tent I am in, hurrying to keep warm I head towards it. I push through the open flap to stop and stare in amazement.

Rows of seating on raised platforms curve around the tent from left to right. Steps in front of me lead down to the open sand-covered stage in the middle. Big grey bricks circle around the stage, clearly dividing it from the audience. A tightrope sways above my head, as do some platforms. The noise comes again making me step in further. There, in the back corner, a man stands throwing knives at a large red and black wheel. Curiosity has me stepping silently down the steps until I'm leaning on the grey bricks.

The man's side is towards me, allowing me to see his back and every inch of it is covered in black tattoos. Too many to make out all the details, but I can see a version of Fluffy on his right shoulder and a large animal on his other one. The rest are clean, sharp black lines and shapes with scrolling words and scattered drawings. His arm flies forward, another knife whizzing through the air to embed in the wheel. I run my eyes over the rest of him, he's trim. Smaller than Rex but bigger than Jesse, his shoulders are strong and narrow down to a muscled back, which ends with two clear dimples above his bum. His black leather pants ride low, allowing me to see his washboard abs and V as he moves with his throws.

His hair is neat, parting just off centre, the dark black hair slicked back to either side. It's cut short, only just reaching his pierced ears. Another piercing glints in his nose as he turns to grab more knives from the table behind him, the blades moving between his fingers with an expertise born from years of practice. I must make some sort of noise when I see his face because his head cranes up and he glares at me. Not even the scowl twisting his pouty lips can detract from his looks. Stubble covers his jaw, more a shadow than anything. His sharp cheekbones and jaw add to his beauty. As do his deep, almost black eyes, surrounded by the longest lashes I have ever seen on a man. The tattoos carry onto his front and up his neck, stopping just below his jaw. I don't get a good look because his sharp voice has me flicking my eyes back to his.

"Great, so not only do we have to save you, it turns out you're a nosey bitch." I realise he's the angry voice from earlier. Didn't Rex call him Blain? Jesse is right, he is grumpy.

I don't know what to say, I'm just staring at him dumbly as he groans.

"You fucking stupid, too?" He snarls at me, making my cheeks heat. I must look like an idiot, just standing there staring at him, but what an asshole.

"It's better than being an insufferable prick." The words leave my mouth before I can stop them, causing my eyes to widen. I've never spoken to anyone like that before. I freeze, waiting for a punishment that never comes. Well, not a physical one anyway.

"Least you're not a total lost cause," muttering he turns back to his board and throws knife after knife.

"What's your problem?" I shout, his lack of anger at my outburst spurring me on. He spins to me, a knife in his hand ready to throw.

"What's my fucking problem, you ask?" he stalks towards me, the knife still clutched in his hand, making me take a step back and hesitate. My eyes are glued to the weapon shimmering in the light. He frowns and stops before dropping his arm with the knife.

"Fuck, you think I'm going to stab you or something? Crazy bitch," he yells before turning in disgust and throwing the knife the length of the tent to the board. It strikes the bullseye, but he doesn't even spare it a glance; like he expected nothing less; as he turns back to me, his eyes flashing.

"You're my problem. Not only did we have to interfere with a settlement matter, but now, we are going to have the fucking assholes who run this place gunning for us all because of you and what's between your legs. You put us all at risk."

"And that's my problem, how?" I shout, crossing my arms. "I didn't ask you to save me and I sure as hell didn't ask to be born a woman."

"Start taking responsibility, sweetheart. Now get the fuck away from me, I don't need to look at you. Bloody trouble is all you are." He growls as he walks back to his table, collecting his knives in a leather bundle.

"Listen here, asshole, I've had men tell me all my life that everything's my fault. Do this, do that, don't speak, don't fight. Spread your legs and think of England. I was fine keeping my head down as I worked my way to freedom before I stepped in to save your friends. So don't blame everything on me just because it got a little bit hairy." My rant runs out, my frustrations and anger at the situation and my whole life coming out like the blades in his hands. His attitude only spurring me on. "I didn't ask for them to save me, but I'm glad they did. I owe them my life, so I guess that means you better suck it up, sweetheart," I sneer the last word.

He glares at me, his mouth opening to throw out more of his bad attitude and unwelcome opinions, before he looks behind me and storms out of the other side of the tent without another word.

I am left fuming at Blain and his shitty behavior. I shouldn't expect anything else, men have never treated me with anything other than disdain. I am so caught up in my anger and frustration that at first, I don't notice that I'm not alone anymore.

My body stills as I realize that someone has entered the big top. I spin, thinking that Blain has come back for more, my temper flaring. I don't know what it is about him that makes me so mad. I am used to being quiet around men, subservient in actions if not in character. It was how I was raised, but something about these men has me acting differently, more reckless, and Blain makes me so mad that I'm acting completely out of character, against my better judgement.

I am good at adapting, I have to be to survive in this male-dominated world that is constantly changing. The only way that I have made it alive and intact to this point in my life is by keeping on my toes and adapting to the situation. My powers have also helped keep me alive, but they also put my life at risk. So I hide them, keep my head down, adapt, and survive.

"So, you are the woman that has caused my men so much trouble?" A rich accented voice greets me.

Not Blain then. The voice sounds cultured, and although the words may be harsh, I can hear a playful edge around them. His men, he said. So this must be the man in charge of the group. I straighten my back, searching the shadows for the source of this new voice. I don't want to look too defiant; these guys did rescue me after all, but I am not going to jump from one bad situation to another. I have no idea why they decided to help me, and I have learnt the hard way that nothing comes for free in this world.

Squinting across the darkened room, I try to get a better look at the man addressing me. There is no doubt from his voice that that's what he is, his rich voice runs over me as he takes a few steps towards me.

"I-" My voice cracks. I clear my throat, not wanting to sound weak. "I didn't mean to cause any trouble," I tell him, my voice low.

I am unsure how to act around the man who now holds my fate in his hands. Jesse and Rex just treated me like a normal human, they were easy to be around. Blain made me so mad that I acted before I could think. But this unknown stranger made me realise that once again, I have no control.

As the stranger comes closer I drop to my knees, head bowed in a position of subservience. That little part of me that has slowly been growing is screaming at me to stand up, not to let myself be used. But a lifetime of being taught that you are a second-class citizen makes certain habits hard to break. The footsteps stop instantly.

"Shit," the smooth voice utters, his slight accent making the word sound different. Exotic.

"Stand up, Cariñoa, we don't do that here." He sounds angry, but I get the feeling that the anger is not directed at me.

Standing, I look up at the man for the first time. He is tall, over six foot, with dark hair shaved short on the sides and styled longer on the top. His icy blue eyes widen slightly as he takes in everything about me, his plush lips quirking up into a smile. He has a short, neatly trimmed beard that does nothing to hide his strong jawline. He looks older than the others, perhaps early thirties? Frankly, this guy is gorgeous. They all are, where did he find these guys?

Striding closer to me, he circles around me, appraising me as if I am cattle at the market. My temper flares again. This man is contradicting himself; one minute telling me not to show subservience and the next, examining my body like an asset for him to sell. Crossing my arms, I spin, glaring at him. He is wearing tight leather trousers which show off his defined legs, and a fitted red jacket with golden trim. He reminds me of the old circus ringmasters I saw in a magazine I stole from Frederick once. I can't help but admire the way it fits him, accenting his powerful male body. He notices my interest, winking at me as he continues his perusal. This just makes me angrier, but at myself more than him.

"Are you done assessing me?" I ask, sarcasm dripping from my voice, and a blush staining my cheeks.

He stops his perusal and a grin spreads across his face, then looks me up and down again, as if reassessing me.

"The boys chose well. I think you will fit in nicely here, but you will need to be able to hold your own," he tells me. "Jesse told me what you did for him. That you risked your neck for us. You even have Rex trying to convince me that you should stay. You must have made an impression."

My heart starts to race as he speaks, not out of fear, but out of hope. It sounded like...like they were asking me to stay with them. A chance at a life outside of Cinders. Like any girl born into this world, I had always dreamed of more, of something better, but I had never imagined that I might get to experience it.

"What are you saying?" I ask, my voice raspy as I fight back my emotions. I am not the type of girl to cry, I never have been, but this is a whole different ball game.

"I am saying, Cariñoa, that if you want it, there is a place for you here." He smiles and runs his eyes fondly over the room. "We could do with a woman's touch around here. Besides, Blain's cooking is terrible," he says with a chuckle before turning to leave.

My heart stills, dread filling my stomach. I have not escaped from a life of slavery to do the same here.

"No," I tell him, thankful that my voice didn't waver.

He turns and raises an eyebrow at me. "And how do you expect to earn your keep, Cariñoa? Nothing in this world is free." His words have an edge to them now and mirror what I had been thinking earlier.

"Let me perform," I tell him, anger rising as I see the condescending smile begin to cross his lips. "I have powers, like your other performers." He frowns and I quickly carry on. "I heard the whispers, I know they are like me."

This stops him in his tracks, the smile dropping as a thoughtful look crosses his face. His eyes snap back up to mine. "What can you do?" He asks, eyeing up my unusual hair and eye colour, all possible thanks to the radiation passing through our DNA from the bombings all those years ago.

I bite my lip. I am so used to hiding my powers from everyone that admitting to them goes against my nature. Sighing, the ringmaster turns away from me.

"A pretty face and strange hair are not enough to perform in my circus," he calls to me, and I can tell this is meant as a dismissal.

Fear clenches my gut, they can't turn me away. "I adapt," I blurt out. I stride toward him where he has stopped, assessing me again. I can tell he is about to give me a smart-ass comment, when I grab at the knife that was concealed at his waist. He tries to grab my arm and I unleash my power, causing my skin to ripple into sharp spines along my arm. He jerks his hand away, staring at my arm in shock. I take the knife and slash along my other arm, only I turn the skin to marble before the knife can slice through it, causing the blade to bounce off harmlessly.

"I can adapt," I tell him again, my voice calmer now.

A grin spreads across his face as he accepts the blade from me. He nods once before a thoughtful look settles on his face.

"Every one of my performers has earned their place here. They are family. You will have to earn your place too. If you do, you are one of us. If not, you are out."

I gulp at this, but nod. I wouldn't expect to just fit in straight away. I have to earn my spot and prove that I can belong here.

"My name is Alcide, I am in charge here. What I say goes, that is the same for everyone. You cause trouble and you're out. You will have to leave everything behind, we can't go back to your settlement."

I nod my understanding, I have nothing to go back for anyway. Other than a few meagre coins I earned from Frederick, I didn't have any possessions of my own.

"There is nothing there for me," I tell him, seeing his eyes soften as he nods.

"Take tomorrow to look around, get to know your fellow colleagues whilst I figure out what your act is going to be," he tells me as he runs his hand through his hair, his tone clearly dismissing me.

I start to walk away when I hear him call my name, which I don't remember telling him. Turning around, I raise my eyebrow in question.

"Welcome to the Circus."

CIRCUS
CIRCUS
THE GREATEST SHOW

Chapter Four

Happy to be dismissed, I slip back out into the night, the breeze cooling my heated skin. All the nerves I should have felt before come rushing back, making me want to be somewhere familiar to gather my thoughts. Racking my brain, I find myself heading back to the tent I woke up in. Sliding back through the opening, I freeze halfway through the flap at the sight of a man bent over, rummaging through a trunk. When he straightens, I realise who it is, so I relax and slip inside, smiling in recognition.

"Hi," I say softly, as he jumps, banging his head on the lid.

"Fuck," he shouts before turning and staring at me in shock, his cheeks instantly heating.

"I mean shit, oh man, I'm so sorry, I didn't mean to swear. My mama always told me it was rude to talk like that in front of a woman, but I didn't mean to, so I guess-" he snaps his mouth shut. Rex's shoulders slump as his face turns the same red as Fluffy's markings, he looks at the ground obviously embarrassed. "Sorry, I'm babbling again, I'll just shut up," he mutters, more to himself.

Frowning at him knowing he feels the need to censor himself with me, I debate how to make him comfortable. Smiling when I see the charcoal clutched in his hands, I look from him to the open sketchbook.

"Your drawings are amazing."

His head snaps up again before he looks at the open sketchbook as if only just realising it was there, before going pale he scrambles over, clutching it to his chest protectively. Startled, I watch him, bemused by his behavior. Have I offended him?

"I'm sorry, I didn't mean to invade your privacy! I didn't realise what it was at first, and when I did I couldn't stop myself, the drawings were that amazing and lifelike…" I trail off as he watches me, his eyes searching mine as if trying to see if I'm sincere.

"Really?" He asks, his voice soft, his insecurities clear in his voice. Nodding, I make myself sit on the edge of the bed.

"Really. Could I see some more?" I ask, smiling at his hopeful expression.

Grinning he rushes over, almost tripping on the rug in his haste.

I have to stifle my giggles as he blushes again, he really is adorable. Smiling in embarrassment, he plops down next to me, causing me to roll into him a bit when the bed moves under his massive size. It's my turn to blush now as I catch myself by grabbing his arm, his impressive muscle flexing under my hand as my eyes find his. My breath catches as he watches me. Quickly, I let go and shuffle back a bit, trying to put some space between us. He looks down, fiddling with the sketchbook.

"Do you draw just animals?" I ask curiously, trying to cover for my awkward moment.

"No, I mean not always. I like drawing living things, people included. There's not much difference to me between animals and us, they are both just as expressive, but in unique ways. I love trying to capture that." He opens the book as he carries on explaining, and I find myself watching him, entranced.

He loses all shyness and doesn't even blush as he points out sketches of animals and flips through, showing me his drawings. His face becomes more animated, and his eyes sparkle. It's clear he loves drawing, the confidence in the strokes on the page is astounding. There's something about this big man holding this tiny sketchbook that has my heart speeding up and my stomach flipping. I look back down at what he's showing me before he catches me staring, smiling when he flips to the drawing of me, before he slams the cover shut. This time his cheeks do heat as he stares at the sketchbook like it's betrayed him.

"I, er-" he starts.

"Can I see? It's beautiful, when did you draw it?" Something in my voice must make him want to trust me because he opens it again, and answers without looking at me.

"It's not finished yet, sorry, I don't want you to think I'm weird and watch people sleep. I just couldn't resist, you were so beautiful, so peaceful that I itched to draw you." His voice is quiet, like he's not sure how I will take that. My chest feels like a butterfly is taking flight and my heart softens.

"Feel free to anytime, especially if I can keep one."

We share a soft smile as he goes back to showing me his work.

"So, where did you go?" he asks when he runs out of drawings. Turning, he puts his knee on the bed between us and leans back on his arm. Shrugging, I play with the sheet on the bed, twisting it between my fingers in a nervous gesture.

"I couldn't sleep, so I went to explore. I met Blain and Alcide."

His eyes widen as he grins, his cheeks are slightly tinted but he obviously feels more comfortable with me.

"And?"

I twist my face and he laughs.

"Alcide is nice, a bit intimidating, but seems okay. Blain is…" I trail off unsure, I don't want him to think I'm bad mouthing the people who helped me.

"An ass?" he supplies, still grinning, his beautiful eyes sparkling.

"Pretty much," I giggle. He nods.

"Don't take it to heart, he's like that with everyone."

"Really?" I ask feeling relieved, I thought it was just me.

"Yup, so are you staying?"

"In here?" I ask, my bravery from earlier returning.

It's so easy to tease him and I feel so at ease with him, like I've known him forever. He blushes but his smile widens, flashing bright white teeth at me.

"If you like." He straightens up, his hand resting on the bed near mine, mere inches separating them.

"Alcide said I could, he doesn't know where I will fit, but it seems like I am."

He tilts his head watching me. "But?"

"It just feels like a dream, some amazing men coming in to rescue me when I needed it most, and now offering me a place to stay and a chance to prove myself." He nods in understanding as his face softens.

"It's more than a chance or a job wildcat, it's home."

Licking my lips I blurt out the next truth, "I've never had one."

"A job?" he says in question. Shaking my head I watch him as I let him have a little piece of me. My hopes and dreams in these two little words.

"A home."

He sucks in a breath and obviously gathers his courage as he grabs my hand and squeezes reassuringly.

"Well, now you do." We smile at each other again, he clears his throat.

"Just don't say I didn't warn you when you realise how weird we all are."

Laughing I reply, "Don't worry, so am I."

We go quiet for a while, each lost in our thoughts even as our hands are still clasped. I'm scared of moving in case he takes his hand away, the warmth and comfort are nice.

"Do you want me to show you around tomorrow?" His voice booms out making me jump, he winces, lowering his eyes again. It's my turn to squeeze his hand this time.

"I'd love that."

I didn't think I would sleep, but I must have nodded off, only to be woken up by voices and laughter drifting through the tent flap as it moves in the breeze. Rays of sun poke through, making me realise it's morning. Yawning, I stretch beneath the comfy sheets and force myself to get up. I can't remember the last time I wasn't up with the sun. If I wasn't, a bell would sound as the masters woke up, and a punishment soon followed. Only when I stand do I realise I'm only in a long shirt, did I really wear that last night when meeting them? Groaning, I look around for something to wear, remembering my usual tunic got ruined yesterday. Spotting some folded clothing at the end of the bed, I grab it and hold it up. I end up looking at the material for a while, unsure how to wear it before shrugging.

Pulling off the borrowed shirt, I fold it neatly and lay it on the bed. I pick up the red silky material and slip it over my head. Next, I grab what looks like pants and pull them over my curvy hips, having to jiggle a little to pull them on. Frowning down at myself I walk over to the mirror, what in the world?

The shirt is a beautiful shade of red, like the flowers that grow in the water oasis, but it's too short. Ending halfway down my ribs, it shows off my stomach which is tight and flat from all the physical labour. The red material fits around my chest tightly with a deep v neckline, nearly allowing my boobs to fall out. The sleeves are long and billowy, which contrasts to the fitted bodice. Pulling at the bottom of the top, I try to cover my exposed skin, to no avail. Trying to hike the pants up, I groan when they don't move.

They cinch in at my waist, mold tight at my hips and then billow out until they cuff at the bottom, matching the sleeves. When I turn, the material moves with me, soft and light. Nibbling on my lip, I can appreciate their beauty. The pattern of gold and red mandala shapes covering each leg and flowing along the belt at the waist, as a deep navy blue blends in with the rest. The voices get louder making me panic, surely I can't go out there like this? Hunting around the room I tug at the top again in frustration. I can't find any other clothes in the whole tent, breathing deeply I square my shoulders. I throw myself one last look in the mirror and before I can chicken out, I exit the tent.

Once outside, the sun beats down on me, warming me. Shielding my eyes with my hand, I squint and try to pinpoint the voices I heard. I know I need to make a good first impression and prove I can fit in. So, if I have to suck it up and wear these clothes, I will. When a loud booming laugh sounds, I follow it around the back of the tent until I see the people sitting there.

A large wooden picnic table sits on the long grass, a red gazebo shielding its occupants from the sun. A smaller table sits a couple of feet away, covered in food.

Blain is eating with a knife and fork, the knife looking extremely sharp. Rex sits next to him, nudging him and laughing, even as he rolls his eyes and keeps eating. Jesse is sitting with his back to me, laughing at whatever they are discussing, his black hair curling today and moving with the breeze. A woman sits on the other end, watching them all with a speculative look on her face and turns to whisper to the man next to her.

Curious, I look her over. It's not often I see other women, especially an older one, which she clearly is. Her mouth has lines around it and wrinkles sit at the corner of each mud brown eye. Her hair is a similar shade to Jesse but hangs past her narrow shoulders. Whereas his is curly, hers seems more frizzy and is very large, the front held back by a red ribbon. A multicolored feather hangs from one ear, reaching the purple cloth covering her thin frame. From here, I can't see if it's a dress or a top, but the material looks thicker than what I'm wearing but looser, too. The fabric appears more coarse as it cups her small breasts and then flows out of sight. Her lips are thin and her nose a touch too big for her face. She's different but pretty in her own way. The man next to her reminds me of one of Frederick's lackeys. A bad feeling seems to ooze from him, the one I get around violent men. His yellow eyes are filled with intelligence as he watches everything around him, constantly scanning. Eventually, they come to rest on me, and he stops talking, his skinny shoulders rounding. He has a long sharp nose and a slightly pudgy face with orange, short spiky hair. He looks like a mismatched person, his eyes clashing with his hair.

The woman next to him follows his gaze and freezes when she spots me, her face turning cold. Swallowing, I pull my eyes away as Jesse seems to sense me, turning and flashing me a huge smile. His beautiful face marred only by a few cuts from the fight yesterday. He jumps up and only then do I realise he's shirtless, his muscles bunching as he moves. He comes towards me, smiling that cheeky smile.

"There you are, sleepyhead, want some breakfast?"

His smooth voice washes through me, cooling my insecurities that the woman raised.

"Oh, I'm sorry! I slept so much longer than I usually do." I tug on the material of my top again, my nerves returning. Will they punish me for not being awake, did they need me to do something? Alcide mentioned I was free today to meet everyone and explore, but that doesn't mean his men knew that.

He frowns before his eyes drop to where my hands are abusing my poor top, he stops mid-step his eyes bulging from his head as he takes in my state of dress. His scrutiny has me fidgeting before I see the look of awe and shock.

"Holy hell, Rhea!" he shouts, rushing to me and walking around me in a circle. His shout has the others looking up and I blush as all eyes are on me. Blain looks me over before grunting and looking back down at his food, Rex runs his eyes over me as his cheeks heat. He smiles at me, but his eyes keep dropping to every inch of exposed skin as if he can't help himself. Blain looks from him to me, and then back to him with disgust before coughing. Rex drops his eyes instantly and rubs the back of his neck, his eyes determinedly staring at his food.

Jesse ends his tour at my front again, a different kind of smile on his face.

"You look absolutely amazing, like some sort of otherworldly being," he says as he grabs a stray wave of my hair and pushes it behind my ear. My skin erupts in goosebumps at his touch, but he doesn't seem to notice as he grabs my hand and tugs me to the table.

"Yeah, like a fucking harpy," Blain snarls. Reluctantly, I let Jesse lead me, still feeling shy about the outfit. Perching myself on the edge of the bench seat, Jesse scoots close until our arms are touching. Rex instantly jumps up, banging his knee on the table as he goes. Blain laughs cruelly.

"Clumsy oaf," he mutters, my eyes narrow as Rex looks sad.

"At least he's not an asshole," I spit, angry that he could hurt someone as kind and sweet as Rex. Blain's head snaps up even as Rex throws me a small smile and hurries over to the other table.

"Feeling brave today are we, or maybe you just want all the attention to be on you."

My mouth drops open before anger flares through me, making my arms prickle as my power tries to reach the surface.

"Or maybe I'm just not into self-righteous, egotistical men who obviously have nothing better to do than put someone else down because they are incapable of being nice."

Jesse snorts as laughter has him doubling over and banging on the table.

"Oh, she has you down to a T, man," he says wiping his eyes. Blain stands, obviously done with his food.

"Sure, whatever you say, Harpy, but I saw you checking me out last night and now Jesse this morning. So, say whatever you want, but your true colours will show eventually and when they do, I will be there to tell them I told you so." He spins before I can come up with a retort and strides away, the black pants clinging to him. Angry I checked him out again, I glare down at the table.

"Hey, ignore him and feel free to check me out anytime, Firecracker," Jesse murmurs to me before picking up his food again. My cheeks heat and I jump when a plate drops down before me, filled to the brim with meats, cheese and bread.

"Thanks, Wildcat," Rex whispers before his hand squeezes my shoulder. He waits for me to nod before walking back around to his side and carries on eating. I pick at my food, I am unaccustomed to eating so much and the anger still burns in my gut. I knew it wouldn't be easy fitting in with people who have obviously been together a while, but Blain doesn't even seem to want to give me a chance. Instead, he seems to want to watch me fail, it only makes me more determined to prove myself.

"Eat, you have a busy day ahead," Rex says softly, watching me until I add some meat to a bit of bread and take a big bite. He offers me that big smile again as he munches on his own.

"So boys, who is this new creature? Did Al find her on the side of the road, she looks like a child."

My head snaps up, looking at the woman before I drop my eyes, scared of the almost vulture like expression on her face.

"Be nice Esme, and no, she saved my life and then Fluffy's," Jessie says proudly.

"Stupid name," she mutters before carrying on louder, "Is that right? So what are you here to do, cook? Clean? That looks like all you're good for."

Gritting my teeth, I hold in my snark, not wanting to piss off another member of Alcide's family, unwilling to give him any reason to turn me away.

"He said he was going to figure out an act for me today," I say softly. The whole table goes quiet before Jesse whoops and hugs me to his side, his hand landing on my exposed stomach.

"I knew you were one of us, Rhea!" He cries happily as Rex nods and smiles.

"An act?!" The woman's voice turns shrill as she grips the table until her hands turn white. I gasp when her plate starts to levitate before she throws it a dirty look and lets go of the table, the plate banging back down again. I look from her to it with wide eyes.

"Did you just-" I ask in awe, completely amazed by her powers.

Her face turns dark like a thunderstorm as she pushes away from the table.

"What's the matter, never seen a freak before, girl? If not, maybe you should run back to where ever you came from and spread your legs for your master like a good little girl."

I flinch at her words as she storms away, the man looking at me oddly before he follows her. Turning to the guys, I feel tears clawing at the back of my eyes before I swallow them back. I've been here one morning and it looks like that's all it's going to be if they all hate me so much. My hopes deflate as my shoulders slump. I knew it was too good to be true.

"Hey," Rex reaches over and lifts my chin, his face filled with anger, but when he looks at me it softens.

"Ignore her. It took her a year to get an act. She's just jealous." I drop my eyes again.

"Seriously Rhea, don't listen, okay, we all know you belong here and she will just have to live with it," Jesse adds, squeezing my side in reassurance.

"And Blain?" I ask, needing to know if they are going to kick me out. Jesse snorts.

"He's a grumpy bastard to everyone, but it's only because he wants to protect his family, he will see you belong here soon." I nod at his words, but deep down I wonder what will happen if they all think I don't. If eventually they change their minds and he's right. If that's the case, I plan on trying my hardest and will treasure the time I have with the two men trying to comfort me. Smiling a little I play with my food until Rex drops his fork and stands, his arm outstretched to me.

"Come on, let me show you around." Smiling slightly, I throw Jesse a soft look before standing and accepting the hand Rex offers me.

Rex and I walk in companionable silence for a while. I get the impression from the others that Rex isn't usually much of a talker, preferring the company of animals over people. Before I met these guys I would have said I preferred the same thing. Well, perhaps not Blain. I definitely still prefer animals over him. Maybe I could feed him to Fluffy. I smirk at that thought.

Rex looks across at me as I chuckle quietly, a questioning smile spreading across his face.

"Care to share?" He asks, nodding to one of the workers that we pass.

"I was just thinking about feeding Blain to Fluffy," I tell him with an evil smile, before biting my lip.

This was his friend I was talking about, perhaps I have taken it too far, I've only just met them after all. However, Rex takes on a thoughtful look, like he is actually considering my comment.

"Hmm. Well him and Fluffy really don't get on, so that wouldn't be too far a stretch," he says, before smiling at me in a way so I know he is joking. "You're going to make Fluffy fat if you keep spoiling him. Besides, I'm trying to train him not to eat people, you're going to undo all my hard work."

I laugh at Rex's idea that spoiling Fluffy is allowing him to eat one of his friends. I had been convinced that he would scold me for plotting Blain's murder. I am busy plotting some more inventive ideas for his demise when I feel Rex's eyes on me. I look across at him and smile at his expression when he realises he has been caught looking at me. Blushing, he rubs a hand across the back of his neck.

"Sorry, Wildcat. That outfit is distracting," he mumbles, trying to keep his eyes on anything but me.

He introduces me to a couple of other crew members, so far all of them have been men except for me and Esme. This isn't all that surprising given the universal male-to-female ratio, but their expressions are what surprise me. Is it really that unusual for a woman to join the Circus? Not that they had been unwelcoming, just surprised. I had been worried that I would not be welcomed here. I was walking into a family and trying to find my place. However, other than Blain, Esme, and that creepy guy at breakfast, everyone had been polite and willing to trust Alcide's judgement of me.

That said a lot to me about the kind of leader he would be. If they were willing to put away their prejudices against women and give me a chance because Alcide told them to, then he must be a fair leader. I think back to what he told me last night when I fell to my knees before him. He told me to get up, that they 'don't do that here.' What did he mean by that? That women are treated differently here? He seemed angry at my behavior, but that anger had not felt directed at me. Well, I guess only time would tell.

Rex was just telling me about this new animal that they had saved as we walked around a corner, his voice soft, but I can see the excitement in his eyes. He is so cute. I stop myself from going any further. *Come on Rhea, you are not in a position to be checking out your new colleagues, you are supposed to be earning your place here!* That is damn hard, though, when all of the guys looked like they had walked out of one of those magazines.

I hear a loud thud as we continue walking, like something heavy has been dropped to the floor. I go to ask Rex what it was when the largest man I have ever seen walks into view. He makes all of the other guys look like children in comparison, and I have to crane my neck to keep looking at his face as he walks towards us. His blond hair is shorn close to his head and he has a smattering of stubble across his chin. I swallow as I look away from his face and find I am staring at his shirt-less chest. Feeling flustered, I take a step back and bump into Rex. *Boy, is it hot out here or is it just me?* His hazel eyes take everything in, and I'm sure from his slight smile that he knows I was checking him out. Turning his focus to Rex, he just raises a questioning eyebrow.

Rex seems to find this whole thing amusing, but decides to rescue me.

"Nixon, this is Rhea. Alcide is giving her an act in the show," he explains to the silent giant. Nixon doesn't seem to be as surprised as the others, just nods at me with a small half smile.

"Fluffy likes her," Rex adds.

This comment does surprise Nixon as he looks at me again, his mouth opens slightly in a silent 'oh'. He looks like he is reassessing me. Personally, I am totally confused and starting to get a bit cranky. I try to push away these feelings, but my run-in with Blain this morning has me fired up.

"Why does everyone keep getting that look on their face? What is so strange about me to cause that look?" I demand, gesturing to both of their faces.

Rex smiles apologetically, rubbing the back of his neck again at being caught. Nixon finally smiles fully for the first time. It only lasts for a few seconds, but it is blinding, easily making him the most handsome man I have ever laid eyes on.

"I like her," his deep rumbling voice reminds me of an earthquake before he turns around and stalks off. I look back at Rex to see him standing with his mouth hanging open.

"I- He...He spoke. He hardly ever speaks," Rex stutters out.

Huh. He does look like the silent and brooding type. We continue our walk in friendly silence, Rex's mind clearly on something else.

Shouting and banging from around the corner greets us, making Rex frown.

"Fucking freaks!"

A loud bellow reaches us and I sprint towards the noise before I can think that it's a bad idea.

Rounding the corner I see that Nixon had been training on some mats in what looks like a sparring ring, and what I see has me stopping in my tracks. His muscles strain as he lifts the rusted remains of an old car above his head. He doesn't even seem to be breaking a sweat as he does this, making it look easy. He looks like he is about to throw it at someone. But this is not what has me stopping. With his back to me like this, I can see his back is covered in scars that look suspiciously like the whip marks that marr my back. Lead lines my stomach and I find myself walking towards the silent giant.

"Nixon," I call softly, seeing him flinch as I call out to him.

"Rhea! Wait!" I hear Rex call out, his voice sounding panicked. In the background I can hear people hurrying about and raised voices, someone shouts something about a trigger, but I pay no attention, my eyes on Nixon. Nixon turns his head to look at me, his face set in a hard mask, but he doesn't scare me, not right now.

"Nixon. It's okay."

He drops the car to the floor next to him with a crash, his breathing is rough, his hands clenched into fists. People are running around and I am aware that we are being watched, I ignore them.

Keeping my attention fully on Nixon, I treat him like I would a wounded animal. I walk slowly towards him, my hand outstretched. As he watches me I think I can see him beginning to calm. I have a hunch at what has set him off. In the short time since I arrived, I have seen that everyone here considers each other as family. From the sounds of it, someone has threatened his family. If the scars on his back are anything to go by, Nixon has had a tough past, and now he has made a life for himself here, which he would do anything to protect.

"We are okay. Everyone is safe."

I place my hand on his arm. He looks at my hand, it looks tiny in comparison to his own. I briefly wonder if he is going to throw my hand off, his body is so stiff. Something in his eyes softens and I see the tension leave his body.

I smile at him and am rewarded when the side of his lips twitch. It's the best I am going to get, and I'm happy about that. Nodding at me, he ambles off without a word, glaring at those who are too close.

Hearing a noise, I turn around to where I left Rex, only to find a small crowd watching with gaping mouths.

"Bloody hell, Rhea, I have never seen someone calm Nixon when he gets triggered. We just usually run and hide," Jesse shouts out to me, the tension in the crowd breaking at his words. I shrug as I walk towards them.

"What happened?" I ask.

"Some locals broke in. We always get a couple of people who take offence at our 'abilities' and try to cause trouble. Nixon was about to go after one of them and pulverize them when you showed up," Jesse explains.

I glance at Rex who is nodding in agreement. *Huh. Maybe I should have let him at them?* I look at those still around me, the looks of shock still on their faces. In fact, the only person who doesn't seem shocked is Alcide, who is leaning against a carriage with his arms crossed. He seems amused. As if sensing my eyes on him, he looks my way with a knowing smile. Clapping his hands to get everyone's attention, he takes a step forward.

"Right, you bunch of gossiping biddies. Less gawking and more action. It's time to start training," he announces to the group in a loud voice, but he says this whilst looking at me. Why do I feel like I'm going to regret this?

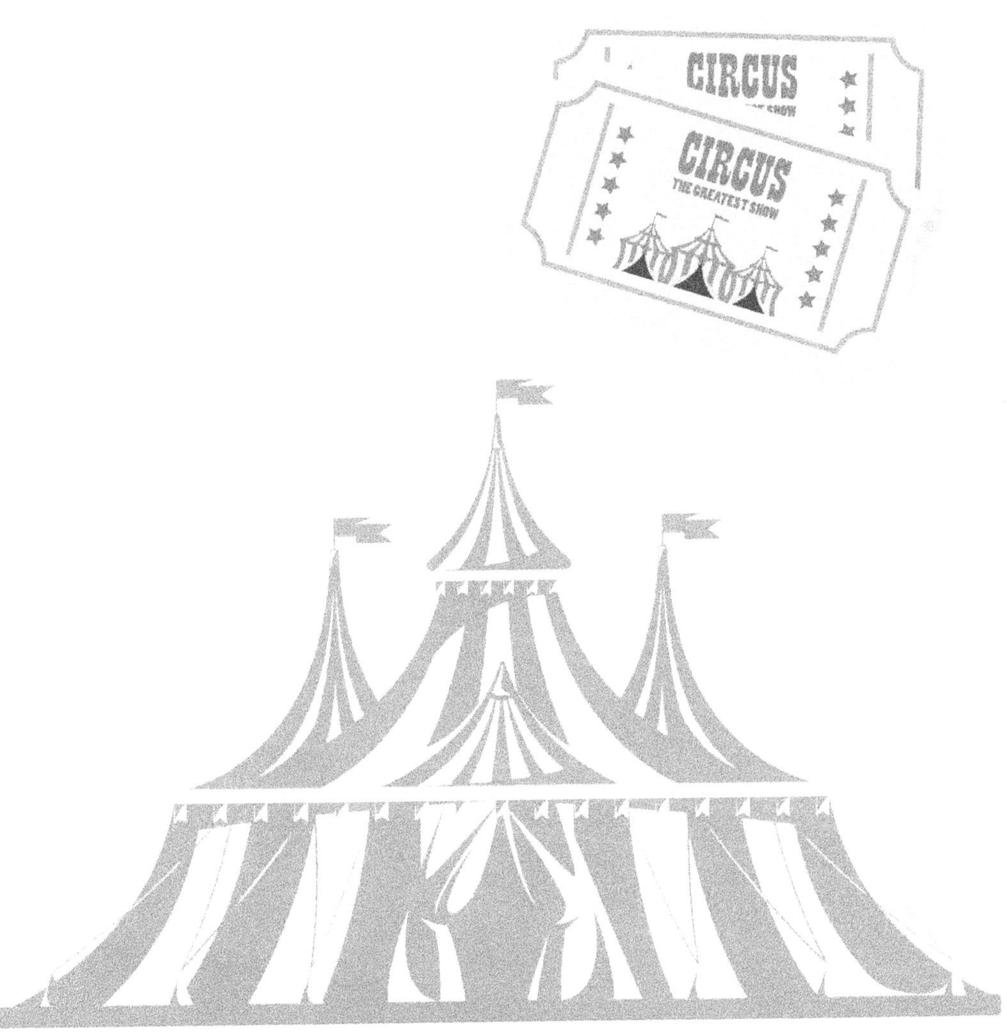

Chapter Five

Rex sits me down with a small smile before he strides into the ring on Alcide's heels; sitting in the rows of seats in the big top my knee bounces as I wait nervously.

Now, they are whispering among themselves as I wait to see what sort of performance Rex has. Jesse plops down on the seat next to me and throws his arm over my shoulder. Esme is leaning against the far corner watching everything intently. I don't know where Nixon and Blain are but I'm too excited to worry at the moment.

"What's wrong, Firecracker?" Jesse asks. His eyes are too intense, so I keep mine focused on the sand in the middle.

"Nothing, just excited to see what you all do."

He goes to say something but stops when Alcide claps his hands and wanders over to Esme. My eyes track him, both intrigued and nervous. Soon they are in a heated argument, his face darkening by the second. Feeling weird for watching them, I turn my attention back to Rex. He stands in the middle of the sanded stage, his arms loose at his sides and confidence in his stance. The sweet bumbling man from last night disappears as a true performer comes forward. The confidence and straightening of his shoulders make him seem bigger than ever.

Following his eye line, I notice the curtain moving before Fluffy comes bounding through, followed by the man with the yellow eyes, who I didn't get introduced to this morning. Frowning at the stick in his hands, I don't spot the giant predator stalking towards me.

"Fluffy," Rex warns, but by the time I turn my head I'm already enveloped by a staggering, purring beast. Grunting, I try to grab something to hold onto as I slip from the chair and land on the ground with a thud.

"Fluffy!" Comes a shout as running feet head my way, not that I can see them over the head, which is knocking into me demanding affection.

Grinning now, I stroke him, letting my hands run through his coarse fur.

"Just wanted a cuddle didn't you, baby?" I coo, scratching between his ears which twitch as his purr increases in volume. It's silent, so much so you could hear crickets, which makes me look up. Everyone, including a silent Nixon, is standing in a circle around me watching in shock. I smile to show I'm okay before petting the needy cat.

"Come on, boy. You've seen the pretty girl, now it's time to work," Rex says sternly, standing over Fluffy with his lips twitching as he takes us in.

Fluffy huffs at him before laying down on me, almost crushing my legs; watching in amusement I see Rex frown.

"Come on, boy," he says, more stern this time. Ignoring him, Fluffy rolls over, his belly facing up as his tail swishes between his spread legs. Rex scratches his head and looks at me for help, obviously unsure how to get him up. Holding in my giggles, I give the cat's belly a quick scratch before patting him.

"Tell you what pretty boy, I'll come and sit in the sand and watch you, okay?"

I probably look crazy talking to him like he's human, but I believe that animals are smarter than we give them credit for. Not only that, but they are quick learners. He rolls his head to look at me, his tongue lolling out.

"Pretty please," I coo again. He shoots forward and licks my cheek before jumping up. My legs instantly fill with pins and needles, making me groan. Rex shakes his head and offers me a hand up, which I gratefully accept. Once I am upright again, I pat the cat's head, my eyes meeting Alcide's. He offers me a grin, but his eyes hold an edge to them. I must be moving too slow for Fluffy because he head-butts my legs, nearly buckling them, to get me going.

"Alright, I'm coming."

Rex keeps his hand in mine, our fingers twined. Fluffy makes a noise and when I look, he's staring at our clasped palms. Confused, I watch as he looks from me to his paw before trotting to my side. My eyes flare in shock when his tail curls around my hand, as if trying to hold it. Staring down at my hand wrapped up in his tail I make a noise, Rex follows my eyes and grins.

"Fluffy is very smart, and apparently he has decided to use that to impress you. Show off," he says, genuine affection for the cat in his voice.

Deciding to go with the flow I follow them to the ring. Rex helps me over the bricks before I delicately sit on the edge. Fluffy watches me as Rex strides back to the middle again.

"Come on now, boy," he shouts. Fluffy turns giving me a look before trotting away, then stops halfway to Rex turning again as if to see if I'm still there. When he sees I am, he continues on until he stands opposite the big man. Hiding my grin by biting my lip, I watch as Rex smiles at the cat before turning to face me. Fluffy turns at the same time, the pair completely in sync and at ease with each other. Rex bows at the waist, his leg pushed forward and Fluffy does the same. His tail thrashing behind him happily as he sticks his front paws out and drops his head. They both straighten again. I don't spot any platforms or props for their performance, making me wonder what they are going to do.

"Jump," Rex declares.

Fluffy instantly runs and leaps. Flinging his lithe body through the air, jumping nearly high enough to touch the ceiling. He lands gracefully on the floor, strutting back to Rex and sitting down in front of him again. I can almost feel something coming, the air thick with tension as Rex stretches his hand out and lays it gently on the big cat's head. They stare at each other for a moment and I swear I see Rex's eyes flash orange before he turns and runs. Leaping into the air the same way Fluffy did, he touches the top of the tent before landing lightly on the balls of his feet and walking back to Fluffy. I know my mouth is open as I watch, unable to comprehend what just happened.

"Claws," he says with no flourish, his act genuine not needing the extra showmanship on top.

Fluffy instantly stands on his back legs, his paws held in the air. Slowly needlepoint blades smoothly emerge from his paws, reaching almost as long as my forearm. Rex repeats the same process, putting his hand on Fluffy's head and watching him. This time, I definitely see his eyes change before he drops his hand and steps back. Fluffy retracts his claws and sits back down as Rex holds his arms out to the sides. The same claws emerging through his skin on his knuckles, I wince thinking it must hurt, but no blood covers his hands.

Something flies past my face, heading for Rex. He slices out with his claws, splitting what I realise is a fruit. It lands on the floor at his feet in pieces. More fly through the air, faster and faster. With every swipe of his claws the ground is littered in sliced fruit.

The claws slowly retract into his skin. I know my eyes should be watching but I'm too terrified that it's hurting him so instead, I inspect his face for any signs of pain. When I see none, I relax a little. He faces Fluffy again and issues a command.

"Speed."

Fluffy yaps and sprints away, his four legs pushing him faster and faster until I can barely see him, more a blur of colour as he races around the circle. Slowing, he stops before Rex, not even out of breath, his powerful muscles waiting.

Rex drops his hand again, the process faster each time. Barely a second later he is copying Fluffy, his powerful body pushing him around in circles. My eyes strain trying to make him out, but it's no use, he's too fast. Sliding to a stop, he grins at Fluffy and reaches out, leaving his hand waiting mid-air. Fluffy yips again and jumps up kicking his back legs at his hand in a high five. Laughing, I clap excitedly, as they both turn to me, almost identical grins and happiness in their eyes. Side by side like this, it is obvious how human Rex makes Fluffy, and how feral Fluffy makes Rex. More clapping comes from behind me as Alcide strides into the circle, his presence instantly filling it up.

"Good, I still feel like you can push yourself more. All you need is the confidence," Alcide claps him on the shoulder and Rex nods. "Okay, try another." Alcide steps back again, returning to his seat as I wait eagerly for more.

I'm totally entranced by Rex's power. I know he mentioned he was more comfortable with animals, and it makes complete sense now. Rex seemed to deflate a little at Alcide's words and I ache to comfort him. Ignoring my usual restraint, I jump up and race to his side.

"That was amazing, Rex, honestly I couldn't breathe watching you. Your power is incredible!" I gush, he turns red under my praise, but his smile widens again, once more filled with confidence.

"Wait until you meet Tiny!"

Fluffy growls before curling himself around my legs; grinning I rub his head.

"You were amazing too, baby." He bares his teeth in his grin, but a commotion has me turning to look at the flap I didn't know was there, towards the back of the tent.

The man with the yellow eyes is hitting an animal with a stick, the huge animal raises itself on its thick, grey back legs, his front two legs suspended in the air. It's body is grey and wrinkly, with a giant head and big floppy ears, it even has a cute, little tail. A long circular trunk straightens as it toots at the man, the sound reverberating around the room. It almost touches the ceiling of the tent, and what looks like plates of armour slide across its skin as the man prods it harshly again.

Without thinking I rush forward, flinging my body in front of the animal. I get deja vu but don't hesitate to stand there and take the beating meant for the creature.

"NO!" Someone screams as I see the stick, which I now notice has a needle in the top, descending towards me. Looking at the man, I know he could stop it or change direction, but a flare of hate lets me know he won't. The rush of my powers races through my blood. Usually, I would push it down but this time I let it come. Embracing it with open arms, I keep my eyes open waiting for the pain that never comes. The stick hits me across the face, snapping on impact and falling from the man's hand as he stares at me in shock. Blinking, I look down, holding my hand out I turn it from side to side marveling at the change.

My skin shines, catching the light like a precious stone I saw in Frederick's room. Almost see-through, with a clear tint, all clean lines and sharp edges. A diamond, I think it was called. My fingers move as I will them to, catching on each other, creating a grating noise. Grabbing my other wrist, I squeeze, nothing even budges. Looking up I meet the eyes of everyone, lingering on Alcide as he watches me with a hungry look. Rex doesn't even hesitate to rush forward and grab my face, twisting it from side to side to inspect for damage. His concern and my adrenaline leaving have my power retreating until I'm once again pale and human. I watch as Jesse approaches the man and punches him, watching as he falls to the floor with a pained moan, before turning to me and hurrying to my side. His handsome face twisted in concern.

"I'm okay, is the animal?" I ask, worried for the wounds I know it must have from the end of that stick. Sadness hits me for not being able to protect it sooner.

"Tiny's fine, looks like him and you have something in common," Jesse says with a soft smile.

"What do you mean?"

Rex lets me go so I can turn and look at...Tiny?

Where there should be blood and cuts, thick, dark grey plating rests. Like snake scales or armour. In awe, I step forward, not for a moment worried it will hurt me. It gently lowers itself to the floor, sitting on the ground with its front legs in the air. I hold my hand out and gently run it across the plates of armour; the texture is hard, like packed earth. Gently, I rap my knuckles against it, the sound reverberating across the other plates. Raising my eyes, I look into Tiny's, an astounding amount of intelligence reflects back, it's like looking into a human's eyes.

"We are similar," I whisper still in awe. My world has turned upside down, so much so that I don't even question it when he nods his big head. The plates slowly retract, sliding away into the animal's body.

"I'm Rhea," I say softly, feeling silly when a snort of derision comes from behind me. My cheeks turn red as Blain strolls into view.

"Great, she is crazy."

Esme laughs as does the man on the floor, he throws them a dirty look before turning to me with his eyebrow raised. Yelping, my arms and legs pinwheel as I'm picked up and held to Tiny's body, my face squished into his chest. He wraps his trunk around me, to hold me securely.

"Er, guys?"

I let out a squeak as we fall, Tiny lays back on the floor with me still clutched to his chest like a toy. Lifting my head, I stare at the creature, before trying to push up. Grunting, I wiggle until he lets me go with a sad noise. On all fours on his huge belly, I stare at the ground next to me and then back at Tiny. Laughter has me looking over my shoulder as Rex and Jesse lean on each other, wiping tears from their eyes. Even Blain has a smile before he notices me looking, then it changes to a scowl. Growling at their lack of help, I turn to face the cuddle monster.

"Hey, you're lovely and all but would you be able to help me down?" he lifts his head and watches me.

"Please, you could go and hug mean ole Blainy instead?" I grin as a snigger tumbles out.

"Harpy..." Comes the warning.

Tiny wraps his trunk around me again and gently lowers me to the floor. It's a strange experience, I'll give you that. Patting his trunk, I turn to the others.

"I think I have an idea," Alcide grins.

After a fifteen-minute argument, Alcide declares that I need to find my place here, after all a person without an act can't be part of the circus. So, now I find myself strapped to the wheel used for Blain's practices. I have never seen him so happy, he is practically humming with pleasure while I shake with nerves, the bands on my wrists rattling against the board. My arms are the only ones tied at the moment, which leaves me thankful for little mercies. Rex comes to a stop in front of me, his eyes stormy as he watches.

"You don't have to do this, Wildcat," he says softly, I try to reel my nerves in knowing I am only upsetting him. Smiling, I look anywhere but at Blain.

"He can't hurt me, we already tested his knife on my skin and it changes to protect me." Blowing out a breath, I force myself to make eye contact with him, feigning the confidence I don't feel. "Alcide is right, so don't worry about me."

Nodding, he steps to the side, but he's twisting his hands nervously.

In all honesty, I'm scared. I've never tested my powers this far before, and never on purpose, but I need to prove I can do what needs to be done. Plus, if I chickened out, it would only give Blain more fuel to use against me, so instead, I stand and wait for the knives to fly.

"You ready, Harpy?" He grins, bouncing two knives up in the air as he watches me. Narrowing my eyes, the nerves take a back seat as the anger I always feel around him surges forward.

"Give it your best shot… Blainy."

His smile turns into a scowl and before I can scream a knife is embedded in the board next to my arm. He throws the next one slower, so I can see it coming. He throws three more, all getting closer and closer each time to my face. Unwilling to show any weakness, I stare at him and try to keep my shaking to a minimum, my power waiting just below my skin, obviously reacting to my heightened emotions.

"That all you got, Blainy? All talk and no trousers," I tease, using the cook's line from my previous Master's house.

A blade comes whizzing through the air, heading straight for my chest. Panic claws at me as I let the power in me run free, chasing across my skin, changing it just as the blade hits. It bounces harmlessly off my chest and some of the tension I was carrying falls with it, now that I know I can change on command. I'm the one scowling now, though, when I realise he didn't give me any warning. I could have died! The pleased smirk on his handsome face only enrages me further.

Something in me snaps, maybe the adrenaline from near death or my anger finally getting the better of me, either way, I hurl insult after insult his way. Each word dripping with disdain, the anger pushing me, not letting me give up. All the pain and humiliation sustained in my life fueling me until I'm shouting them at him. My tongue wicked and sharp as venomous words flow from them at the man who riles me like no one else.

He yells wordlessly, fury emanating from his shaking body until a blade forms in his hand as if slinking from his body. The blade is shiny and sharp, forming from his skin into his palm. He doesn't even hesitate, as he throws it at me. It embeds in the board inches from my face. I hang here panting, our eyes locked as we try to figure out what the hell happened. He stares at his hand like it's an alien, or if it grew a second head.

"I've never seen him do that before, have you?" Comes a whisper from the side.

Looking at Blain, I can believe it's true, he looks like his whole world just shifted and found out the boogeyman was real. He stumbles back, falling into the table with his knives. He lifts his head and meets my eyes, his reflecting how shocked I must be.

"I'm sorry." Spinning on his heel he flees the tent as if Fluffy is chasing him.

Alcide gives me an unreadable look and follows him. I drop my eyes to the floor, not wanting to look at anyone after my outbursts. I bet they think I am crazy now. My body starts to shiver as the power and anger settle down, leaving me cold and tired. A click has my hand falling down, then one on my other side. Looking up, I meet the worried eyes of Jesse and Rex.

"You okay, Wildcat?"

Nodding, I accept both of their hands to help me down from the board. Not letting go of my hands, they lead me over to the chairs and help me sit. Jesse kneels in front of me and watches me worriedly.

"Are you really okay, Firecracker? You're really pale. Well, paler than normal." He brushes my hair away from my face gently as he watches me. Blowing out a breath I force myself to nod.

"I'm okay." My voice is rough and quiet and it's obvious he doesn't believe me, but he doesn't call me on it, and for that, I'm grateful.

"You know, you're fucking hot when you get all riled up. Want to see if I can rile you up later?" He wiggles his eyebrows at me, making me burst out in laughter. It's slightly hysterical, but I honestly feel better now.

"In your dreams," I say around a smile.

"That's what I'm worried about, Wildcat," Rex says, his hand dropping on my shoulder. Smiling up at him I see his cheeks heat under my gaze.

"What are we standing around for? Nixon, it's your turn, let's show our newest member what you can do," Alcide calls as he strides back into the tent.

Nixon has been watching me throughout the training session, and I can feel his eyes on me now. I turn to look at the silent wall of muscle and give him a slight smile. It's difficult to tell what he is thinking, his blank expression giving nothing away, but I can't help but feel that he is trying to convince himself that I am okay. I haven't had the chance to talk to him since his episode earlier, but I overheard from some of the stagehands that this is not the first time that he has gone into a rage. Something will trigger him, and he will be unstoppable. I don't know for sure, but I have a sneaking suspicion that I know what his trigger is. Especially, when he calmed down once I reassured him that everyone was safe.

Nodding once at me, Nixon rises from the bench where he was sitting alone and strides into the ring. The stagehands give him a wide berth but I see Jesse jog over to Nixon's side. He says something with a grin that I can't hear from my seat, but it has Nixon giving him a ghost of a smile. Jesse laughs and claps the taller man on the shoulder before bounding towards me.

With a flourish, Jesse throws himself onto the bench next to me, his ever-present grin firmly in place. He brushes a stray strand of my wild hair from my face and tucks it behind my ear.

"So, Firecracker. Earlier was pretty dramatic," he says this lightly, but I can see some tension in his posture as he leans his arms on his knees.

Shrugging, I look back over at Nixon, seeing that the big man is warming up in the arena. His shirt is off again, and I can see the sweat glistening off his muscles as he does his punishing warm-up routine. He is making me thirsty just watching him. A slight cough gains my attention and I turn back to look at Jesse, who has a knowing look on his face. My cheeks flame, I'm not used to being around so many good-looking men. Even if I was, I have never felt safe enough to be able to appreciate someone's beauty. Back in Cinders, they were either someone to avoid, or someone to keep an eye on, looks had been merely something to identify a person by. If anything, I had learnt that beauty was dangerous, at least, it was if you were a woman. I had known several girls who had deliberately scarred themselves to make them more unappealing to men. Unfortunately, these girls tended to then end up on the streets, turfed out of their lodgings as they were 'no longer of use.' They were not seen for long after. No longer offered protection from one of the houses, they were fair game. Frederick may have been an asshole, but he was a hell of a lot better than some of the scum that walked the streets of Cinders, or worse, the wanderers from outside of the settlement.

"I can understand that he wants to protect his family," I reply to Jesse's comment, defending Nixon's actions. Jesse barks out a humourless laugh and shakes his head.

"I wasn't talking about Nixon. I was talking about you. You walked up to a nearly seven-foot-tall rampaging wall of muscle. You could have been hurt! No one can calm down Nixon once he gets triggered, and you just waltzed up to him like you were asking him for afternoon tea. And you touched him! Just touching him is enough to set him off," he rants, his voice getting louder the more agitated he gets.

I haven't known Jesse for long, but he has always seemed like the joker of the group, never taking anything seriously. Even when he was being attacked in Cinders, he still flirted with me. I was starting to understand that these guys are not just colleagues or even friends, they are family. And from Jesse's reaction, he was acting like I could be part of that family. I wonder when this happened, we have known each other for just over a day.

"You sound like you care what happens to me," I state quietly, unable to hide the shock in my voice.

"Of course, I care Firecracker! You're family!" His matter-of-fact tone has me blinking back tears.

"But, Alcide said I had to earn my place-" I'm cut off as Jesse makes a rude noise at the back of his throat.

"I don't care what Alcide says. You saved my life. You're my family now," he tells me, glancing up at Rex who was looking in our direction with a slight frown. "I would go as far to say that Rex considers you family now as well."

I have no words for him, so I just nod, a happy smile on my face as my heart fills with a feeling I've never experienced before. Belonging. I look around the tent at the people who are quickly gaining a place in my heart and I let out a small chuckle as I spot one of Blain's knives on the floor.

"I'm not so sure that Blain feels the same way," I say in a conspiratorial tone, grimacing slightly. All of my interactions with him so far have been...eventful.

Jesse laughs and pulls a face.

"Yeah, Blain can be difficult. He is just really protective of us. He will get used to you. Just ignore him."

I snort at this comment. I'm good at ignoring bad behaviour, I have put up with it all my life, but something about Blain just rubs me the wrong way and brings out a fierce, argumentative side of me that I didn't know existed.

My attention is brought back to Nixon, who is proceeding to pummel large stone pillars into small pieces. I wince at the sounds of flesh hitting stone, he must be hurting his hands. I notice that Jesse has fallen quiet, watching the big man in the ring.

"So, what's the story with Nixon?" I ask, curious.

"He was one of the first to join after Alcide founded the circus, I think they knew each other from before. I don't know much, but from what Alcide has told me, he had a pretty shitty life. There is a reason he doesn't speak much, you know?" he tells me, my heart sinking for the silent man.

No one's life after the bombs have been good, life is hard. And those scars....

"So, his power is strength?" I ask, trying to keep my eyes from the raised scars crisscrossing Nixon's back.

Jesse shrugs. "So, they say."

I look at him, surprised. Nixon is obviously strong, stronger than any person I have ever seen, what else could it be?

"Sure, he is strong, and he probably was mutated to become stronger." His voice drops to a whisper and he meets my eyes with his. "He may not speak much, but when he does, he seems to know stuff." He emphasises 'know.'

I raise my eyebrows, leaning back in shock. "He knows the future?!" I ask quietly.

"No, I don't think it's that simple, and everyone will think you're crazy if you say anything. I tried to talk to Alcide about it once."

I look into the ring again and see Alcide is pacing around with a thoughtful look on his face. He steps up to Nixon and says something which makes him stop and look up at me. *Uh-oh.*

"Alcide has been pushing us all recently to develop our powers, so who knows," Jesse continues, oblivious to the conversation going on in the ring.

"Rhea. Come over here for a moment," Alcide's voice carries over to me and I don't really feel I have an option but to go over to him. Although after the last fiasco with Blain, I'm not quite as eager to trust him as I was earlier. Walking over towards the two men, I try to guess what he is going to ask me to do.

"Rhea, can you please turn into your stone form?" Alcide phrases it as a question but I get the feeling I don't have much of a choice.

I close my eyes and try to find the place within me that controls my powers. This is only the second time trying to do it on command and this time I don't have knifes flying at me, so it takes several tries. I can hear impatient voices around me and I try to tune these out. After what must be about five minutes, but what feels like an hour, I feel my body change. I open my eyes to see that I have turned to marble, not stone.

Alcide frowns, but then shrugs and looks to Nixon.

"This will still work. Right, Nixon, pick her up." He tells the tall man.

"Woah, wait. Pick me up?" I ask, panic starting to rise in my voice.

"Yes, Rhea, you will be fine. Your body will protect you if anything goes wrong," he states in a matter of fact way.

I stare at him, bug-eyed at his comment. Whilst he is telling the truth, I still don't like the idea of anything going wrong. But I'm still trying to earn my place here, as Alcide keeps pointing out. I nod to Nixon. He gently reaches towards me and gives me a ghost of a smile which reassures me a little, I don't think he would let anything truly bad happen to me. I guess there is only one way to find out. Without so much as a grunt of effort, Nixon picks me up, cradling me in his arms like precious cargo. *Man, it's a long way up here.*

"Perfect. Now throw her," Alcide orders.

My head whips round to look at him.

"Wha-" I'm cut off as I am hurtled high into the air, so high that I almost reach the top of the tent, rivaling Rex's jump earlier. My breath is taken away from me by the force of the throw. My flight begins to slow as I arc through the air and begin my descent towards the ground. Panic hits me. I'm falling. In this form, I am heavier, so I am falling much quicker, a scream leaves my throat.

"Rhea!" I hear my name shouted by someone, but I can't register who it is in my panic.

I wheel my arms in the air, trying to slow my stop. I'm falling too fast. Nixon looks like he is trying to catch me but at this speed, I am going to crush him. Panic races through my body and I can feel myself begin to change. My limbs lengthen slightly and I feel a large weight leave me as I turn from marble to something else. I glance at my fingers as I feel them tingle and I see webbing form in between them. I can see something else forming on my skin, but I don't have a chance to look before instinct has me shooting my arms out wide. I am jerked back slightly, pain pulling at my shoulders and arms, but I am shocked to see that my fall has slowed, and I'm now gliding to the ground.

When I reach it, I bend my knees to absorb the impact, but I land funny and roll across the ground. *Ouch.* My fall may have been slowed but it certainly wasn't graceful.

I stand up and spin to glare at Alcide, who is wearing a smug expression.

"What the hell were you thinking?!" I shout at the ringmaster, my anger making me forget that this is a man I should be grateful to.

His expression changes and I see a flicker of annoyance cross his features before he masters it back into his usual controlled mask.

"Rhea, you need to push yourself to see what you can do, what your limits are. You were never in any danger," he tells me, his voice even and smooth.

Rex and Jesse come running into the ring, both looking me over to check I'm alright. Jesse runs his hand along my arm.

"Woah, Firecracker, your arms."

His tone of quiet wonder distracts me from my anger at Alcide and I look down at my arms. My limbs are longer and lighter, willowy, and my skin looks different. I squint my eyes and bring my arm closer. My eyes widen in shock. Feathers.

What. The. Hell.

Before my widened eyes the feathers disappear as my limbs return to normal length. I stumble as my usual weight settles across me, leaning into Jesse for support. I look into his eyes, fear at what is happening to me plain to see on my face. Jesse's eyes soften as he pulls me into his arms for a hug. I stiffen initially, I don't think I have ever been hugged before, but I feel safe in his arms, so I quickly sink into it.

Rex has been quiet for this whole exchange, watching me with worried eyes. I glance over at him from my position in Jesse's arms and give him a small shaky smile. I see something in his eyes harden and hear a noise that sounds suspiciously like a growl. I'm worried that he is angry at me as his eyes flash orange until he spins around and strides towards Alcide. Walking right up to the ringmaster, the gentle man that I was beginning to think of as family stops just inches from Alcide. Fists clenching at his sides he looks furious.

"What are you thinking Alcide?! You could have killed her," he spits out.

"She was never in any danger. She needs to push herself to see what she can do," he retorts, and I can see that being questioned by his men is beginning to wear on his temper. "What I say, goes. I could throw her out on the streets if I so wished. Besides, she needs to earn her place here, you know that. And so far, she hasn't." he ends harshly.

A flicker of fear runs through me, he is right, he could snap his fingers and I would be out. I need to work harder. I bury my face is Jesse's chest and I feel his arms tighten around me.

I don't see what happens next, but Jesse's shout of alarm has me glancing up.

"Rex, no!"

I gasp as Rex shoves the palms of his hands into Alcide's chest and pushes the man away from him. My jaw drops as Alcide is thrown to the other side of the tent. I am not the only one shocked, as the room is filled with whispered comments.

"Did you see his eyes?"

"He didn't touch an animal but still had their strength!"

"Will Alcide punish him?"

I try not to listen to these comments as my eyes focus on Rex, who is staring at his hands like they don't belong to him. He looks lost. I take a step towards him.

"Rex."

He looks up when I call his name, his eyes a mixture of shock and sorrow. He turns on his heel and walks from the tent.

I turn to see Alcide on his feet, brushing down his jacket as he watches Rex with a contemplative expression on his face. I'm surprised. If I had just been pushed by one of my men, I would be angry, but he doesn't look that way. More like he is trying to figure something out. He then turns to look at the gathered crowd, his gaze stopping when it lands on me. I swallow, uh oh, this can't be good.

"Back to work everyone. Jesse, you're up," he announces.

People jump to action. I go to walk back to my bench to watch, Jesse is already in the centre of the ring warming up when a hand lands on my arm. I turn to look at the owner of the hand, surprised to see Nixon. He looks like he wants to say something. I smile at him softly in understanding, knowing that he was probably feeling bad about what had happened.

"I wouldn't have let you get hurt," he tells me, his deep voice running over me.

I look at the big man in front of me properly, and I believe him. He would have caught me in my marble form, even though it would have caused him injury to catch marble at that speed, even with his strength. This silent giant would put himself at risk to make sure I wasn't hurt. He had begun to turn away, but I stop him with a gentle hand on his chest. He looks down at my hand in confusion, then to my face. He expression softens at something he sees in my gaze.

"I know. Thank you, Nixon."

He nods at me and lumbers away. I watch him as he exits the tent until I feel someone watching me. I turn and see Alcide watching me again. Winking at me he turns back to the ring to watch Jesse.

The rest of the afternoon I watch Jesse and the other acts of the show practice. I am mesmerised by Jesse. His act is acrobatics and he has to be one of the most flexible people I have ever seen. After doing a summersault that had me holding my breath, he looks over at me and winks. My heart does a summersault as if trying to mimic Jesse. I have to admit, he looks good in his tight leggings, shirtless with his hair slicked back.

Taking a run up, he powers along the circle performing an incredible series of tumbles and somersaults; when he lands he goes down to one knee, and claps his hands together as a large column of flame comes bursting from his mouth. I jump to my feet and run towards him, amazed. I didn't see him use a flame, this must be his power!

"Jesse, that was amazing, I didn't know you could fire breathe!" I say breathlessly.

"That's me, too hot to handle," he flirts with a wink, blowing a tiny flame in my direction.

I curse as I fall to the ground again, before standing and brushing myself off for what feels like the one-hundredth time. The rest of the afternoon had passed in a blur. Alcide had decided that I needed to get in better shape and learn some of Jesse's moves. I don't think that I will ever be able to do what he can, my powers won't be able to help me either. But at a look from Alcide, I did as I was told, I'm still on probation here after all.

Which is why I'm in the dark on my own practicing my new moves. I really am terrible at this, but at least there is a nice view. When I was looking for somewhere to practice, I didn't want anyone to see me, so I walked to the edge of the camp and found a flat space near a ravine. The land may be scorched and dying, but the orange sunset looks stunning out here.

With a sigh, I try to work through my stretches again, I am determined to get this. I will prove myself and earn a place here.

Facing the setting sun, I run through my routine again, I start to feel like I may be able to do this. A smile spreads across my face until a shock of pain hits the back of my head. Bright lights flash across my eyes and my vision starts to go black around the edges. I stumble, trying to gain my footing until I am shoved hard in the back and I feel myself tumble off the edge of the ravine.

The feeling of falling greets me for the second time today and I only have time to scream as terror fills me, my vision flashing again as the ground rushes up to meet me.

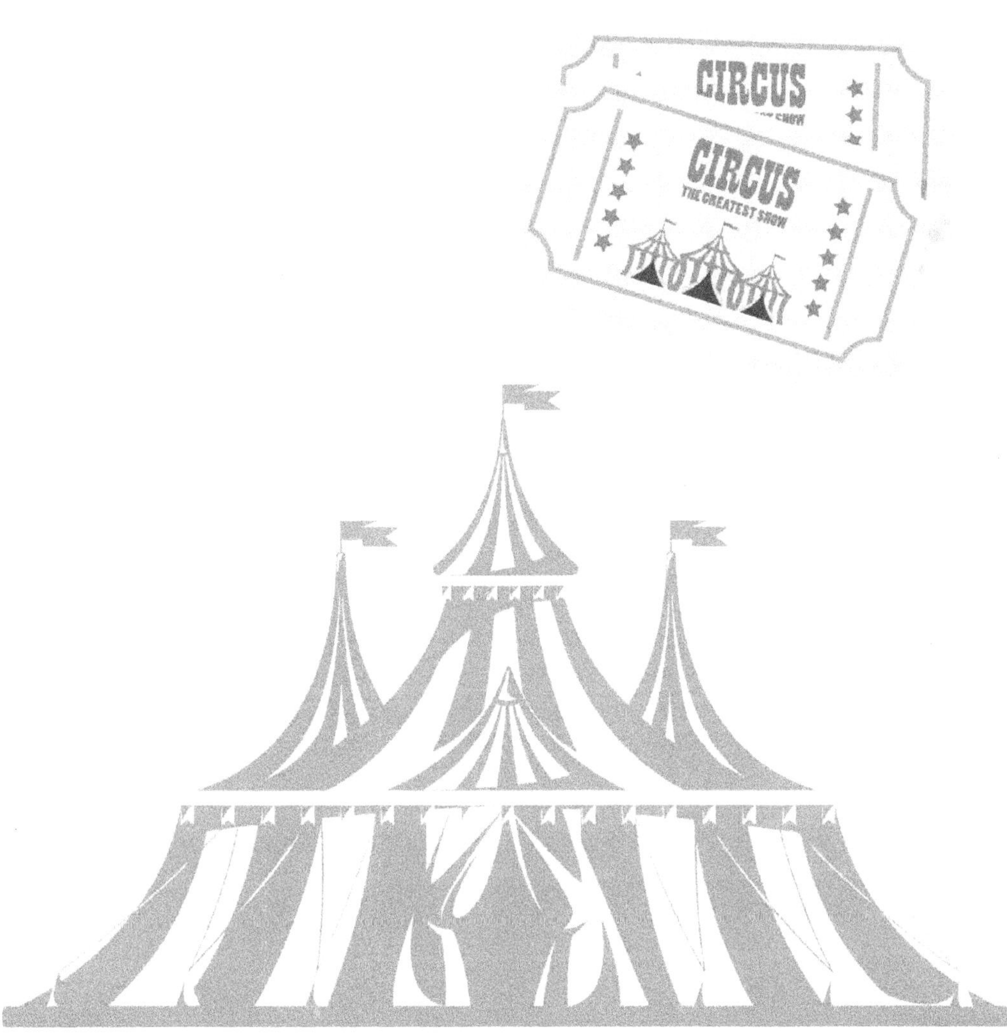

Chapter Six

I jerk awake, the feeling of falling following me into consciousness. I look around and realise I am not where I thought I was, this is not Rex's tent. I seem to be at the bottom of a ravine. Everything comes back to me in a rush. The Circus, Alcide, practicing my moves, falling. No, I didn't just fall, someone pushed me. Looking up to the top of the ravine it is easy to see that fall would have killed a normal person. I take stock of my body, checking it over for injuries. Apart from my head, which is pounding from where I was hit, I can't see any damage. But my body feels strange. My legs are in rock form, my arms are covered in a leathery material and my shoulders ache like there has been a heavy weight hanging from them. I close my eyes and try to pull my powers back inside me. It's hard work, and I'm exhausted once it's done. I've never changed into multiple forms at the same time before. I don't even know what I changed into. Hearing an animal howl in the distance causes fear to rush through me, and I know I need to get back to the circus soon, there are worse things out here than just wolves. Especially, if you're a lone woman.

Pushing to my feet, I look around for the best route out of here. I am starting to panic, the feeling rising at the back of my throat and threatening to consume me. I've never been on my own outside of a compound before, it's too dangerous. I try to put more faith in my powers, I adapt to survive, I will make it back to my guys. I laugh, which sounds loud compared to the silence of the wilderness. *My guys, since when did they become that?* I shake my head, I need to focus if I'm going to get out of this alive.

I look around again, and for some reason, I feel compelled to go left, following a little dirt track that an animal must have made.

I stop walking as I hear a noise, a rustling coming from the tall grass on my right. I crouch down into a defensive position, ready for what might be lurking in the darkness. Two green, glowing orbs peer back at me from within. I stay as still as I can, unsure of who or what the glowing eyes belong to. I don't know much about the animals of the wilderness, I've only heard tales from the folks in the taverns, although I wouldn't pay much attention to what comes out of their mouths. The rustling gets louder and I feel my fear rising up once more. I keep as still as I can, like my life depends on it, even my breathing is shallow. Then out of the grass, an animal slinks towards me. It stands at about knee height, has the appearance of a cat, and has short black fur all over its body. In fact, it would look like a normal cat if not for the size, with its glowing green eyes and two tails. The cat continues to stalk towards me, but at this point, I don't think it means me any harm. I know I am right when the creature rubs up against my legs, making a deep purring noise. I let out a small laugh and drop into a crouch, offering my hand for the cat to smell. Once my hand has been sniffed, I gently place it on its head, rubbing behind its ears. The purring noise gets louder and a smile crosses my face.

A howl sounds again, closer this time, which has me jumping to my feet. The cat spins around and hisses in the direction of the howl.

"Come on cat, we need to get out of here," I say in a shaky voice.

The creature looks up at me as if it understands, and I swear I see it nod its head. I start walking in the direction I had felt pulled towards, glancing over my shoulder to see the cat is following me. A small smile crosses my lips again.

"You should have a name," I say out loud as I walk through the bottom of the ravine. I walk for a while, losing track of time. I'm pondering over names as I begin climbing up a rocky incline.

"How about Sid?" I ask. I know I sound slightly hysterical, but talking to Sid is helping to keep me sane and not over think that someone just tried to kill me.

I don't know how long I walk with my silent companion, but my feet are sore and my arms are scratched up from where I stumbled on the rocky ground. I may be used to hours of physical labour, but I'm not used to falling down ravines and walking in the wilderness. Suddenly, I can see lights in the distance and before I know it I am running.

I'm running blind, my breathing ragged, just following that instinctive part of me that has never lead me astray. I can't see Sid, but I can feel his presence behind me as if watching my back.

"Rhea," a deep voice calls to me.

I look up and have never been so glad to see someone in all my life. I don't question why Nixon is out here in the wilderness, maybe he just knew that he needed to be here? I run towards him, stopping only a few feet from where he is standing. I look up at him to see him frowning at me, a worried expression written across his face, and before I know what is happening he pulls me into his arms and holds me close. Finally feeling safe, I let the emotions of the evening take over, tears running from my eyes as I bury my face in his shirt. I'm aware that at some point Sid has gone, but I don't want to pull away from Nixon's comforting embrace.

They find us like this an hour later, in the wilderness at the edge of the camp, with me clutched tightly in Nixon's arms, just the two of us in the dark.

"Why the fuck have you woken me up. Because Harpy over there fell over? What, did she get a boo-boo?" Blain sneers at me, where I am sitting in between Nixon and Rex. Both of them holding a hand each.

"I was pushed," I grind out. Once again Blain has managed to rile me up and he has only just walked into the tent. My fear turning into anger, the kind that burns deep, just waiting to explode. At least I am not shaking now, instead, I'm fighting the need to fling myself across the table and punch his smug, handsome face. Rex grunts, making me look down to see my hand has turned to stone around his. Shocked, the change retracts until my pale skin is revealed. As I look up at him, he offers me a smile before turning back to the table where we all sit for a 'family meeting' as Alcide calls it. The man himself sits at the head of the table, watching it all unfold with an unreadable expression on his face.

"I've called you all here because one of our own was attacked," Alcide begins, looking down at the group assembled in the tent. My heart warms a little that he classes me as 'one of their own.'

"Tonight, Rhea was hit across the head and pushed off the edge of the ravine. Had she been anyone else she would have died." His words are becoming more clipped, and I can see he is beginning to get angry.

"Did anybody see anything? Hear anything?" he asks the room. No one answers and he seems to get more annoyed.

"Who would attack Rhea, though?" Rex asks, his face twisted in worry.

"I'd push her if I thought it would get rid of her. Stupid wench seems to be unhurt," Blain mutters. Alcide throws him a tired glare before looking at all of us. Just then Esme comes sweeping through the flap.

"Sorry I am late, darlings, I had to get dressed," she says as she runs her hands over the back of Blain's shoulders on the way past. He throws her a scowl as she sits down next to Alcide. Her hand landing on his arm on the table. He frowns down at it, before pulling his arm off the table and dislodging her hand.

"What did I miss?" she asks Alcide, fluttering her lashes at him.

"We were discussing who attacked Rhea," he declares. Her face twists in shock, and I can't help but wonder if it's real.

"Oh, did someone hurt our little slave?"

I grind my teeth, what is her problem?

"If anyone lays a hand on Rhea, I'll deal with them," comes a deep grumble from my left.

I look up at the large, usually silent man next to me. I smile up at Nixon, pleased that I have him on my side. I notice that the tent has fallen silent, everyone looking at Nixon in varying degrees of shock. Jesse's mouth has fallen open, which causes me to laugh.

"Don't see why everyone is so worked up, she's obviously fine!" Esme calls, gesturing her hand at me dismissively.

I have a bad feeling about Esme and I'm going to try and stay clear of her. Well, as best I can, we will be working together after all.

"Well, this is getting us far. Someone is hardly going to step forward. It was probably a townie anyway, she did piss off the locals!" Blain scowls, leaning back in his chair, obviously done with this meeting.

Alcide rubs his head, his usual controlled demeanor cracking to show the tired man underneath.

"Very well, I want everyone on guard, though. Do not go out alone, and watch each other's backs." He waits as we all nod. "I can't wait to leave this town behind," he mutters as he stands. "Alright everyone, try and get some sleep."

Esme stands and flounces out of the tent, Alcide watching her. When she and a few of the other workers have gone, leaving just: Me, Rex, Blain, Nixon, and Jesse, he turns to us.

"Guys, I want you to keep an eye on Rhea. Someone obviously is out to get her. I don't know if it's townspeople or one of our own. She stirred up a lot of people, joining like she did. I would hate to think our family would betray us, but we need to prepare in case it's true."

"Since when did she become one of us? She just joined!" Blain spits out.

"Shut up, Blain. She is one of us, and she shouldn't have to put up with your issues," Jesse says angrily, glaring at the tattooed asshole.

"Jesse, it's okay," I say softly, offering him a reassuring smile.

"Fucking hell! Do you even see how pussy whipped you are right now?" he laughs, "'Jesse, it's okay'," he mimics my voice, making me throw daggers at him with my eyes.

"Who's to say you didn't push me?" I ask, throwing my hands in the air. He growls and steps forward, bracing his hands on the table as he leans in towards me.

"If I had tried to kill you, Harpy, I would have made sure the job was done." With that, he grins at me, flashing his teeth before storming out.

The men all turn to look at me, Alcide smirking.

"You really get under his skin," he chuckles tiredly, before sighing and rubbing his face with his hand. "Right, I've said what I needed to say. Get some sleep," he says before getting up and walking out of the tent.

Jesse gets to his feet and walks up to me, his ever-present smile looking strained.

"Are you really okay, Firecracker?" he asks, his voice soft.

I take stock, trying to figure out how I feel, his question demanding nothing but honesty.

"I'm not sure. But I will be," I answer, looking at the men surrounding me.

Nixon gives me that ghost of a smile I am beginning to love and squeezes my hand, before getting up and heading to the exit of the tent.

"Keep an eye on her," Nixon's deep voice fills the space before walking out.

"Come on Rhea, you can stay in my tent again," Rex says softly. Nodding, I grab his hand and with a smile at Jesse, follow him out. I don't know where Sid slinked off to, but I will try and find him tomorrow.

We slip out into the night, the stars shining down on us. My shoulders tense, as if someone might be watching me. It is probably just nerves from everything that has happened tonight, but I cling to Rex's hand harder, just in case. He glances down at me with a worried frown, before his face clears.

"Want to come and meet some of the animals and check on them before we sleep?"

My smile is instantaneous, my love of animals overpowering every worry and doubt.

"I'd love to!" I gush, he squeezes my hand and we start walking around the big top.

"What other animals do you have?" I ask, the excitement evident in my voice.

"We have a snake, a hunter, and a white croc." My eyes widen as I look ahead, pulling on his hand to hurry up. He laughs, sending shivers down my spine as he pulls me to a stop.

"I love that you care about the animals like I do," he says softly, brushing my hair away from my face.

"The stick," I gasp, he frowns and drops his hand.

"Stick?" He asks, puzzled.

"Do you hurt them? That man earlier had a stick with a needle on it." I like Rex, I really do, but if I find out he hurts the animals to make them perform, there's nothing he can say to redeem himself. My worries disappear when he stumbles back and looks like he might be sick.

"Never! I don't even know where he got that from, I spoke to Alcide right after to sort it out. My animals are my family, just as much as anyone else here." He frowns, obviously upset that I would think that about him. I cling to his hand and drop my eyes in shame.

"I'm sorry, I just-" I lock my eyes on the ground. Stupid Rhea, questioning the people who are looking after you. He lifts my chin gently until I am forced to look at him.

"Don't do that. Don't ever look away from me. Here you are equal, you can question me all you want. Shout, scream, I don't care. Just don't ever think you are less just because of who you are."

"But, that's what I was taught." He grips my chin a little harder to stop my words.

"Forget all that, I know it won't be easy but try. We aren't like them, I'm hoping one day you will realise that." He searches my eyes before dropping his hand, taking his heat with him.

"Come on, let's meet them."

I think over his words as we walk in comfortable silence. Does he really mean it? I've been here a couple of days and yet they have flipped everything upside down. My exhaustion is pushed back in my eagerness to meet the animals.

I follow him into another tent, this one larger, roughly the same size as the big top. There's no seating and stage here though, instead it's an open space filled with cushions and raised platforms. There's a rubber square filled with water in the corner and meat hanging from different areas. It looks like a paradise for animals, and better yet? There's no cages or locks.

Grinning, I watch as Fluffy jumps and grabs a raw steak before laying down and tearing into it.

"Don't they try and escape?" I whisper, not wanting to disturb them.

"No. They bond with us, plus they are free to go at any time. They choose to stay."

Tiny spots us first, he rolls to his feet and bumbles over to us. He pats Rex's head with his trunk before wrapping it around me.

"Oh, no! Not again!" I cry as he gently pulls me. I flop onto his back as he wanders back into the room, he grabs me again pulling me to face him as he drops to the floor on his back legs. He puts my back to his chest, his trunk wrapped around me as my bum hits the floor between his legs.

I blink over to Rex before laughing.

"You really like cuddles, eh big guy?" I stroke his trunk as Rex watches him, his face tender, his smile so big I fear it might crack.

"I should rename you cuddle monster," I mutter. He lays his trunk in my lap, as I run my fingers softly over it.

A hiss has me looking up. A couple of feet away a giant snake is curled, watching me warily. His body is pure white, like the colour of the moon on a clear night. His body is wider than mine and as long as Tiny's. Following up its body, I gasp as it splits off into two separate heads. Both staring at me, one with pitch black eyes and the other with red. The one with the black eyes and mouth open wide showing me it's impressive fangs, which are at least the size of my face.

"Rumple." Comes Rex's warning, he steps slowly over to me but stops when the snake head with the black eyes swings his way and a forked tongue sticks out.

"Erm, Rex?" I ask a little worried as red eyes peer at me, unmoving.

"I know he looks mean, but he's a softie, I promise. He just doesn't like strangers, he's quite protective of me."

He doesn't look like a softie, he looks like he wants to rip me to pieces. Tiny toots at him angrily, which makes Rumple hiss at him. With a human-sounding grumble, Tiny releases me and trudges to his feet. Leaving me to face the snake. Before I can move, its giant body is circling around mine. Coils and coils of scales shining as it stops before me, its faces inches away.

"Don't move. Don't scream," Rex warns. "Rumple, leave her alone. If you do, I'll get Jesse to come and sing a lullaby for you."

The red-eyed head swings his way, as he lolls out his tongue happily. The beady black eyes continue to stare into me, and I find myself unable to look away. I remind myself that if it attacks I can always change into something else, it dampens my fear a bit.

"I'm not afraid of you, I don't want to hurt you," I say softly, the red-eyed head looks back to me. It swings from looking at the black-eyed head to me before darting forward and licking my face. I giggle but stop when the other one hisses and darts forward, its fangs inches from my face. I don't know what makes me do it, but I grab the head and hold it.

"No. Bad snake." Its eyes narrow as I hear a choked sound from Rex.

"Now, I only want to be your friend. You are being mean; if you can't be nice, Jesse won't sing to you," I threaten. Its eyes are barely slits now, but it stops hissing.

"I'm going to let you go, and you are not going to bite me," I say sternly. I gently let go and it moves back slowly, watching me.

"Good boy," I praise, the red eyed head pushes my face obviously wanting praise too.

"Yes, you're a good boy, too," I coo, rubbing along its scaley head. The black-eyed one darts forward and I'm not sure what to do, but red eyes darts to it. The heads twine as the body uncurls from around me and starts thrashing.

Are they fighting?

"Rex, it clearly has different personalities. Why the one name?" I watch it to make sure it's not getting close, but it seems distracted by biting each other.

"Oh erm, I just like the name." He mummers, scratching his head. His cheeks heat and I grin.

"Rumple?"

"It's short for Rumplesnakeskin." He mutters, my eyes round before I burst out in laughter. Every time I think I might stop, I remember what he said and it starts again, at this point tears are streaming down my face.

A hiss, louder than any before has my laughter drying up as I frown at the snake. An idea forms in my head, making me nibble on my lip in indecision. Deciding what the hell, I get to my feet and storm over to the snake.

"Right, if you can't play nice you get punished!" I shout, both heads stop and look at me. They are twisted around each other. The red-eyed one un-twines from the other and lowers its head to the floor, clearly sad.

"I think it's time we gave you another name." Pointing at the red-eyed one I carry on. "You can stay Rumple because you were good." I point at the black-eyed one. "You, I am renaming. Because you can't play nice, I'm going to make it very embarrassing." Racking my head I look around, spotting the water I grin.

"Bubbles," I call cheerfully. He narrows his eyes at me and flashes his fangs again. "Oh, behave Bubbles, you still don't scare me!"

With one more hiss, he turns and slithers into the corner, looking like a sulking child.

"Well, that's one way to do it." Rex laughs, I turn back to see him approach a rock. Confused, I nearly jump out of my skin when he strokes it and it moves. Stepping closer, I try to figure out what it is, it isn't until it uncurls that the long, thick tail with barbs running on the top that I know. This must be the Croc. Its body is probably the same length as Nixon if he laid down, and half as thick. It has four webbed feet ending in four long claws, and its head is nearly as long as its body. Its jaws powerful and deadly. Two beady eyes are on either side of its head, one is a lovely blue and the other yellow. It's the only colour on its body, the rest is pale white. Whereas Rumple/Bubbles has shades and lines around his scales, nothing separates this one. Ribs and dots line its body, as it hovers barely over the ground.

"Come meet Rodger, don't worry he's an old man. All he wants is naps and food."

"How old is he?" I ask, watching as he doesn't even move as Rex pets him.

"I think he is as old as the blasts, he has a damaged scale underneath that's burnt away."

"That would make him over thirty!" I step to his side and crouch down, his double eyelid flicks open before closing again.

"Do any of the animals have powers?"

"Rumple, as you can see, is bigger than any snake and well, there's two of him. His venom also causes paralysis in people or it kills them," I raise my eyebrows at that as Rex looks embarrassed. "He paralyzed Blain once." Rex looks around like Blain might pop out and get angry for him telling me. "He called Rumple a wuss because he's scared of kids, so he bit him."

"Wow, I think I just might love him. He really bit Blain?" Rex nods.

"Good." I grin, Rex grins back. I hear a slither and look over my shoulder to see Rumple/Bubbles behind me. Rumple rubs on my shoulder as Bubbles hisses and looks away, turning his face away from me.

"Rodger here can turn invisible, Fluffy is a mutated Lion and well, Tiny is super smart."

"Wow." I don't know what else to say.

Rex pats Rodger once and stands, offering me his hand. I pat Rumple's head and stick my tongue out at Bubbles when he hisses. Rex pulls me up and to his side.

"Right, night guys. Be good!" He calls; a chorus of animal replies surge and I grin. My night started out horrible, but right now? I've never been so happy.

"Good night cuties, I will see you in the morning," I offer, they all reply again apart from Bubbles, who flicks his tongue at me.

Turning, we slip out of the tent, and back into the night. The camp is quiet, I'm guessing we spent more time there than I thought.

We stroll through the camp, hand in hand. When we reach his tent, he hesitates.

"What's wrong?" I ask, tilting my head back to look at him. He avoids my eye contact, once again shy.

"So, I guess this is goodnight?" He mutters rubbing the back of his head.

"Wait, I thought- I mean, I guess." Blowing out a breath I try to push out what I want without being embarrassed. "I thought you would be staying in here, with me."

His head snaps to me, his eyes searching my face.

"You want me to stay with you?" He says slowly, as if to be sure. My cheeks heat, both of us matching right now.

"Yes," I whisper "If you want to, I just… I don't want to be alone."

He seems to slump at that and I almost kick myself.

"What I am trying to say, and failing horribly is… I want you to stay tonight with me, I feel safe with you. I trust you." He seems to cheer up at that, his shoulders straightening and his smile flashing at me.

He doesn't reply but tugs me through the flap, into the tent. Once there he seems unsure what to do. Braver now that I know no one can see us, I let go of his hand and walk towards the bed.

"Do you have a shirt I can borrow again? I don't want to sleep in this." I ask pulling on the top which was a little worse for wear now. His eyes run over me, heating as he licks his lips. His eyes dart back to mine before he averts them quickly.

"Sure, one sec." He stumbles over to the trunks. Lifting the top one, he sets it aside before rummaging in the one below. He pulls out some black material. Standing he walks towards me, offering it. I grab it with a smile and wait. Blinking, he watches me before red creeps across his face.

"Sorry!" He shouts, spinning around to offer me privacy to change. Grinning, I quickly strip and pull the shirt down, it hangs to my knees like a dress.

"You can turn." I quickly climb into bed, under the cover and scoot over to the wall. Leaving room for him. He turns slowly and sighs when he sees me in bed. He grabs the bottom of his shirt and hesitates again.

"I usually sleep in just my pants," he says.

"Okay."

He pulls his shirt off and throws it to the side. I gawk at the muscles, my eyes running over his magnificent form. He turns to the side pulling off his boots and socks. I watch the muscles play in his back, and have to clench my fingers on the bed to stop myself from reaching out and touching him. He's like the animals he adores, soft on the inside but so deadly looking on the outside. He grabs his trousers and strips them off before jumping into bed. I bite my lip and shuffle back further as his wide, tall frame takes over the bed. He wiggles before turning on his side to face me, his hands cushioning his head. Our legs are touching and our torsos and head only inches apart. My nerves return at being so close, it's not like I have ever been this close to a man before, at least not in this context. I've certainly never had feelings like this for anyone and no one has ever made me feel things like this. His warmth seems to seep into me, and when I meet his eyes, they reassure me. This is Rex, after all, the giant softie who prefers animals to humans. I know he won't hurt me, and my instincts have never led me wrong. I settle on my side, our heads sharing a pillow.

"Where did you sleep last night?" I ask softly.

"I slept in the animal tent," his voice is soft and deep and has me shivering as it seems to play over my skin. This close, I can't escape my growing attraction to him or the feelings he seems to stir in me.

"When did you join the circus?" I find myself wanting to know everything about him.

"Erm, 2055."

I try to add it up in my head, that would make him a kid.

"Did you volunteer or...?"

"No. Alcide found me, my mum was a whore. She wasn't allowed to have a child but raised me in secret, when they found out, she abandoned me out in the middle of nowhere when I was young." The pain in his voice has me reaching across, grabbing his hand and holding it. He offers me a smile, his eyes filled with pain and memories.

"I was supposed to die. I remember I had been walking for what felt like forever when I finally found some food. I was just about to eat it when I heard a tiny cry. It called to something in me, so I found myself looking for what made it." He strokes my hand as he speaks, like you would stroke an animal. "It was Fluffy, well, baby Fluffy. He was skinny as hell and had obviously been left as well. I spent the whole day getting him to trust me enough to share my food. I spent the next two gaining the rest of his trust. When I went to sleep that night, he was on the other side of the tree from me. When I woke up, he was in my lap." A tear slips down my cheek and he catches it, wiping it away.

"It's not all bad Rhea. We've been inseparable ever since, we became each other's family. He taught me how to hunt and survive and I helped him. When Alcide found me, I was more animal than man. He offered me a home, a family. For me and Fluffy." He runs his eyes over my face like he's memorising it.

"I slept that first year in the same tent as Fluffy. In some ways, I changed, but in others I am still the same." Frowning I try to understand what he is hinting at.

"What do you mean?" He looks at my hand in his, my hand almost completely dwarfed by his larger one.

"I am still more animal than man. I might be able to act human, but I will always be more comfortable around them. I'm not like Jesse, always knowing the right thing to say. Or Alcide, who can charm the pants off of anyone. I'm just… me."

I tug at his hand, which is still clutched in mine and I wait until he looks at me.

"I like you. I don't need pretty words, or charm. I love that you look after all the animals as family, I love how you managed to survive when so many would not. You are perfect the way you are." He grins at me, his heart in his eyes. "Plus, it's not like I'm perfect either. I barely know how to be human myself, being taught for so many years to be nothing changes people."

He draws in a breath. "So, we will learn together," he offers softly.

My eyes drop to his lips, so close to mine. I've never kissed someone before, but right now I've never wanted anything more.

Before I can lose my nerve, I lean my head toward him, pushing my lips against his. I freeze once there, unsure how he will react. I have never done this before, and I briefly panic that I am kissing him wrong. I almost pull back, but he grabs the back of my head gently as he kisses me back. All thoughts disappear from my head, my focus purely on our lips and the feelings it is evoking inside me. Featherlight and soft. We explore each other before he nips on my bottom lip, making me gasp as he slips his tongue in my open mouth.

Fisting my hands on his chest, I moan as he strokes his tongue with mine. Not wanting to waste my opportunity, I run my hands down his impressive chest. He shivers and pulls me closer. Our kiss picks up speed before we are forced to part, both gasping for air. We watch each other before his chest rumbles and he yanks me to him. As he rolls on top of me, our bodies crash against each other. My legs fall open, cradling him. He darts his mouth back to mine as I stroke along his chest and back. Everywhere I can reach.

A smash has us breaking apart, staring at each other in confusion. Another louder bang sounds, as Fluffy roars. Voices shout as people wake up.

"What's that?" I ask breathlessly.

Rex shakes his head, obviously to clear it before jumping off me. Leaving me cold and alone.

"Stay here, I will go and see." He pulls on his jeans as he talks, not bothering with a shirt he runs outside. The flap shows me shadows moving and flames. Jumping out of bed, I stumble over to my clothes and yank on my trousers, my back to the flap of the tent.

"Well, look what we have here. Frederick's bitch." The sneer has me spinning, almost losing my balance as I face the man standing in the flap entrance. Two more flank behind him, all running their eyes over me. My eyes dart between them as I start to panic.

"Please get out," I beg.

The man ignores me and walks inside, his friends following, the flap closing behind them. My eyes dart everywhere, trying to look for a way out.

"Frederick's not here now bitch, so how about we play?"

Horrified, I watch his eyes light with lust as he licks his lips. I can hear Rex, but he sounds far away. It looks like I am all on my own. Stumbling back I try to search for a weapon without losing eye contact.

"How about you make it easy for us slave. Bend over like the whore you are." His friends cackle behind him as I tremble in fear, but I won't be that meek little slave anymore.

"You're going to have to make me," I say with more confidence than I feel.

"Gladly." He grins, stepping towards me. His friends following as the lust and anger rolls off them in waves. I'm trapped at the back of the tent, as they advance on me.

CIRCUS
CIRCUS
THE GREATEST SHOW

growl has me looking towards the tent flap, to see Sid standing there. Grabbing the hairbrush next to me, I watch in horror as the cat jumps at one of the men, teeth flashing. I don't have time to help, as the man at the front rushes me. Grabbing me by the hair, he flings me harshly on the bed. Scrambling back, I kick out when he grabs my legs. Screaming, I smash the brush down on his head.

He scowls as he snatches it out of my hands and flings it over his shoulder. Chest heaving, the next scream sticks in my throat as I watch the way he grins at me, his eyes alight with lust.

The ripping of my top is loud in the room, my breasts tumbling out of the now torn material. Tears drip down my face, as I kick and fight, trying my hardest to get him off me. It's no use, he's too big. The scream finally erupts from my mouth, long and ragged as I thrash. He pins down my hips and tugs at my pants.

I can hear Sid clawing and growling as the other two men swear, trying to stop them. I don't know where he came from but I have never been more grateful for him showing up, almost like he knows I need him. *God, I hope they don't hurt him.* Shame and terror race through my veins as the man above me backhands me. My head snaps to the side, ringing with the force. It stills my movements, and he's able to get my trousers down to my ankles before I start kicking again. It only seems to help him get them off, eagerly he presses his hips to mine.

Rubbing his dick across me, making me cry out in revulsion, my stomach lurching at the thought of what is about to happen.

My power rushes forward finally, but there's not much it can do to stop this from happening. My soul cries out at what I know is going to come. I promised myself I would never let this happen, but now I'm powerless. I hate it. My hand hardens as I pummel at the man's head, trying to stop him as he fumbles with his trousers. He groans in pain before he looks up at me. Freezing at the hate in his eyes, I don't see the fist aimed at my head. My powers retreat, leaving me human as it slowly descends towards my unprotected face.

I refuse to let my eyes close, but I flinch as it gets closer, only for it to stop just above my face. Blinking, my chest heaving as tears stream down my face, I look up and straight into Blain's enraged face. His eyes are burning and his face hardened, so different from the anger he shows me. The look he gives the man is terrifying.

Grabbing the back of the man's neck he pulls him off me and throws him to the floor. Scrambling back, I clutch the edges of my shirt together over my breasts as I watch Blain. The need to cover my nakedness after what almost just happened is running fiercely through me. I try to pull my pants back up; they are ripped, but they will do for now. He glances at my terrified face before moving in front of me and facing the man.

"You okay, Harpy?" he asks.

I nod before trying to talk.

"Fi-" I clear my throat before carrying on, "Fine." My voice shaky and filled with tears.

"Get up," He commands before kicking the man. The man stumbles to his feet and rushes Blain. Unsure what to do to help, I sit hesitating on the bed as Blain destroys the man. The fight is over before I can even move. The man falls to the floor, unconscious. Blain stands there, his chest heaving in and out with his fast breaths, his hands fisted at his sides as he looks at the other two men. One is on the floor, Sid on top of him as the other darts in trying to hit the cat.

"Get out before I kill you," Blain warns, his voice deadly. A knife appears in each hand and the men must see it. The one trying to hit Sid sprints out, the man on the floor crawling after him.

Blain still has his back to me, I can almost feel his fraying control as the knives slowly disappear. Sid looks at me and nods before jumping on the end of the bed and curling up in a ball, licking himself.

"Blainy?" I ask softly, my nickname for him which I usually use to piss him off sounds more like an endearment, although my voice is rough from screaming. He hunches his shoulders before turning to me. I see the fury and malice on his face before he wipes them away with his usual scowl.

"Harpy-" I don't let him finish, I throw myself into his arms with a cry. He catches me with a grunt and stands stiffly as I wrap my arms and legs around him. I don't even care at the moment that it's Blain, I need to be held and he just saved my life. Slowly, as if unsure, his hand drops to my back and he rubs it, causing fresh tears to fall.

"Damn, Harpy, you're okay." His voice is the softest I've ever heard it. Pulling my head from where I buried it in his shoulder I look at him. When I continue to cry he grimaces.

"What's the matter princess, wishing it was Rex or maybe Jesse who was here? Sorry, looks like you are stuck with me, guess you will just have to suck it up. Now stop fucking crying, it's pathetic."

It's my turn to scowl, my fear and panic turning to anger like it always does around him. Why does he always have to be an asshole?

"Can't you just be nice for one fucking second?" I shout in his face.

"Why? Can't deal with the truth?" He sneers.

"God, you're such an asshole! Stupid fucking man, can't you see how glad I am that you were here!"

Ugh! I want to smack him, hit him so hard it might knock some manners into his stupid pig-headed...

Our eyes lock as both our chests heave from anger, my body still wrapped around his. My eyes round before sliding shut as his lips smash to mine.

Groaning, he devours my mouth, nipping and sucking until I'm panting. He pulls away as quickly as he started. He untangles my legs from around him and steps back from me so fast I fall back onto my ass on the floor. He leans across me to grab something and throws it at me.

"Put some fucking clothes on, will you?" he demands, his tone harsh but I think I can see something softening in them as he looks over me again.

He strides out of the tent, leaving me laying on the floor looking bewildered, my mouth red from our kiss. I look at my lap at what had been thrown at me, it's some of Rex's leggings. It will be huge on me, but right now I will just be happy to be covered. Sid yawns, making me look at him, he looks at the flap then to me.

"Hell, if I know," I say stiffly, grumbling as I climb to my feet. Yelling outside has me hesitating, I need to go out there and check on everyone, but not like this. I hurry into the clothes Blain had 'supplied', me with before slipping out and looking around.

The ground near the big tent is scorched and a fire is still raging near the entrance to the camp. Men are running back and forth, some with buckets of water. Spotting Alcide, I slowly walk over. He stands with his back to me, men gathered around in front of him.

Stopping behind him, I gently put my hand on his back, he looks over his shoulder and throws me a smile before turning to face forward again.

"Gentleman, you will forget you ever came here. Forget about the slave girl and go back to your pathetic lives. Nod if you understand," his voice is strong and sends shivers down my spine. My power rushes forward like it recognises something in him.

Peeking around him, I frown at the group of townspeople in front of him. Their faces are slack, their eyes empty. They all nod at the same time.

"Good. Now leave," Alcide says, his voice filled with something intangible.

They all turn and walk away, lumbering out of the camp and back to Cinders.

"What was that?" I whisper in awe.

Alcide turns to me, dislodging my hand and making me take a step back.

"You didn't think I would be in charge if I wasn't one of you, did you?" He goes to say something else but frowns at me instead.

"What happened to you?" He growls looking me over, his expression dark. I cross my arms across my chest. Even though I am mostly covered, my torn shirt still makes me feel exposed, evidence of what nearly happened clear for all to see.

"Some men came in my tent. Blain fought them off," I mutter.

"Blain?" Alcide says, his eyebrow raising. Nodding, I watch him; did he mean that he used a power on those people somehow?

"Interesting. Here." He pulls his shirt off and offers it to me. Smiling in thanks, I take it and pull it over my ruined one. Once it covers me, I try to pull the tatters of the other one out. Grunting, I yank trying to tear it. Alcide's hands still me.

"Let me," he murmurs. His long cold fingers work under his shirt and collect the tattered remains of the other one. With a pull, it comes out and he drops it on the ground.

"You okay?" He asks quietly. I look at the ground, how do I answer that? Why is it so hard to talk to him? Even outside he seems to fill up the space, his power and personality taking over, making me shy.

"Rhea," he demands, making my head pull back up. I look at everything on his face but his eyes, trying to ignore the questions in them.

"I'm fine."

"Bullshit." He cups my cheek, forcing my eyes to his. They beg me to trust him, to never lie to him.

"I will be okay. They didn't-" I force out a shaky breath and swallow the tears I can feel pooling again, "I will be," I answer honestly.

"You don't have to hide anything with us, Cariñoa. We are your family now, trust us." Nodding, I watch as his face transforms from solemn to smiling.

"Did you mean you have a power?" I ask, being brave.

"Yes, I will tell you about it sometime. For now, I need to check on everyone, will you come with me?" He waits for my answer as if it is important.

"Yes."

He grins at me, those brilliant eyes catching me and keeping me staring at him like an idiot. My kiss with Blain has me blushing and pulling away from him, looking around at everything but him. He chuckles before wrapping his arm around my waist, his large hand resting on my hip.

"Come on then, Cariñoa. You look very fetching in my shirt by the way." My cheeks have just cooled but instantly heat again. *What is happening to me?*

By the time we have checked on everyone, including the animals, I am exhausted. The last two days are catching up with me, leaving me a walking zombie.

"You need to rest," Alcide murmurs as he picks up a crate that had been flung out into the middle of the camp, its contents spilled in the yard. He turns it over and packs it back up as I watch, almost swaying in the wind, my eyes like sawdust.

"I'm okay, I can help," but even to me, my voice sounds tired. He grunts before standing and assessing me with that eyebrow arched. He looks me up and down. I shiver and cross my arms, trying to hide my reaction considering what almost just happened. Smiling at me, he saunters up and grabs me by the back of the legs. I let out a little scream as he flings me over his shoulder. Yelping, I smack his back, where I hang like a sack of clothes. He smacks my leg back as he starts to walk away.

"Alcide, put me down!" I shout.

"Hush, Cariñoa, you will wake everyone."

Gritting my teeth, I blame my tiredness for smacking his ass next. He stops on a laugh.

"Is that how you want to play? Game on."

I can almost see his grin.

"No, wait-" Yelping, I try to sit up as he spanks me.

"Alcide!"

He ignores me and starts walking again. "Come on, we need to get some sleep. We are leaving tomorrow."

"What?" I ask, shocked.

"We aren't staying here, it's too dangerous. We leave at first light, that's why everyone is packing up. You can stay with me for a few hours, so I can keep my eye on you. That should stop you from getting into trouble."

"I do not get into trouble," I grumble.

"Yes, you do. Regular little troublemaker, it's a good thing you're cute."

He gently sets me down on a wide bed, I throw a glare at him and then look around at his tent.

Books cover nearly every surface, they are the only decorations in here apart from the bed. The tent is bigger than Rex's, but it feels empty. In Rex's, you can feel him, the drawings, the colours, every-thing. Here? It feels like someone just passing through.

"Where are your things?" I wonder as I scoot to the back of the bed. He blinks and looks around.

"It's all here, I never had much. Makes it easier to move, when needed. I guess that stuck." He says it casually, but my heart breaks a little. I know exactly what he means, but surely now with his family, he can start to collect things he wants. I don't say any of this though, noticing the lines of exhaustion on his face. I do plan to buy him something in the next town.

"Get some sleep, Rhea. It's going to be a long morning." He crawls in next to me, laying on his back. His eyes closing instantly. Unsure, I hesitate, curling my fingers into the bedding. He cracks an eye open, looks at me, and groans. Darting up, he grabs me and yanks me to his chest. I grunt when my head hits it.

"What-"

"Shh."

His arms band around me, holding me to his chest. I start to wiggle, trying to get away.

"Go to sleep Rhea, before I spank you again." Freezing, I try to decide if he's serious. Giving up trying to get away, I lay my head on his chest and close my eyes. My body is rigid and I don't think I will fall asleep, but soon sleep claims me. Curled up in my ringmaster's arms.

Alcide wasn't joking. We leave at first light, me still half asleep helping to pack everything up. Sid sticks close to my side, I guess he is joining the circus. I will have to introduce him to Rex. I end up in the wagon with Alcide and Blain. The air is filled with Blain's anger and Alcide's unasked questions. Trying to ignore them, I curl up on the back bench, Sid in my lap.

"Wake up, Harpy." Comes a quiet murmur. I ignore it.

A hand shakes me roughly.

"I said wake the fuck up, bloody lazy princess."

I sit bolt upright, my dreams filled with the town's men reaching for me. My head connects to his where he was crouched over me. He falls back, clutching his head

"Fucking shit, Harpy!" he yells. Shocked, my hands hover over him, unsure how to help.

"Sorry!" I offer. He glares at me, making me draw my arms back. He gets up and sits on the wooden bench opposite me. Glaring at me as he sulks. Rolling my eyes, I look out of the window as we slow down. The sound of rushing water has me sticking my head out of the window.

Blain mutters something but I ignore him. Once I see the settlement we are going to camp outside of, I gawk. The settlement has a large wooden sign proudly declaring 'Falls Town'. The houses seem smaller than Cinders', and farther apart. It's probably half the size of my old settlement but has a charm that I can't explain. We pass through, children racing alongside us crying happily. Some people wave at us, others watch us curiously, but no one throws us dirty looks. We drive for five more minutes before we reach where we are going to set up.

When we stop, I jump out and stretch my legs. People instantly jump out of the other wagons as I wander further across the hill we are on. From up here, I can see all of the shops and people. As they mill around, talking, shopping, and laughing. There's no punishment post in sight and I can spot at least one woman down there. A new place, a new family. The last of my restraints fall away, crumbling to the ground below. I suddenly feel free, maybe it's knowing Frederick is miles behind us in the dust, or just that these people around me accept me for who I really am? Either way, my smile is bigger, my walk more confident. Turning around, I watch as everyone starts to unpack, the black mountains behind us casting shade on half of the camp. Trees line the bottom of them, and that must be the source of the running water I hear. Dragging my eyes away, trying to stop myself from exploring, I take in the rest of the camp.

Everyone is working together to set everything up like a well-oiled machine, knowing what they are doing and what needs to be done. I feel out of place. I've been told that I'm 'one of them' now, but I still feel like I have something to prove. I wander through the camp and come across my guys setting up the tents. Jesse sees me first and bounds over to me, wrapping his arm around my shoulders and walks me towards the tent they are gathered around.

"Rhea, perfect timing, we have something to show you," he tells me excitedly, practically bouncing as we walk into the tent.

Rex and Nixon are already in there, arguing over some scatter cushions. Well, when I say arguing, Rex keeps trying to put more cushions on the freshly made bed, whilst Nixon keeps taking them off.

"No," he says again, hugging a sequined cushion to his chest so Rex can't take it from him.

Seeing this huge muscled man clutching a decorative cushion has me smiling and shaking my head at their antics.

"But ladies like cushions!" Rex argues. Seeing that I have walked into the tent, he throws his arm out to me. "Rhea, help me out on this one. Ladies like cushions right?"

I try to hide the laugh that is building as I watch these men that have come to mean so much to me in such a short space of time. I look to the bed, the mound of cushions there, and then back to Rex. He looks so hopeful and proud of what he has done, I don't want to shatter his happiness.

"Well, I guess many do, but it depends who it's for," I say carefully.

At Frederick's, I was given a folded up blanket that I used for a pillow in the summer, and in the winter when the temperatures dropped, I would be forced to use the blanket as extra coverage to avoid freezing. My first experience of using a pillow was when I stayed in Rex's tent. I had even made a comment about how soft it was.

I look over the bed again. "Well, perhaps ten cushions is a little much? Whoever the lady is, she won't be able to fit on the bed if there are too many," I say, and wince as I see Rex's face fall.

Nixon lets out a snort of amusement and throws the cushion at Rex, which makes him smile. I can't hold back the laugh as I watch them. This is exactly what I needed after last night, and I can feel the tension and frustrations of the attack start to ease. It will take a while, but these guys have started the healing process.

"So, what do you think?" Jesse asks as he goes to stand by the other guys, gesturing his arms at the tent, a hopeful look on his face which is shared by Rex, and even Nixon has a cheerful gleam in his eyes.

I look around the tent again, wondering why they think my opinion on this tent is so important.

"It's beautiful," I tell them honestly. "Who does it belong to?" I ask, wondering at their smirking expressions.

Alcide strides into the tent and casts his eyes over the interior, nodding in approval.

"Good, Rhea's tent is all set up. Are you happy with it?" He asks me and I think I can hear a slight note of uncertainty in his tone, his eyes alight with anticipation.

No, that can't be right, Alcide is always sure of everything. I'm smiling and nodding until I take in what he has said. Rhea's tent. My tent. My eyes fill with tears of happiness and I look around the tent again with a renewed sense of appreciation.

"This is all for me?" I ask, my voice rough with emotions that I can't place right now. "My Master- I mean, in my last place, I slept in a dingy cellar, I've never had anything that was truly mine before..." I trail off as the tears threaten to fall again.

A grumbling noise makes me look up and I see all of the men in the room with varying stages of anger written on their faces. Nixon looks like he is about to start punching something, so I give them a beatific smile.

"I love it," I tell them honestly. I can't wait to go through everything once they are gone, there is so much here, and it's all mine. "I can't believe you did all this for me."

This seems to appease them.

"We just wanted to do something for you, since you've had a difficult couple of days. Now you have a space that is all yours," Jesse tells me, his smile tender.

Alcide claps his hands and looks around the tent.

"Right, now that everything is set up, you all have the remainder of the day off. Rest, explore, do what you want. Rhea, make sure you're with one of the guys. I think we are safe here, but it doesn't hurt to be cautious," he says before walking out of the tent again.

I look around at the guys, a little overwhelmed with everything. Jesse is grinning and looking from Rex to me.

"A whole day off! I know the perfect place."

The roar of the waterfall fills the air as we come across the most beautiful view I have ever seen. I have never left Cinders before, but what I have seen of Falls Town makes my previous settlement look like a dump in comparison. When Jesse had said he was taking me somewhere to spend the afternoon, I thought he had meant the town. He had told me to wait in the tent whilst they sorted out some things and to make sure I was wearing some shorts. While the guys were gone, I snooped around my tent, marveling at the items they had filled it with. There was a chest filled to the brim with clothing so bright, I didn't even know the colours existed.

I had decided to get changed as I was still wearing Alcide's shirt from the night before. I settled on a pair of blue embroidered shorts with what looked like little mirrors sewn into the waistband. There was a matching top, but like the day before it ended just below my rib cage, leaving my midriff exposed. I look in the mirror, which was also a novelty for me, and found that although I feel a little uncomfortable in it, the whole effect is pleasing, and it makes me feel pretty.

Rex had picked that moment to enter my tent. His mouth dropped open as he looked at me, causing me to anxiously tug at the hem of the top.

"Does it look okay?" I asked nervously, his stare making me feel self-conscious.

This seemed to shake him out of his stare and he blushed, rubbing his hand across the back of his neck.

"You look amazing, Rhea," he gushes, making me blush. "The guys are ready, let's go."

Which is how I ended up staring at the most beautiful waterfall with my guys. They took me to a clearing by the base of the falls and brought a picnic. They had to explain what a picnic was, as this is a new experience for me, and now we are sitting on a blanket after enjoying our food. I'm not sure where they got most of the food from, but it was delicious. Bite-sized foods both sweet and savoury, but my favourite had to be the pieces of cake.

Others from the circus also came down to the lake at the bottom of the falls, and I can see Blain and Alcide swimming in the water. Jesse jumps to his feet and pulls his top off, throwing it down on the blanket.

"Time for a swim! Come on!" He shouts before running to the water and jumping in.

Rex and I laugh and even Nixon has a smile on his face. Nixon stands and offers me his hand to help me to my feet. They both remove their tops and I suddenly find myself surrounded by half-naked men. I can feel my cheeks flush as we walk to the water's edge. Nixon jumps in, nearly drowning Jesse in the process. Jesse tries to retaliate by jumping onto Nixon's back, which ends up with the two of them thrashing in the water.

I laugh watching the two of them, feeling happier than I can ever remember being. I sit at the water's edge and dangle my feet in, pulling them away slightly at the cold temperature of the water. Once I am used to it, I submerge my feet. I look around to see where Rex has gotten to, and see him standing just behind me, watching me. I raise my eyebrows in question and he just blushes before taking a running jump into the water.

"Aren't you coming in, Firecracker?" Jesse calls out from the water, attempting to swim away from where Nixon is trying to grab him.

I laugh and shake my head.

"No, I'm just happy to watch," I call out and I'm telling the truth.

They don't need to know I can't swim. Cinders had a small lake at the edge of the settlement, but the water was polluted, and no one actually swam in it because it would kill them. So, I never learnt how to swim.

I spend the next hour watching the guys splash about in the water with a smile on my face. They seem so carefree, even Nixon seems to be having a good time. I am so busy watching them, I don't see Blain swimming over until he is by my feet.

"What's wrong, Harpy, don't want to get your hair wet?" he calls out, startling me from my happy daze.

"God, Blain, didn't anyone ever teach you not to sneak up on someone?"

"What, too busy perving on my brothers? One of us not good enough for you?" He sneers, making my blood boil.

"Why do you have to be such a dick?" I fire back.

"Right, I think you need to cool off." He says with a smirk and before I can stop him he grabs my ankles and pulls me into the water.

I go to scream but I'm already under the water. I desperately kick and flail around, trying to find the surface of the water. After what feels like a lifetime, I burst to the surface, gasping for breath before sinking under the water again.

Blain is looking on, with a look of half of disgust and half of amusement.

"God, Harpy, you're acting like you've never been in water before," he comments with a smirk before realising what he says is the truth. "Shit." I hear him curse under his breath before diving under the water and swimming to me. I have drifted away from him but he is fast, and I soon feel his arms around me.

I grip on to him tightly and wrap my legs around his torso. We surface from the water and I bury my face in the crook of his neck.

"Pl-please don't dr-drop me," I stutter, the sudden shock and the cold water making me stutter and shiver.

Pulling me tighter, Blain hugs one arm around me tightly as he treads water.

"Don't worry, Harpy, I won't let you fall," he tells me as he begins swimming to the shore. I almost don't catch the last bit, and it's so out of character for Blain that I could almost believe that I was hearing things.

"Blain, what you doing with our Firecracker?" Jesse remarks, swimming towards us with a grin. I can feel him go rigid in my arms.

"Saving her useless ass, again. Fucking Harpy can't swim," he retorts, swimming right up to Jesse, unhooking me from his body and practically throws me at him. "Be useful and teach her. I'm not always going to be around to save her."

I feel a sting at his comments; I thought we had connected, especially after last night, but he has gone right back to being asshole Blain.

Jesse just cradles me in his arms, it must be shallow enough here that he can touch the ground. He grins at me.

"Just where I wanted you!" His grin falters when he sees my expression. "Just ignore Blain, he's a dick."

I spend the rest of the afternoon with Nixon, Jesse, and Rex trying to teach me how to swim, even Alcide joins in for a bit. He isn't very good at teaching me, though, and keeps getting distracted when I'm in his arms. Eventually, he returns to the shoreline, reminding us that I will be performing my act tonight for the first time.

Now, I am pacing in the back of the main tent, waiting for my entrance. My costume feels tight, just like my chest, as I try to take deep, calming breaths. The fitted one piece shows off my figure, and under the lights I know that I glitter and sparkle. My makeup is bright and over the top, but Jesse assures me that under the spotlights it will look perfect. With the guys help I have been practicing ever since we got back, but I can't help but feel underprepared.

I hear my cue and I take one last, deep breath before fixing a smile on my face and pushing through the tent flaps into the bright lights and waiting crowd.

Chapter Eight

The first thing I see are the spotlights blinding me as I walk into the big top, although with the lights like that, I can't really see the crowd, which helps calm my nerves a little. If I can't see them, I can pretend this is just like when I practiced with the guys earlier. I am momentarily distracted by little lights shimmering across my skin until I realise that it's my costume glittering and reflecting the light. A large cheer from the audience sounds out as I walk into the ring and I smile and wave like I was taught.

Tonight I am to be the assistant for the acts. Alcide decided that whilst I am still in training and developing my act, that I would assist with the others. He said it would be good to add a female to the mix when they already had plenty of male acts, and this was a good way to introduce me to the audience.

I walk further into the ring and up to Alcide's side, hoping my nerves aren't showing. My eyes run over him and I can't help but think he looks amazing tonight. His jacket is tight across his broad shoulders and the leather trousers show off his muscular thighs. Unfortunately, the tails of the jacket cover his butt, but I'm sure it looks just as amazing. *Focus, Rhea!* I have no idea where these thoughts are coming from but being around all these good-looking guys is wreaking havoc on my hormones. Taking his offered hand, I take a bow as rehearsed.

"Tonight, we have a very special treat for you. Introducing our newest member of the troupe. Rhea the Immortal!" The crowd cheers loudly as I am quickly lead to my position for the first act.

The rest of the show passes in a blur. In Blain's act, I am strapped to the board again, just like in rehearsals, but I am shocked at the transformation in him. Stick him in front of a crowd and gone is the surly man that I have gotten to know. Sure, he isn't all smiles and waves, but once the scowl is gone from his face, I am reminded how handsome he is. His eyes pierce into me during the act, sharper than any of his blades. It was decided that Blain would use his knives for this act, as he was still working on summoning his own blades. So far he has only been able to do it when feeling intense emotion.

He throws his last blade and the crowd cheers, calling out for more. Blain stalks up to me and slowly runs his hand over my bound arms, his fingers trailing along my skin, making the hair on my arms stand on end. His eyes don't leave mine the whole time and my surroundings drop away, I am only aware of Blain and his touch. Leaning closer to me his lips come closer to my ear and I shiver as his cool breath brushes over my flushed skin.

"Don't get carried away Harpy, I'm playing up to the crowd," he whispers in my ear, and I would almost believe him if it wasn't for the arousal shining clear on his face. Releasing me from my bonds, he steps away and bows to the crowd, walking away from me. My thoughts are a mess.

"Rhea." I hear him call my name.

I spin around and see a blade materialise in his hand. I barely have time to register him changing his position as he hurls the knife towards me, straight towards my heart. I stick my hands out to protect me and pray my powers can react in time. I feel a ripple across my skin and watch as the blade bounces harmlessly off my body. My body, which has turned to diamond, glittering brightly under the spotlights. I stare at Blain, rage and confusion running riot through me. That was not part of the act. The crowd, however, loves it, they are roaring with applause. Alcide, sensing that he needs to intervene before something else 'spontaneous' happens, runs into the ring.

"What an act! Why not give another round of applause for our very own diamond, Rhea the Immortal!" He announces loudly, effectively snapping me out of my staring match with Blain. With a shaky bow, I leave the ring.

The other acts go as planned, although Nixon doesn't throw me again, I just assist with his act. I had offered, but Nixon just said no and stared down Alcide until he agreed. Rex and I paired up with the animal act, and I am still left so gobsmacked watching him take on the animals abilities, that I am clapping along with the crowd as he demonstrates.

Jesse's act is the last one of the show. This is the one I am most nervous about. Turns out acrobatics is not one of my natural talents. Jesse wows the audience from above on the tightrope, doing tricks that should be impossible, especially at such heights. A hoop is also suspended from the top of the tent, which he uses to amaze the crowd with aerial moves, his muscles straining as he hangs precariously above the ground, whilst I go through a series of tumbles and flips on the ground when he is in between moves. The final part of the act involves both of us suspended in the hoop above the audience. I can feel myself shaking, I'm not a great fan of heights, as my only experiences have involved falling. I climb into the lowered hoop, clinging onto Jesse as it's raised back up.

"You've got this, Firecracker," he whispers to me, his eyes glittering with excitement.

I nod at him, a smile spreading across my face, I can't help it, his happiness is infectious. I know I am safe with Jesse. There are no safety nets or harnesses here, but I trust him.

The act goes well, and for the finale, I hook my legs over the hoop and drop down so I am suspended upside down. Jesse spins the hoop and drops down into the same position so we are back to back and breathes fire. I haven't seen it myself, but I have been told that with the ring spinning it looks like we are encased in flames. I hear the crowd roar with approval. There is a screech from above us as the hoop shudders and we drop a couple of inches. Jesse looks around at me in horror, we both know what's going to happen. I look around but there is nothing soft to land on. I should survive a fall from this height, but

Jesse might not. I twist from my position and throw myself at him. Our combined weight causes him to lose his grip.

"Rhea!" He shouts as we hurtle to the floor.

I wrap myself around him and try to turn us in the air so my back is facing the ground. I close my eyes just before the impact and feel my body change to protect us. There is a loud bang and the impact smashes through my body, a loud crashing sounds seconds after.

A stunned silence fills the air. I open my eyes to see a stunned Jesse in my arms, looked down at me in wonder. I am in my diamond form again. I sit up and frantically look over Jesse.

"Are you okay?!" I ask, he looks a little scratched up, but no major damage.

"You sacrificed yourself to save me," he whispers, his hand running over my face.

I feel myself turn back to my human form and shrug at his comment. I knew my powers would protect me, in my mind, there was no choice.

"Come on, let's get out of here," he says as he tugs on my hand.

I look around at his comment and realise we are in a crater in the ground. The impact of my landing created it. We climb out of the hole in the ground to the sound of shocked applause.

Alcide comes on stage and smooths things over, making it seem like everything happened just like it was supposed to. However, I know from his look over at the mangled hoop, which is now laying on the ground, that he knows this wasn't just an accident.

I stand in Alcide's tent waiting for him nervously. After the show, he pulled me aside to check if I was okay and then told me to wait in his tent as he had something he needed to talk to me about. I tug anxiously at my now ruined costume. The fabric is covered in dirt and is torn up from our landing. I've been here less than a week and I've already caused so much trouble. Not to mention the massive hole in the middle of the circus ring. Alcide is probably going to tell me I need to leave.

I'm pacing the tent, biting down on my lower lip when the ringmaster walks in. He stops dead when he sees me and I walk towards him.

"I'm really sorry. I'll fill the hole in the ground, and I'll pay you back for the costume. I'll work really hard on my act so I can earn my place here properly. Please, Alcide, don't throw me out, I just feel like I'm learning who I'm meant to be," I say in a rush, my hair has fallen out of it's bun, so it is hanging in wild waves around my face.

Alcide laughs and closes the gap between us, tucking a curl of my bright hair behind my ear. I bite down on my lower lip as I wait for his response, my heartbeat loud in my head.

"Rhea, why on earth would you think I am going to kick you out? You saved Jesse tonight and didn't think once about the fact you could have died in the process," he tells me sincerely, his hand resting against my cheek. His eyes focus on my lips and he groans, taking a small step away from me. "Rhea, you're going to have to stop biting that lip of yours, I only have so much control."

I stare at him in shock, the desire in his voice is clear. I find myself taking a step towards him, closing the distance between us.

"Welcome to the family," he says breathlessly, staring down at me and I think he is going to say something else.

There is a noise from outside the tent which startles both of us. Alcide curses and steps away, running a hand over his face before turning away from me. I watch him as he strides to the tent entrance and glances at me over his shoulder before exiting the tent.

"Oh, Rhea. You look stunning in that costume," he says with a grin, winking at me as he walks out.

I am left standing here with a blush colouring my cheeks, wondering what on earth just happened.

I walk back to my tent in a daze, quickly strip out of my costume and look through my new clothes. Grabbing a dress, I shimmy into it and spin in front of the mirror. The thin, floaty material moves around me, with a split up both legs reaching my thighs, showing off my pale skin. The pattern is beautiful, with white flowers scattered all over the emerald material. The front is cut into a low v, and the back swoops low to the base of my spine, causing me to hesitate. However, seeing as

I just performed in front of a whole town in a skin-tight costume, I think I can make this work.

"Firecracker, you ready to-" I grin at Jesse's dumbfounded expression and twirl for him.

"What do you think?" I say softly. His face is shocked but soon clears to a burning desire, his usual charm and smile nowhere to be seen. He prowls towards me, all graceful and smooth, and I find myself frozen on the spot waiting for him.

"You look perfect, almost too beautiful to touch. I don't know how we got so lucky as to find you," he says in awe, his honeyed voice making me swallow nervously. Every word has me building up to something, but it's a fall I wouldn't know how to survive.

"I'm not-" I start, he stops when we are touching, my dress twining with his legs.

"Don't. Just listen for a minute," he waits for me to nod, and then cups my cheek softly. "That day you saved me, when I met your eyes for the first time, I knew you were going to change my world. I'd never seen anyone so beautiful, so fierce, so brave. Then you come here, you join my family, and you care. You push us, ask us for more in the best way. I've never seen Rex so happy, so confident, you drew the animal out of his shell. Alcide has never smiled so much, or let go of that careful control he has to keep us all in line. He might have been the leader, but it pushed him away from us. Left a distance I don't think he knew how to bridge between family and duty, but you did. You bridged that. Don't even get me started on Nixon and Blain... And me. You saved me again tonight, not even worrying about yourself. You're bringing our family even closer together, and you don't even know it. I believe in destiny, always have, and you, Rhea? You're ours."

His head lowers to mine, my heart bursting from his words. He's all I want at the moment, and if he doesn't kiss me I feel like I might explode.

"Where's Rhea, party's starting." I hear someone call from outside, breaking our moment.

We watch one another, breathing each other in, our mouths inches away. Need and something I have never seen before, something close to love, shines in his beautiful eyes.

"We better get the star to her celebration party," he whispers, but he doesn't move away and neither do I.

"Yeah," I murmur, still watching him. He closes his eyes as if in pain, but when they open they are soft again and he smiles before kissing my cheek, his lips lingering there. Slowly pulling away he steps back and offers me a weak smile.

"Come on, Firecracker, let's not keep your adoring fans waiting."

Disappointment has me slumping a little, but I wind my arm through his and follow him out of my tent.

The outside seating area has been transformed. Dangling lights are strung around, the table is covered in a beautiful multicoloured cloth, music is playing loudly as everyone mingles and drinks. The moon shines down on us, and for a moment I just watch as my family enjoys themselves. I never thought I would find a place to belong, now I would do anything to stay here.

"There you are," Rex says as he jogs over to us, his cheeks flushed and smile massive. I smile back and he watches me happily.

"You ready to celebrate? Dancing, drinking, Blain scowling."

I laugh along with Jesse until he pulls me over to the table and plops me down.

"I'll get you a drink, save me a dance,'" he kisses my head and wanders off as Rex sits next to me, his thigh pressing to mine.

"You look stunning, Wildcat."

I lean my head on his shoulder, watching as Jesse teases Blain. "Thank you."

"Will you dance with me, I mean I'm not great but I try, I mean you don't-." I giggle as he starts to ramble nervously again.

"I can't dance." My cheeks heat with the confession.

"What?" he asks, his head moving making me lift mine as he watches me in shock. I shrug.

"Never had the chance to learn."

A drink bangs down on the table in front of me as Jesse slouches on the bench opposite.

"Did I hear that right? Firecracker can't dance?" He clutches his chest dramatically making me roll my eyes.

"Yesss." I drag the word out, unsure why he is asking.

He grins before jumping up. "I'll teach you, come on it will be fun." He pouts his lower lip when I don't instantly move. I look to Rex for help but he smiles at me before sliding off the bench and wandering away, leaving me to Jesse's mercy. Groaning, I put my hand in his and let him pull me to my feet. We walk over to a section of grass where Esme is dancing. Her hips are moving as she dances slowly in front of all the others. I start to get nervous, realising everyone will see me. I tug on Jesse's hand.

"Maybe later."

He spins me until I'm in his arms. "Ignore them all, it's just you and me," he says softly.

"But I won't be able to dance like Esme- what if..."

He puts his finger to my lip. "Esme dances like a hooker, come on, Firecracker, I didn't think you were scared of anything. Live a little."

Giving in, I let him move me to the sultry music, his hands on my hips.

"That's it, follow the music, just let go. Don't overthink it, just move your hips the way they want to."

Giving myself over to the experience, like everything since coming here, I copy his movements. He moves like he performs, all graceful and sultry. Twisting and moving my hips to the beat, I lose myself in the music, forgetting about the audience as we twist and dip around the grass. Our bodies move against each other, each slide making me heat up as I feel all of his hard muscle.

My smile is free and uncaring as we grin at each other. His pelvis is level with mine as he sways, taking us lower to the floor. I follow him down, moving with him, our eyes locked. We sway, each movement making me wish for things I shouldn't think of as desire races through my veins.

He bands his arm over my back and dips me low to the ground, my leg instantly comes up and into the air as I giggle. He smiles down at me, that same heat coming into his eyes from earlier. Clapping makes me jump and he groans before pulling me up and into his arms again. He spins me around into a bow in front of the others. Alcide winks at me, as Rex grins shyly. Nixon nods, but I see the softness on his face. My cheeks heat from all the attention as I fidget nervously. Blain isn't scowling for once, but he does quirk his eyebrow at me. Esme stands at the end, her eyes narrowed and her arms crossed.

"Well, at least you dance better than you perform, even if it was like watching a child following its parents." She laughs.

My eyes drop to the ground, was I really that bad? I try to pull away from Jesse, but he locks his arm around me. I roll my eyes up and watch as he glares at Esme before pulling me after him as he walks away.

I follow, happy to be out of the spotlight, so embarrassed that I was that bad at dancing. I'm silent as he tugs me after him until we are at the back of the closest tent. Then he spins and faces me, his eyes hard.

"Don't listen to her, Firecracker. She's jealous."

I play with a rock at my feet, unable to meet his eyes. "Jealous?"

"Fuck, yes. You didn't see it, but you were breathtaking. You had us all hypnotized, not one of those men looked away as you danced. You had the same confidence about you as when you perform. The one you hide away, don't let her ruin that."

I drag my eyes to his, needing his words like the earth needs rain. I soak them up and use them to build back my confidence. Until I am the person I always want to be, watching the man I want. I haven't been able to get the idea of kissing him out of my mind, I know it will lead to problems and I have already kissed Rex and Blain. But I don't care, how could I not want him? The man who pushes me to be more, who always has my back and makes me remember that above all else, I am a woman.

"Kiss me."

He looks shocked before he grins at me, his eyes alight like the fire next to us. "With pleasure, Firecracker."

I don't know who moves first, but our lips meet as the whole world seems to explode. I grab onto his hair and hold as he presses our bodies together. His tongue slips into my mouth as I beg for more. One of his hands cups my cheek as the other slips down my body and cups my ass, pulling me close so nothing is left between us. I can feel his length hardening, and it only makes me needier. Maybe what he said is true, they are... he is my destiny. All I know is before them I had never felt so alive, and right now I need him. I pull away, panting. He kisses the corner of my lips and down to my neck. I tilt my head to the side on a moan as he licks up the sensitive flesh and leaves a trail of stinging bites. I grab his hair harder and pull his head, needing his lips back on mine. He complies happily, kissing me like there is no tomorrow. His hips move against mine, making me gasp into his mouth. He uses his hand on my ass to move me against him. He swallows my moans as we move together, a different kind of dance now.

Breaking away, he watches me. His lips puffy from our kiss, and his face flushed.

"I'm crazy about you, Rhea, please don't hurt me."

Before I can respond he kisses me gently and pulls away.

"Come on, let's get back to the party before people start missing you."

Nodding, I twine my hands with his.

I spent the rest of the night dancing and laughing. Even Blain dances with me, scowling the whole time, but he spins me around for a couple of minutes before flinging me at Rex for a dance, and stalking off to get another drink. It's an amazing night, and under the full moon, I finally feel at home. My heart now belongs to these five men, I just hope they are always there to catch me when I fall.

CIRCUS
CIRCUS
THE GREATEST SHOW

I fell into a deep sleep, alone in my new tent last night. I did miss laying with someone, but I am not brave enough to ask anyone to join me yet. I wake up automatically at dawn, old habits are hard to break even after the late night I had. No one mentioned anything we had to do today, and Jesse told me they usually have a day of rest. It leaves my day wide open. Staring at the tent ceiling, an idea hits me. Grinning, I jump up and quickly dress in some loose pants and a coloured crop top. I make sure to grab a cover-up, a cape, but unlike my old one, this one fits and only seems to showcase my body. Black, with fur at the top, it cinches at the middle with a bow and flows at different lengths down my body. I grab my coin purse and shoes and slip out of the tent.

Quietly, I sneak through the camp, not wanting to be caught. When I reach the edge of the camp, I grin and make my way down the hill, using the dirty road trodden by feet and wagons.

When I reach the outskirts of the town, I can hear the hustle and bustle of people coming and going about their daily life. It's so much louder than camp, leaving the peace behind. My old insecurities and worries return making me hesitate before I straighten my back and stride through the gate with purpose. I am not someone's property or slave anymore, it means they can't touch me. Plus, most of the town came to see us perform last night so they will know I am part of the circus.

The big wooden gate opens up right into the main street of town. Shops and stalls line the stone road, with houses poking up behind them. Laughter and music reach me, making me relax even more. Cinders was the complete opposite, if you heard laughing it was because of the rich men hurting a slave. Here children run happily through the street, men watch and smile as they work. I take my time looking at everything, trying to decide where to go for what I want.

Spotting a stall with trinkets and treasures, I hurry across the road, smiling at a child who runs past me. I offer the old man behind the stall a small smile before looking over his wares. From jewelry to books, this stall seems to have everything.

I debate what to buy Alcide, I need something he can decorate his tent with.

"Looking for something in particular, miss?" The man croaks. I look up at him.

"Ah-yes. I need something for a man. A present of sorts, something he can put in his room."

He coughs then struggles to his feet and looks over the options. "Brother, father, or master?"

"None. Friend."

He blinks at me incredulously before looking down again. "How about a good book?"

Frowning, I scan again until my eyes land on a beautiful hand carved frame. Animals of all shapes and sizes dot around the rectangular frame and my heart jumps. It's perfect. Now I just need something to fill it. Nibbling on my lip I look around. It needs to be personal, something for his family. I know! I could get Rex to draw something. Grinning, happy with myself I gently grab it.

"How much is this?"

"Thirty-five coins."

Nodding, I grab my purse and count them out before handing them over.

"Thank you, it's beautiful," I gush, he smiles at me before offering me a brown wrapping. I gently wrap it and then frown, damn why didn't I bring anything to carry it.

"Here, miss. My son carved that, you have a good eye. He is one lucky friend." He passes me a bag and I smile gratefully. I safely put the frame away before looking at the man.

"Thank you, tell your son he is as talented as his father is kind."

The man ducks his head. "Thank you, miss, have a good day."

I smile before wandering away. I look through the shops and stalls for a while, and my eye catches on one filled with paper and paints. Hurrying over, I pick some out for Rex before paying. As I am putting them in my bag, I spot a large man looking at me from the next stall. Frowning, I nod at the man who served me and walk away. At the stall a couple of doors down I find a necklace for Jesse. I also find Nixon some leather gloves to protect his hands when performing.

I spot the same man again and start to get paranoid. I go inside the next shop and watch to see if he follows. When he doesn't, I breathe easier.

Silly girl, I chastise. Looking around the shop I spot a fluffy teddy section. I pick up a little bear and an evil thought of giving it to Rumple/Bubbles has me giggling as I look around again. I don't need to get Tiny anything to cuddle with as I seem to be his cuddle buddy. I go to pay for it when next to the desk I see a magnificent knife. The handle is gold with beautiful carvings on it and the blade itself has words written on it. I must stare at it for too long.

"Do you like it?" The man behind the desk asks.

"It's amazing," I say softly.

He nods and stands, pulling it down he offers it to me. I put the teddy down on the desk and hold it delicately. Trying to make out the words I run my fingers along them.

Carpe Noctem

"What does it mean?" I ask curiously

"Seize the night," he answers.

Debating whether or not to buy it for Blain I give in. "I'll take it and the teddy please."

He nods and adds them up before handing them over. I pay with the money Alcide gave me and leave the store. Wandering down the road I try to think if I need anything else.

I stop. I can feel someone watching me. An itch burning my back where I feel their gaze. Dropping my head, I hurry my steps. Looking up I frown, when I realise that I have turned into an alley next to a shop. Groaning at my own stupidity, I turn around.

The man from before stands at the end of the alley watching me, hunger on his large face. I look behind him spotting the main road. He steps further into the alley and I panic and try to slip past him. He grabs my cape and yanks me back.

"Not so fast. I think it's time you learnt your place," he rumbles.

I don't even have time to raise my power as lights flash before my eyes and something hits the side of my head. The world tilts sideways as I fall and my vision edges in black. I can only blink as he crouches down next to me.

"Oh yes, you will do perfectly."

I try to cry out, but the black overtakes my eyes and I pass out.

I push through the darkness clinging to me, trying to drag me back under. Flickering my eyes open I groan and slam them shut. Allowing myself time to adjust, I squint before opening them fully. Blinking at the unfamiliar ceiling I try to remember what happened, where I am. When everything rushes back I gasp and sit up. My eyes search the barren bedroom I am in. A wooden door sits shut at the end of the single bed I am on. Other than that, no other furniture graces the room. I scoot to the side of the bed, stumbling to my feet and start toward walk to check if the door is locked. Crying out, I fall back on the bed as something pulls at my leg.

Looking down, I stare at the chain around my ankle. My eyes follow it to the corner of the bed where it is anchored with a large lock. Panic and terror claw at my throat as I try to control my breathing. Flashbacks of the man who took me start to come back to me, making me panic even more. Frantically, I pull at the chain. The rusted metal links don't creak, and the bed doesn't even move. Dejected, I collapse on the bed out of breath. Tears escape my eyes as I look around the room I am trapped in. Dashing them uselessly, I try to think of a way out of this mess.

Think, Rhea, think! I look around the room again for any clue or hint of where I am. My memory is still fuzzy, and my brain starts playing tricks on me, the room blurring and losing focus. I climb off the bed and inspect it, looking for any loose pieces I could use to escape, or if I needed to, as a weapon. I curse under my breath when I find it intact. I walk around the room as far as my chain will allow me. I can take four steps until it pulls me back, which is about halfway to the door. I scour the room for anything else I could use. It is meticulously clean, not even dust litters the floor. There is a pink blanket and a pillow on the bed which looks like it has seen better days. I sit back on the end of the bed and put my head in my hands.

I can't help but think about all the horror stories Frederick and his men used to tell me, about women that were less fortunate than me. I used to think they were just made up to keep me in line, but now I can't help but wonder if this is what fate has in store for me. Stories about women that are used and sold like cattle, beaten until they were mindless, just empty shells to be used as their owner wished. Frederick once told me of a girl he found out in the barren wilderness when he had been visiting another settlement for a trade deal. She had been like a zombie, and 'defective' had been carved into her skin. She had been stolen from her settlement and taken to a commune in the middle of the barren lands. The commune was run by a group of breeders who believed that it was their mission from God to repopulate the earth. Part of the process would be to make the girls obedient, this would often involve 'breaking in' the girls.

Meaning they would brainwash them and beat them until they would do as commanded. This girl, who was only about sixteen, had been unable to bear children so they had no use for her. They marked her, beat her within an inch of her life, and dumped her in the barren lands to die. Frederick had found her and decided it was kinder to kill her and end her suffering. I had always been horrified by this story, not understanding why he would not help her or bring her back. But I think I can understand now.

There is a noise outside of the room and I can hear voices as they move past. I freeze on the bed, hardly breathing as I try to make out what they are saying. However, they are too quiet, and I clench my fists in frustration. I stand up, wanting to pace the room but I start seeing double as dizziness overcomes me and I sit back down on the bed with a thud. I feel like I'm going to vomit. Clutching my stomach, I roll onto the bed; I'll lay down for a bit until I feel better. I can't escape if I can't see properly.

I close my eyes and wonder how everything has come to this. This might be all I know, but the world didn't used to be like this. Women were classed as equals and fought for their place next to men. The cook at my first Master's household had been from before the blasts. She used to whisper stories to me, about marches that women used to do to demand equal rights. She would tell me of the government, who were once in control of the countries, and how they made bad decisions which lead to a world war. Advancements in technology had led to weapons of mass destruction which were unleashed upon each other, which left us with the wastelands we live in now. She explained to me that the nuclear blasts destroyed the ozone, which caused the planet to heat up, so any plants that survived the blasts died in the drought. The world became a brutal place after the blasts, with the government collapsing leaving no one to rule them, people became unruly and crime rates rose. Then the plague hit and decimated the remaining population, unfortunately, women suffered worse than men. Apparently, after that, the world was such a harsh place to survive only the strongest or most resourceful were left. Which left us with about one female to a hundred males.

Fertility rates dropped due to all the excess radiation and women became something to possess, to own. I don't remember my mother, she dumped me outside of the settlement at Cinders when I was only a baby. I have no idea who my father was. Which was how I came to live in Cinders. I lived with my first Master until I was twelve, and then I was bought by Frederick. I once tried to visit the cook who used to tell me of a better time, but I found her body strung up outside the property with a sign nailed to her body which read 'traitor.' I never spoke of her again for fear of the repercussions.

A loud bang has my eyes shooting open and I jerk to a sitting position. Standing in the doorway is the same man from the market who cornered me in the alley. He stands still, his disgusting, beady eyes running over my body. My breathing speeds up and I contemplate what might happen next. He stalks towards me, his eyes never leaving me as he licks his lips. I scoot back on the bed, trying to get as far away from him as I can.

"Who are you? Where am I? You have to let me go," I demand, wishing my voice didn't sound so weak.

The man laughs like what I have said is hilarious. "I don't have to do anything, girl. You have forgotten your place, which we will remind you of."

I bite my lip from saying anything that will get me into more trouble than I am already in, although I struggle to push the anger away. I glare at the man, meeting his gaze so he knows I am not some meek girl who will be pushed around.

"My, my, you are a pretty one. We were lucky to find you. If it wasn't for the tip-off from that freak, we might have missed you. You are too well protected at the circus. But we got a message saying you had come to the market, alone. And lo and behold, there you were! Walking around like you belong here, practically begging to be taken."

My blood turns to ice as he confirms my fears, someone in the circus has betrayed me. But who? Sure, Esme hates me, but would she really betray a fellow woman? I didn't really know anyone else in the circus except for the guys and they wouldn't do this to me, would they?

"Why am I here?" I ask, dreading the answer that I know is coming.

"You are here to answer your calling," he tells me with a smile I'm sure he thinks is charming, but actually comes across as creepy. "Our population is dying, and you will help us save it. If you're a good girl then this can be beneficial to you, but you have no choice in this," he tells me and horror fills me as he walks towards me, adjusting the bulge in his crotch as he nears.

I've been caught by the breeders. *Stupid Rhea.* I had felt safe in this town, so I had ignored Alcide's advice and came out on my own, and walked straight into their hands.

The man crawls onto the bed and grabs my shoulders. I try to twist to get away from him, but he is too strong, tearing at my clothes. I cry out as they rip. I kick my legs and try to claw at his arms.

"You're feisty! I like my girls with a bit of fight to them," he says and laughs as he backhands my cheek. I cry out, thinking I can hear sounds of fighting in another room, but my full focus is on trying to keep the man on top of me as far away as possible.

He tears at my loose trousers and I can't stop the angry tears that roll down my cheeks.

"Get off me!" I scream, using all of my energy to try and fight this man off me.

"Rhea!" I hear a deep booming voice bellow.

I manage to push the man's face away from mine and turn my head. In the doorway, like an avenging angel, is Nixon.

Chapter Ten

"Nixon!" I cry out, never more glad to see someone in all my life.

Except the gentle giant that I have come to care for isn't there. A rage that I have never seen before clouds his face and I know that he has been triggered. I need to get up so I can calm him down.

The weight of the man above me disappears, as he is thrown from me with a yell. I prop myself up and watch as the man goes to fight Nixon before realising how big he is.

"Hey now, this girl is my property. Go get your own," he says angrily, gesturing towards me chained to the bed.

I can see the exact moment that he realises that he made a mistake by saying those words. His eyes widen as Nixon roars at him, sounding more beast than man. Grabbing the man by his shirt, Nixon lifts him up and looks him dead in the eye.

"Rhea belongs to no one but herself," he utters, his words coming out clipped like he is struggling to speak.

I am shocked, this is the most I have heard him speak since I have met him. If I wasn't chained to a bed I would have wrapped my arms around him at his statement. I have always been owned, someone's property, but no longer.

Nixon moves before I have a chance to shout out, his hands going to the man's neck, snapping it like a twig. He then throws the man's lifeless body to the floor. His breathing is still rapid and he stares at the body like it might jump from the ground and attack me.

"Nixon," I call, but he doesn't move, it's like he can't hear me.

"Nix," I call gently, walking slowly towards him as far as my chain allows.

I place my hand gently on his arm and he spins, hand raised as if to hit me. I flinch, eyes wide, but I know that he wouldn't hurt me.

"Nixon, it's me," I keep my voice quiet and my tone soft.

I can see he is still deep in his trigger, but the Nixon that I know is starting to come back.

"You think you could help me, big guy?" I ask, pointing to the chain attached to my ankle.

He growls as he sees that I am chained to a bed and notices the state of my clothing. Removing his shirt, he passes it to me, and I gratefully put it on. Crouching down he looks at my ankle, before grasping the chain and ripping it from the band around my leg. The cuff is still firmly in place, but I am no longer bound. I take another step towards him but my knees buckle, the events of the day taking their toll on me. Nixon immediately catches me and picks me up, cradling me in his big arms. He begins to leave the room, walking through the dimly lit building. I have a thought as we leave.

"Wait. Are there other girls here?" I ask with horror.

We can't leave anyone here, I refuse to. I won't let anyone else be treated the same way. Nixon shakes his head and I feel relieved.

"They killed them," he tells me, bursting my bubble of relief.

"Why would they do that?!" I ask, horrified.

They were stealing girls to breed because there wasn't enough women, so why would they kill them? It makes no sense to me. It apparently doesn't to Nixon either as he shakes his head.

"Something about them being 'defective'." His voice is layered with rage and I'm worried he is going to go after them again. I am horrified by what he says, and I fall silent, remembering what Frederick had told me about 'defective' girls who weren't able to fall pregnant.

I look up at the big man and see his eyes have returned back to normal, my Nixon is back. I feel safe in his arms and as he wanders back to the circus I feel my eyelids begin to droop, his hand stroking my back reassuringly. A thought comes to me which has me trying to sit up in his arms.

"Wait, how did you find me?" The question feels really important.

He just meets my eyes and shrugs.

"I just knew," he tells me, and I know he is telling the truth. "Rest now, Rhea."

I close my eyes and fall asleep in my protector's arms.

I awaken as I hear the noises of the circus around me, the general hustle and bustle of people working in the camp. I open my eyes and see Nixon peering down at me as he walks through the camp, towards what looks like my tent. I hear several people call out, but none of them are my guys and I wonder where they are.

Pushing through the entrance to my tent, Nixon stops dead and swears under his breath. All of a sudden he drops me, his hands going to his neck, making choking noises as he struggles. I look up from my position on the floor, wondering what the hell is going on. I cry out as I see a person dressed in black hanging off of Nixon's back, a black cord wrapped around his throat.

Nixon roars as he tries to get him off, but the attacker isn't moving. I have to do something, I am not content to sit around and let others keep saving me. I feel a tingling in my hands and look down to see my nails have changed into razor-sharp claws. I look across at Nixon and the attacker again, waiting for their backs to face me. Seeing my opportunity, I run across the tent and slash at the guy on Nixon's back. With a grunt he lets go, clutching at his side which is now bleeding from the scratches I gave him. Nixon uses this as the chance to throw the guy across the tent, where he lands on the bed. I look over and see that someone else is laying on the bed as well.

My eyes have adjusted to the dim light in the tent and I can now see that the other person is dead, a knife still in their chest. I scream, I can't help myself, everything is too much. I hear a commotion outside, and the attacker uses this distraction to slash the side of the tent and run into the night, a trail of blood following him.

"Rhea," Nixon's deep voice calls to me.

I turn to look up at him and am greeted by a stunned expression on his face. I may be in shock over what has happened but right now I want to comfort him. I take a step closer and take his large hand in mine.

"Are you okay, did he hurt you?" I ask, reaching up my other hand and placing in on his neck where I can see an angry red mark forming already. I dimly notice that my hands have turned back to normal, but Nixon's next words take my full attention.

"You saved me. You could have run, but you saved me," he whispers. I've never heard his voice so soft. His eyes look at me like this is the first time anyone has shown him kindness and I wonder what on earth his life was like before the circus.

"Of course I did, you're my-" My words are cut off as he pulls me in close and presses his mouth to mine.

I am stunned for a moment, my body stiff after the shocking events of the day, but knowing it's Nixon and that I am safe with him, I relax into his arms. I would have expected kissing Nixon to be all fiery passion and hard urgent kisses, but his lips are soft and gentle, igniting a desire inside me I hadn't known I possessed. Nixon pulls away and I make a noise of complaint that has a rare smile gracing his lips until I can hear footsteps running towards us.

Nixon wraps his arms around me and pulls me out of the tent, getting me away from the carnage inside. Shouting greets us.

"Rhea! Where did you find her?"

"Are you okay?"

I see Alcide run towards us, his hair disheveled and he looks worried, I've never seen him lose his composure like this.

"Rhea, what happened, what is going on?" he asks, taking my hand in his, worry and frustration clear to see in his expression.

"There is someone in her tent," Nixon tells Alcide, who raises his eyebrows and sends several guys into the tent to check it out.

"The breeders caught me, then Nixon found me and killed the guy and when we got back here, someone attacked Nixon and now there is a body in my bed," I ramble, the words running into one another.

Alcide can see I'm about to have a breakdown and looks to Nixon.

"Take her to my tent, I'll have a look in her tent," he orders, the self-composed Alcide I know coming back. Nixon nods and walks me over to the ringmaster's tent, directing me to the end of the bed.

A few minutes later Alcide walks in, his eyes filled with sorrow as he sits on the end of his desk, facing towards us.

"The body in your bed was Sam, one of the stagehands. He was a good man and didn't deserve to go that way. The question is, who killed him and why was he in your tent?" Alcide asks tiredly, rubbing his hand across his face.

"How did you get away?" he asks, running his eyes over me as if inspecting for injuries.

"I was chained to the bed. Nixon found me and broke the chain," I mutter quietly, my thoughts on the poor man who was killed.

"Wait a second. You were chained? Let me see your leg," he orders, his voice stern as he sees the cuff around my ankle.

I lift my leg to show him where the chain had been attached to the metal cuff.

"Rhea, did you think for even one second that you could use your powers to escape from this?" he asks, dumbfounded, his voice starting to rise.

I look at him in shock. I've had a pretty shitty day, and he is shouting at me?

"What do you mean-"

"What I mean, Rhea, is that you have escaped worse than this before. You grew wings for heaven's sake, you should have been able to change the shape of your foot and escape!" he shouts, his face contorted into an expression of frustration.

"Alcide," Nixon warns.

"No Nixon, if you hadn't gotten there in time, something terrible could have happened, and then we would have lost two people today. You have to start pushing yourself Rhea, you need to learn to master your powers!" His voice is so loud at this point, I flinch away from him.

He is right though, I can't keep hoping my powers will protect me, I need to learn to harness them.

Alcide sighs and walks over crouching down in front of me.

"I'm sorry I shouted, Rhea. I just can't lose you. None of us can," he tells me gently taking my hand is his.

He looks up at Nixon who is nodding in agreement.

"It's time to call a family meeting."

I curl up into Nixon's lap, loving how big he is compared to me and how safe I feel in his arms.

"Someone tipped him off," I say into the silent tent, my men around me waiting.

"What?" Rex asks, his face scrunched.

I tell them everything I remember, ignoring the outcries of anger, and when I finish I snuggle deeper into Nixon's chest.

"Who would betray us?" Jesse asks, voicing what everyone is thinking.

"Anyone got any ideas?" Alcide asks, rubbing his eyes.

I nibble on my lip, unsure whether to say anything but Alcide zones in on it.

"Rhea, do you have something you want to share?" he asks, making my decision for me.

"Esme hates me."

They look between each other, and then every eye focuses on me.

"But enough to betray us?" Jesse asks quietly.

. . .

"Make sure you are certain of accusations you are throwing out, Rhea. Remember, these people are our family," Alcide's voice is stern, making me feel like I have been scolded.

"I am! But someone told that man where I was. If Nixon hadn't found me, we all know how it would have ended. Not everyone is happy with me being here. I am simply listing a person who falls into that category." Pushing out another breath, the anger leaving with it, I look into Alcide's eyes. "I know you don't want to believe your family could betray you, but someone has and pretending it isn't happening won't help."

"Okay, so let's make a list," Jesse says seriously, looking between me and Alcide. Alcide nods but doesn't look away from me.

"Esme, Harold-"

"Wait, who's Harold?" I ask tilting my head to the side.

"The one who follows Esme around," Rex says softly. I nod and they continue throwing names out there. At the end, the list is six people long. It makes me sad to think someone here would betray me, that six people hate me that much.

"Right, so we keep a closer eye on them. Rhea is not to be left alone, ever. She will also not be going into town again while we are here." Alcide throws me a meaningful look and makes eye contact with the others as they nod.

"Great, so we are babysitters now," Blain groans.

"Oh, Wildcat, I forgot to tell you. Here is your bag," Rex passes it over and I jump up in happiness that my gifts haven't been lost.

"All this just because Harpy wanted to go shopping," Blain mutters. Glaring at him, I grab the bag and put it in front of me on the table.

"I guess you don't want your present then," I say snottily. He freezes, his eyes watching me like a mouse in front of snake.

"You bought me a present?" he asks slowly. I nod and he watches me in confusion.

"Why?"

I shrug. "As much as an asshole as you are, you are still my family."

His eyes soften as he looks at me, a small smile on his face. "I've never had a present before," he mutters, and my heart breaks a little bit for him. Searching in the bag I pull his out and slide it across the table.

"Well, now you have." I watch as he unwraps it like it's a precious stone. He stares at the knife so long I start to get nervous. "Is it not okay? I could go back and get you a different one."

He looks up at me and back to the knife. "It's perfect, thank you, Harpy."

I grin at him and he narrows his eyes. "This doesn't mean I like you, though."

"Whatever you tell yourself, Blainy." I blow him a kiss for good measure.

His scowl reappears, but he picks up his knife and tosses it experimentally.

"Do I get anything, Firecracker?" Jesse asks, grinning at me when I look at him. I dig through the bag and pull out his necklace, a stone that looks like fire in the middle hanging on a long silver chain. I offer it to him and he snatches it from my hands with an apologetic smile.

His face looks shocked as he looks from me to the necklace and back. He slips it over his head before launching himself over the table and kissing my lips before sitting back down and admiring the stone. My cheeks heat and I busy myself pulling out the next present. I pass Nixon his gloves and he fingers them softly like he might break them.

"So you don't hurt yourself in your act," I say softly to my protector.

"Thank you," he rumbles.

I smile at him and turn back to the bag. I pull out the teddy and my cheeks turn red before I stuff it back in and grab Rex's paints and paper.

"What was that?" Alcide asks curiously.

"Erm, oh just something I bought for Rumples and Bubbles"

He blinks in confusion and then laughs, shaking his head.

"Here," I offer Rex his supplies and he takes them delicately. His face breaking into a grin.

"Thank you, Wildcat!" he gushes.

"Not that we aren't grateful, but why did you get us these?" Jesse asks.

"To say thank you, for welcoming me into your family," I offer as I look in the bag for Alcide's. I hear them sucking in breaths and some murmurs but ignore them as I pull out the wrapped frame. While the others are distracted showing each other what they got, I walk around the table to Alcide.

"Here, I thought Rex could fill it with a drawing for you. You can hang it in your tent, it's time to start living Alcide. Why don't you start with filling your space with things that make you happy?"

He gently takes it, brushing my fingers with his. He unwraps it, his long fingers making quick work of the brown wrapping. He stares down at the frame and then strokes the animals carved there.

"Do you like it?" I ask impatiently.

"I love it," he says breathlessly. I nod and go to sit back down when he grabs my hand.

"We are the lucky ones to have you as part of our family."

Smiling shyly, I sit down at the end of the bench next to Nixon.

Looking around at the men as they all look at their presents, I notice their happy expressions. I realise none of them have ever received presents before and just how much this means to them. My heart speeds up and my smile feels like it might break, it's that strong.

A scream has us all looking at the tent flap before they bolt outside, me close behind. I run after them and we all skid to a stop outside the big tent, where Esme staggers out. Blood trickles down her head from a cut at her hairline.

"Esme, are you okay? What happened?" Alcide asks, striding up to her. I notice none of the others do, in fact, Nixon steps so close to me, we are touching.

"Someone attacked me. I was walking through and they hit my head and tried to drag me away, but I managed to kick them and run," she says between sobs as she throws herself at Alcide, who catches her and looks uncomfortable as she sobs in his arms.

"Blain, Rex, go check it out," he calls, as they both throw me a look but step through the flap into the tent. I wait anxiously, the only sound is Esme's incessant sobbing. Not to sound mean, I know everyone reacts to situations differently, but it just feels like she is putting on a show for sympathy.

Blain and Rex come out of the tent and shake their head at Alcide.

"Okay everyone, back to your tents. No one stays alone. We are leaving in the morning anyway." Alcide leads Esme away and I get a little jealous.

"Hey, you wanna feed the animals with me, Wildcat?" Rex asks, perking up my mood.

"Yes," I nod enthusiastically making him grin.

"Rhea, I know that after everything that has happened you may not want to share a bed with anyone right now-" Jesse begins, his words blurring into one.

"Jesse, what are you trying to say?" I ask softly. I know they are trying to make me feel comfortable after what happened, but I don't want their sympathy, I just want to be treated like they would treat me normally. I want hugs from them and the little touches that make me feel loved. They make me feel safe and protected, and I know they are nothing like the guys who tried to hurt me.

"Can I stay with you tonight? I really want to make sure you're safe, Firecracker," he says, shocking me as his cheeks flame red.

"Yes, please, I don't want to be alone right now," I reply, not really wanting any of them out of my sight, but I know that's not practical.

"I'll stay in your tent tonight with you then, Firecracker, I'll meet you there when you are done." Jesse winks and walks away. Nixon squeezes my shoulder, causing me to look up at him. He tilts his head in a silent question and I know he is asking if I'm okay. I nod at him, a soft smile on my lips, and watch as follows after Jesse, but a slight sense of panic fills me as I see him walk away.

My expression must change as Rex takes my hand. I jump slightly but relax as I see it's him, feeling safe again, I know that Rex will look after me. We start to walk towards the animal tent when I have a real-isation.

"Oh, wait I need to get Rumples and Bubbles' present," I shout before darting back to the other tent and grabbing it. Jogging back to Rex, I grin and hold up the pink stuffed bear.

"Got him!" I call triumphantly and raise him to the air. Rex groans but grabs my hand.

"This should be fun." He says making me giggle and clutch the bear closer.

Chapter Eleven

I let Rex greet all the other animals, while I make a beeline for Rumple/Bubbles who is curled up in the corner. I plop down into a cross-legged position in front of him, with the bear behind my back.

"Hi."

Rumple lifts his head, his eyes sliding open. His tongue darts out as he rubs his head on my hand. I stroke his head and wait for Bubbles. He doesn't bother to lift his head, but his eyes slit open and watch me.

"I bought you both something," I singsong. Rumple nudges my hand while Bubbles hisses.

"If you're not nice, you can't have him," I say seriously.

Bubbles finally lifts his head but stays a good distance away as if still unsure of me. I am hoping Beary will do the trick. I pull the peace offering from behind my back and put him on the floor in the space between us. Bubbles eyes widen before he darts forward and wraps his neck around the bear, resting his head on it. He starts to nuzzle along it as if trying to cuddle it and I have to bite my lip to stifle my giggle.

He freezes and then slowly lifts his head as he looks from the bear to me.

"Friends?" I offer.

He pauses before nodding. Grinning, I watch as he dives back in to cuddle Beary. Rumple licks my hand before trying to wrestle him away. I stand and leave them to fight over it.

I dust off my bum and walk towards Rex who is under a pile of animals. Tiny is at his back, Fluffy on his belly and Rodger is laid over his feet. Sid, who has been AWOL since the night of the attack comes bounding in and twists around my legs.

"Hey buddy," I say, as I run my hands through his fur before looking up and seeing Rex nearly be suffocated. "Need a hand?" I ask around a smile.

He looks up at me as he scratches Fluffy's head, a massive smile on his handsome face.

"Want to meet Sid?" I ask seriously, bending down to scratch my new friend again. Rex manages to untangle himself from the animals and huffs over to me. He crouches next to me and lays his hand on Sid.

"He's beautiful, yes you are," he coos at the animal. Sid lays and flips onto his back, his belly in the air. Rex strokes him whispering to him as he goes. I don't blame the cat one bit, I would roll on my back if Rex spoke to me like that. My cheeks turn red at the direction my brain is taking me in.

"Where did you find him?" his voice pulling me from my dirty thoughts.

"He found me," I say, stroking his head.

We spend a while playing with the animals before I help Rex feed them. I bid them a sad goodnight and follow Rex out of the tent.

Grabbing Rex's free hand, I twine our fingers, smiling shyly at him when he grins down at me. We walk in comfortable silence to my tent, although at the flap he hesitates. His cheeks heat as he looks at the ground.

"Well, goodnight," he offers.

"Goodnight," I say softly. He lets go of my hand and turns to walk away, I watch him go a little bit disappointed.

"Screw it," he mutters before striding back to me.

He grabs me and lifts me up, his lips smashing to mine. The kiss is quick and over way too soon. He lowers me gently to the floor, his hands cupping my cheeks.

"I couldn't leave without that. I'm going to miss you tonight. Be good, try not to get into any trouble, Wildcat," he says before kissing me again and walking away before my muddled brain can think of a response.

Feeling stupid for just standing outside, I slip through the tent flap to see Jesse already in my bed. He watches me with a soft, sleepy smile.

"Come on, Firecracker, time to get some sleep."

I gesture for Jesse to look away and I quickly strip, putting on one of Nixon's shirts he left me. It acts like a dress and I am not ashamed to say I sniff it. Feeling exposed, I climb over Jesse and slide under the covers. He turns to face me, our heads sharing the same pillow. This close it's easy to remember how beautiful he is, but with his hair all pushed back and him tucked under the covers he looks younger too.

"You okay?" he asks softly.

It's a hard question, so much has happened today, I feel overwhelmed. I've been trying to push it away, to forget, but Jesse's question brings it all back and I burst into tears before I can help myself.

"Hey, it's going to be okay, Firecracker. You're safe now." He grabs me and pulls me into the circle of his arms. He lets me cry it all out on his chest, my hands curled around him like a safety blanket. I bury my head further into his chest, his steady heartbeat calming my tears. He runs his hand through my hair, whispering reassurances until my tears stop and I'm just curled around him.

"Sorry," I mumble, unwilling to move away.

"For what?"

"Your chest is all wet," I hiccup.

He laughs, shaking me as his hand lands on my hip.

"I think I will live, plus I have nothing to complain about. I have a beautiful woman in my arms."

I smile into his chest and run my hands along his side. He sucks in a breath, and I can hear his heartbeat speed up.

"I don't pretend to know how you are feeling right now. What you went through today..." He trails off, a kiss landing on the top of my head.

"If you need to cry, if you need to scream, talk, hit me, whatever. Do it. But holding it in isn't healthy, you need to feel it and then try to move on. We- I- will help you the whole time." His voice is strong and sure and lends me his strength to tackle how I am feeling.

I just feel so violated, two times now a man has thought he had the right to touch me without consent. To take what I didn't offer. To them I was nothing more than an object for their lust. But I don't think talking will help, there's nothing anyone can say that will make this better, that will make me feel less dirty, less used, less powerless. I know what I want, now I just need to be strong enough to take it for myself. I lift my head until my eyes meet his.

He smiles gently, his hand coming up to hold my cheek.

"Help me," I whisper.

"Just tell me how," He pleads, his eyes searching mine for answers.

"Make me forget," I beg, searching his eyes.

He freezes, not even breathing as he watches me. His eyes bore into mine, asking me to tell him I am serious. That this is what I want.

"Rhea, I don't think it's a good idea. You've had a bad couple of days, I don't want to take advantage of you."

I shake my head, "Never. I'm not saying we need to… but just let me forget. For now, help me lose myself so I don't dwell on this pain unfurling inside of me. Screaming at me, cutting me up inside with the feeling of their hands on me, with their mouths and words. I was nothing to them Jesse, just another thing to own. To control and have. I know you're different, I can see the caring in your eyes. You need to help me, so please just… help me forget, just for tonight."

I don't know what he sees in my eyes, but he smiles softly at me.

"Okay, Firecracker," he murmurs. He cups my cheek again, his warmth making me close my eyes.

His lips meet mine, gentle and soft. Like a butterfly, they flutter over mine. Making me chase him before he hardens them. The feeling of his skin against mine pulls a gasp from my lips, and he slips his tongue in. My hand grabs his chest, as he dominates my mouth. All thoughts, memories, everything slips away until it is only me and him.

I pull away panting, his eyes are unfocused when they flutter open and his lips are pink.

Before he can move, I press my lips to his. As we kiss, he moves over me, until I'm lying on my back with him using his forearms to hold his weight off me. He pulls away, his weight comforting me in a foreign way.

"I've never…" I whisper, my cheeks heating for a whole other reason. His eyebrow raises.

"Really? I just mean with you being a woman and… Never mind." He bites his lower lip as he watches me, our bodies still pushed together.

"If I tell you something, promise you won't laugh?" he asks, looking embarrassed.

"Always," I agree instantly.

"I'm a virgin too," he admits, his voice strong even as his face heats.

My eyes widen. "But you always seem so…"

"I know. I just never found the right girl, it's not like there are many options."

"Are you saying that I am the right girl?" I hold my breath as his eyes search mine.

"Yes." His lips descend, and I meet him halfway.

We don't take it any further than that, just spending the night kissing and talking until I fall asleep in Jesse's arms. When I wake up in the morning, I smile at his sleeping face. Wiggling, I sigh sadly before leaving the bed and quickly getting dressed.

"Where are you going?" Jesse's half-asleep voice asks from behind me. I tie my boot and turn to see him. The cover is at his waist, showing off his impressive naked chest. His hair is spiked all over and he is smiling softly. The sight makes me falter at how perfect he looks.

I saunter up to him and drop a kiss on his lips. As I go to pull away, he grabs the back of my head and deepens it. I have to drop my hands to his chest to balance myself as I moan into his mouth.

Squealing, I land on my back as he pulls me down on the bed and hovers over me. I giggle at the mischievous look in his eyes.

"I might keep you here all day," he says through a grin, his lips meeting mine again.

"Time to go! Everyone up!" Comes a shout from outside.

We both groan and look at each other like naughty children.

"Want to hide in here all day?" I whisper. He smiles at me as we hear people starting to move.

"If I thought I could get away with it, I would. Time to get up, Firecracker, stop being lazy will you," he says before kissing me again. I gape at him before grabbing the pillow and hitting him with it.

We both laugh as we fight over the pillow, trying to hit each other.

"Are you two having a pillow fight?"

We freeze and look at the tent flap at the same time to see Rex. He laughs as Jesse jumps up and races at him with it. They both fight over the pillow as I get up and start packing. Eventually, they call a truce and help me.

We pack up quickly, Rex and Jesse helping. Each time they pass me something their touch lingers, and they make sure to throw me smiles every now and again. Even Nixon comes to check on me, even Blain is hovering where he thinks I can't see him. Eventually, everything is ready, and we set off for the next town. I just hope the next settlement is better.

I'm sitting in the back of one of the carriages as we travel to the next settlement, Jesse and Nixon are with me. They think I can't see but they keep throwing me anxious glances when they think I'm not looking. Jesse is regaling Nixon with some story about the first time he rode in a carriage. I'm not really paying attention, my head leaning against the side of the wagon as we travel, my eyes running over the barren landscape as his voice washes over me. I didn't sleep much last night, and I feel weary today. So, I guess it's not that much of a surprise when my eyes droop and the swaying of the carriage lulls me to sleep.

Hands are all over me, holding me down, prying at my clothes, tearing them off of me, and exposing me for all to see. I can feel his hot acrid breath along my neck, making me want to gag as he grinds himself against me. I look around the room and realise I'm back at the breeders building, they got me again. I thrash in the bed and I can hear the clanking of a chain, so I know that I'm trapped again.

"Get off me. You're dead, you can't own me anymore," I cry out, my words sounding desperate.

I watched Nixon kill the man, how could I be back here? I see him lean back and sneer at me, licking his lips as he grinds his arousal against my leg.

"I may be dead, but you're a woman, you will always belong to someone. Today, that someone is me."

His hands grasp at me again, pulling down my leggings and horror fills me at the prospect of what is to come.

"No!"

"Rhea!" A voice shouts my name and I startle awake.

Panting, I look around, unsure where I am or what is going on. Where has the breeder gone? I can hear Jesse talking to me and I focus on his face, his voice.

"Focus, you know us, you are safe. Tell me, who am I?" He asks me.

I take a deep breath and try to centre myself, focus on the things I do know. "You're Jesse, this is Nix." My voice comes out small and scratchy like I've been screaming.

I see him nod, his smile widening. "Good, do you know where we are?"

I look around again and see we are in one of the circus carriages, we were travelling to the next settlement. We have stopped now, so we must have arrived.

"We are travelling with Alcide's Circus, we had to move because of the attack."

Jesse's face drops slightly at the mention of the attack, but he nods, acknowledging my statement. I realise that I am in Nixon's lap, his arms tight around me, his large hand gently stroking my hair.

"Why am I in Nixon's lap?" I ask. I'm not complaining, I feel safe, I'm just unsure how I ended up here.

"You were screaming in your sleep," he tells me, as Nixon rubs his hand up and down my back to comfort me. I lean back in his arms, feeling safe with the giant of a man holding me.

"Alright, we are here, everybody out!" I hear Alcide's voice call, followed by groans as everyone hops out and gets to work.

"Sorry," I whisper as I climb out of Nixon's arms and jump out of the carriage.

Jesse jumps out behind me and puts a hand on my shoulder to stop me before pulling me in for a hug.

"Nothing to be sorry for, Firecracker," he whispers in my ear before rushing off to help unpack.

Several hours later, all of the tents are up, including mine, which has now been fixed. I'm still not sure I can sleep in there alone after everything that happened, but we will see. One day at a time. Alcide interrupts my musing as he strides towards me.

"Cariñoa, meet the others at the training mats," he orders before striding away.

I look over at Nixon who is on Rhea duty and raise my eyebrows in question. He shrugs at me and we walk over to the training area, Nixon gently taking my hand in his. Since the attack, everyone is on what Jesse likes to call 'Rhea duty', so there is someone with me at all times. Ever since Nixon saved me, I have felt the safest around him, but I know he has his own issues, especially about being touched. I probably would have stayed in his tent, but I didn't know how he would react with me being that close to him, invading his space whilst he slept. He instinctively knew where to find me, and I know he won't let anyone hurt me whilst we are together.

The training mats have been moved into a smaller version of the big top. These are usually outside under a cover, so I wonder why we are suddenly training inside a tent. The other guys are here when we arrive, they smile and walk over to me, except Blain who is scowling as usual. Alcide steps forward and claps his hands to get our attention.

"Thank you for coming. We have moved training to the tent to keep your abilities secret. There have been too many 'accidents' and I want to keep everyone's acts and training secret until we know who we can trust again." We all nod in agreement. "We are going to be pushing your abilities. I know you can all do more than you are currently. Ever since Rhea arrived you have been developing your powers, we need to expand these," he continues.

Blain snorts and we all look over at him. "Why? So, you can earn more money from us?" he asks bluntly, and I can see he has struck a nerve with Alcide.

"No. So you can save your own sorry ass. These attacks are coming on thick and fast, you need to know what you can do to protect yourselves," Alcide replies, his voice harsh.

There were grumbles but eventually everyone agreed, we needed to know how we could protect ourselves in case these attacks kept coming. We spend all afternoon in that tent and it's gruelling work. When we are not practicing our powers with Alcide, we are lifting weights with Nixon or fight training. For me, that involves learning self-defense. The old cook that I had known in Cinders had once shown me where to stab a man that would keep him down for good if I was attacked, but I don't want to kill anyone, so I've never used the knowledge.

The guys take turns to teach me how to defend myself. Jesse teaches me how to get out of various holds, using Nixon as an 'attacker.' Rex shows me some grappling training and how to throw a punch without breaking my thumb. Even Blain helps out, showing me how to use a knife, even if he said it's because he didn't trust me with a knife unless he taught me how to use it. I have a couple of flashbacks during the training, usually when I am pinned to the ground or I'm unable to use my arms. The guys help me through it, Nixon just holds me gently whilst Rex and Jesse talk me through it. Their comforting touches and words of reassurance help me ground myself to the here and now.

"Rhea, you're up!" Alcide calls me from across the tent.

I walk over to the makeshift ring and step over the hay bales that line it. There are no lights in here, so lanterns are lined up along the edges of the ring, giving us enough light to train by. I smile nervously at Alcide, I'm a little worried about what he is going to have me do.

My powers revolve around me protecting myself, which means that I have to be put in danger to work on them.

Alcide gestures at someone at the edges of the tent and two stage-hands wheel in a glass tank filled with water. There is a lid on top, which looks like it locks in place. Dread fills me as I look at Alcide.

"Don't look so nervous Cariñoa, everything will be fine and if anything goes wrong, we are here," he says it so simply.

"You're not the one that is going to have to drown though," I mutter, looking at the tank of water again. "I can't swim Alcide, let alone breath underwater!" I cry out, my nerves getting the better of me.

"That has yet to be seen, Cariñoa. I trust in your abilities, you should too. You need to know if you can do this," he tells me, and I can understand where he is coming from.

I bite my lower lip and nod slightly in agreement, walking up to the tank. A small step ladder has been placed there and I climb it, pausing at the top to look at Alcide again.

"Just don't let me drown, okay?" I ask, pleased that my voice doesn't shake with the fear that I am feeling.

"I would never let anything happen to you, Cariñoa," he says softly, for my ears only.

I give him a tight smile and swing my legs into the tank.

"Wait, what is she doing? Why is there a tank of water?" I can hear Rex ask, a note of concern in his voice.

Before I get the chance to back out of it, I jump into the water, pulling the lid with me. The shock of being surrounded by water hits me and I get memories of being back in the lake when I didn't know which way was up. I open my eyes and can see the guys running towards Alcide, their arms waving and even through the water I can hear they are shouting. My eyes sting and my lungs burn, I need air. My feet touch to the bottom of the tank and I push up, arms reaching for the top of the tank. Only to feel glass, the lid is stuck. I can't get out. Panic sets in as I search for a way out, banging against the glass in a futile attempt to break it. A hand appears on the glass next to me and I focus on the face. Blain. He is saying something. I try to get my panicked air deprived brain to pay attention to what he is saying.

"Change! Come on you, lazy bitch! Change!" He is shouting, but his eyes look worried.

That can't be right, I must have water on the brain. *Ha. That's funny...* My vision is starting to go dark and the shouting outside increases when a sharp pain across my neck brings my attention back. All of a sudden, I can breathe, although that's not quite the word for it. I open my eyes and am shocked that I can see better, my eyes not stinging from the water.

Arms reach into the water and pull me out, dropping me on the floor as I cough and splutter, suddenly finding it hard to breathe again. I look down and see my fingers are webbed and when I touch the burning on my neck I find slits there, like...gills. My body tingles and I gasp for breath as my body changes back to my human form. I lay where I am on the floor for a bit, the guys close around me, watching me with nervous eyes.

"I turned into a fish?!" I say, not quite believing what just happened.

The guys let out relieved laughs and Nixon helps me to my feet.

"I knew you could do it, Cariñoa." Alcide's voice calls to me, a pleased smile on his face. "Now let's try-"

"No," I say, spinning on my heel and walking to the side of the ring. "I nearly drowned Alcide! I'm not doing it again," I say, anger filling me. I know it's not his fault, but I am fed up with feeling like my life is constantly in danger.

"Rhea, you need to do this," he says, his voice hardening with command.

"I won't, I need a break." I reach the hay bales and step one leg over.

An arm grabs me, pulling me to a stop and spinning me around. Alcide is about to say something as I lose my balance. I stumble back trying to steady myself when I knock into one of the lanterns. I hear a smash and then everything goes white as I am engulfed in flames.

eat engulfs me, and I can't see anything beyond the fire that is blazing along my skin. The fire roars blocking out any other sound apart from my frantic heartbeat, smashing against my chest like a trapped bird. Panic runs through me until I realise that I'm not in any pain. Sure, the fire is hot, but it's bearable. What on earth is going on?

My clothing was wet when I crashed into the lantern, so it couldn't have caught fire, which means that it must have been *me* that caught on fire. I look down at my skin, although glowing like embers I see that the flames aren't actually touching my skin, they are dancing just above it.

My powers have never reacted like this before. They usually adapt to protect me from any threat, not absorb it. But if this is my power, that means that I can control it. Closing my eyes, I imagine the fire running along my skin and grabbing it with both hands I tug, pulling the flames back a little. Opening my eyes, I can see that it worked, the flames are still large, but not blazing and I can see the guys gathered around me. Nixon is dragging the tank of water over, obviously trying to put out the fire. Jesse is on his knees watching me with pain in his eyes unlike any I have ever witnessed. Blain and Rex are shouting at Alcide who is gesturing towards me.

"Stop shouting and just look at her for a moment! Does she look in pain? Does she look like she is dying?!" He shouts at the two men.

They both turn to look at me and I wave at them slightly. Blain's mouth drops open in shock, I've never seen that expression on his face before. Rex hurries over to me, stopping a little way in front of me before having to back up a bit, placing his hand in front of his eyes to protect them from the heat. I feel strangely empty as I stand engulfed in flames, watching my friends stare at me with varied expressions of shock, fear, and worry.

"Rhea, do you think you could change back? You're pretty hot right now." Rex's comment makes me smile and although I know he can't see my smile, his face colours with a blush as he realises what he just said.

I close my eyes and try to focus on the place where my power resides. I focus on the fact that I don't need protecting anymore and pull my power towards me. A wave of dizziness fills me, causing my knees to buckle as I drop to the ground, hard. I know I have changed back when cool air brushes my skin. A cough has me raising my head weakly and Rex is looking away awkwardly.

"Rhea, your clothes..." He trails off.

"I like this fire form!" Jesse remarks and I look at my clothing, which has apparently burnt off, seeing as I am now completely naked. I also remember that fire is part of Jesse's power. Nixon silently shrugs out of his shirt and kneels down next to me, his arm outstretched as he offers me the clothing. My cheeks heat and I gratefully pull the garment over my body, desperate to cover my nakedness from all of the men staring at me. Now that I am back in my human form various emotions threaten to overwhelm me. I set myself on fire. No, I *was* fire. Having all the guys this close to me whilst I am naked and vulnerable causes my breathing to become rapid and I can feel the panic making my chest tight.

"Everybody take a step back," Nixon's deep voice fills the space and without looking I can feel them obeying his command.

He may not say much, but when he does, they listen. And he was right, I needed space. I know that they would never hurt me in the way those disgusting men tried to, but in that moment of panic I had felt like I was back in that room, chained to the bed and at the whim of whatever disgusting desires the breeder felt.

Nixon has also started to step back, giving me space, but right now I just need to feel safe and one of the only places I feel that is in his arms. I look up and meet his gaze, finally finished fumbling at the buttons of his shirt.

"Nixon..." I begin, how do I tell him that I need to be held after I just freaked out at their proximity?

Thankfully, I don't need to, as he wordlessly stops in his tracks and opens his arms, allowing me to approach him at my speed. I push up onto shaky feet, exhaustion making my movements unsteady, as I slowly make my way towards him. I place my face on his now bare chest and wrap my arms around him, aware of the others silently watching. Nixon wraps his arms around me, one of his hands gently stroking my back and we stay that way for a while.

Once I feel calmer, I pull away and smile up at him softly. Taking his hand in mine, I turn and look at the other guys, expecting to see judgmental looks. I am surprised at what I see. Their expressions range from shock, I'm guessing from Nixon's gentle behaviour towards me, to acceptance and worry. When my gaze falls on Alcide, I see a look that I am beginning to dread.

"I have an idea," he begins, causing the others to groan at the smile on his face.

The next few days pass in a blur of rehearsals. Alcide had finally figured out what my act is. It caused many arguments between the guys, even Blain didn't like it. There haven't been any more attacks on the circus, and we have settled into a routine, although you can still feel the tension around the camp. I am getting stronger every day, and I haven't had any more flashbacks. Although, I am struggling to sleep, and the sleep I do get is plagued with bad dreams. It's better when I stay with one of the guys, so they graciously allow me to rotate between them, sleeping with a different man each night,

Looking in the mirror at my reflection, I almost don't recognise myself. I am in Alcide's tent getting ready for tonight, and whilst I am alone, I don't feel unsafe as we are so close to the main tent that I know someone would be here in a matter of seconds if I needed them. They have been taking turns checking up on me all evening.

My scarlet red hair which fades to orange and then blond at the tips, has been pulled back into a ponytail, with the end curling down over my shoulders. Gold glitter has been added at my hairline, causing it to shimmer. In certain lights, it looks like fire. I have gold eyeshadow on, which contrasts nicely with my bold, dark red lipstick.

I stand and spin, watching my outfit shine in the mirror. I have no idea where Alcide got the dress from, but I have to admit that it is perfect for what he has planned. The tunic of the dress is fitted to my body, the neckline plunging down into my generous cleavage. The fabric is soft and the colours seem to shimmer in the light. From one angle, the dress looks a shade of red, but from a different angle, it changes to orange and gold. The skirt has different layers of the same fabric which falls down to knee level. When I spin, the fabric flares out prettily. Instead of sleeves, there are strings of what look like golden beads from front to back over my shoulders. The whole effect is quite striking. The most shocking thing about the whole outfit...it's fireproof.

I hear a loud cheer from the big top and I smile, one of the guys must have just finished their act. I had helped with the first few acts at the beginning of the show as I had before. I protested at this because I had my own act so why did I need to be in the others? Alcide just said that the others worked harder when I was around and that I was making him a fortune.

Typical Alcide. I can't decide how I feel about him, as it's almost like being around two separate people. When it is just the two of us I can feel the passion burning between us and it is like nothing else matters but us. He is kind, funny, and mischievous. Then there is Alcide, the businessman: pushy, determined, and cold. When he is like that, I can feel him pulling away from us and it makes me sad. I don't know if he does this on purpose, to put some distance between us, but I feel like I don't really know him.

I try to focus my thoughts, it will be my turn to perform soon and I need to have my head in the game. The acts have been moved around, much to the annoyance of some of the performers, and my act is the last one, the grand finale as Alcide likes to call it. I take a deep breath and leave the tent, walking the short distance to the big top. I pause outside, listening to the music, listening for my cue. Jesse jogs out of the tent, the sounds of applause following him, his skin glistening with sweat. His satisfied smile turns into a grin as he sees me, and he comes over to me.

"Hey, Firecracker. You ready for your first solo act?" He asks excitedly.

Of all of the guys, he has been the only one who actively accepted and encouraged it. He trusted in my abilities more than I did, believing that I would not only pull this off but would excel, well and truly cementing my place within the circus.

"I think so," I tell him, biting down on my lip as my nerves surface again.

I am not anxious about performing anymore, I have discovered a love for it, but I find that tonight is the first time my nerves are coming back. This is why I am here, and I am worried that I will fail, disappointing the guys. They have given me everything since my turbulent arrival, and I don't want to let them down. Jesse can see my nerves and his expression softens as he takes a step towards me, placing his hand on my shoulder. My skin tingles where his hand touches me, and I raise my eyes to meet his.

"Hey, Rhea. You've got this, don't look so nervous," he tells me and I nod at his comment but my smile is shaky

I obviously don't convince him of my confidence as he steps even closer, so our bodies are almost touching. His hand moves from my shoulder to cup my face, and I can see the desire burning in his eyes.

"Rhea, are you ready for your entrance?" I startle at the call, pulling away from Jesse as I turn to see one of the stagehands waiting expectantly for my answer.

"Oh, yes. Thank you," I reply with a small smile at the stagehand.

Nodding in acceptance he hurries away, I assume to tell everyone to get ready. Timing has to be perfect for my performance. I look back at Jesse and give him a nervous smile.

"Go get them, Firecracker," he tells me with a wink, causing me to giggle.

Taking one last deep breath, I walk up to the performer's entrance of the big top. I listen to the music inside the tent and Alcide's confident voice over the top.

"And now, Ladies and Gentlemen, we have a special finale for you. Introducing, Rhea the Immortal!"

Polite clapping fills the ring, my name not as well-known as some of the other performers. The applause starts to drop off as nothing happens, and confused murmurs fill the tent. All of a sudden, the lights turn off, plunging the space into darkness. A few screams sound from the shocked audience. Taking my cue, I walk silently into the ring, my powers adapting my eyes to see in the dark easily. Standing in the centre of the ring, I stand tall and extend my arms out to the side of me and call on the power that resides inside of me.

I feel my skin change as I will it and nod in the direction of Alcide, where I know he is giving signals to the stage hands. The lights flood back on and shocked gasps sound around the tent as bright tendrils of light sparkle off me.

My diamond form is easy to see in this costume, clearly showing off my figure. Jesse runs back into the arena and takes my outstretched hand in his. Releasing my hold on my power I turn back to my human form and face him with a smile. Together we perform the dance that we have rehearsed endlessly the last couple of days. It is an emotional dance, full of spins and tumbles, representing the turbulence and hardship in a difficult relationship where the woman is fighting for independence. Jesse pulls me close to his body as we finish our dance, lifting me above his head as I arch my back, before falling into his embrace, clutching him tightly.

Pushing away from him, I struggle as he tries to keep me where I am, before escaping his grasp and running away. He strides away, a menacing look in his eyes as I look at my hands, as if in shock that I am truly free. Shocked cries fill the tent and I look up as if in surprise, seeing Jesse striding towards me with a bow and flaming arrow aimed at my chest. I stare in shock as the arrow flies towards me and hits me.

My powers protect me, but I sink to the ground as the flames rush over my skin, enveloping me in their heat. I stay crouched on the ground for a few seconds, before getting up and looking around the crowd. Letting them see that I haven't let hatred or prejudice beat me.

I stride to the middle of the ring and start spinning. At first, my flames are so hot, it just looks like a ball of flame, but as I start pulling the heat towards my centre, I know that my shape becomes more obvious, until I am glowing softly, staring out at the audience. Jesse runs back in and takes my hand, which I am careful to make sure isn't hot, and leads me into a bow.

There is a stunned silence around the tent, until the crowd bursts into applause, shouting and screaming for more. A smile fills my face as a variety of emotions fill me. Alcide enters the ring again and addresses the audience as we leave the tent.

This act is supposed to be more than just something to entertain, it's to send a message. That I may be a woman, the sex they believe is weak and to be owned, but I am strong, and I will keep adapting to spread my message until I am no longer able. It represents that women don't belong to anyone, and we can survive in this horrible world, but we are going to have to fight. It is going to cause problems, the message we are spreading is not one that many people are going to want to hear. Everyone had disputed, but eventually agreed that we were being hunted anyway, so we might as well try and tell our story at the same time.

"Guess it's my turn to babysit you, Harpy?"

Gritting my teeth, I sit down at the table opposite Blain. He watches me intently, his usual scowl firmly in place. My first performance finished over an hour ago, and I quickly escaped to get changed and take a few seconds to myself. Performing that dance, showing my defiance lent me strength. It allowed me to push myself, to try and fix the broken bits left behind after everything that happened. I'm not perfect, and I never will be. But I am something better...real.

"I thought we had a truce after you saved me. Especially now that..." I trail off, but still unwilling to back down. The mention of my almost rape has his face tightening and his fists clenching, I am right there with him. My whole body turning ramrod straight. At first, I couldn't even think about it, pretending like it didn't happen in hopes I could forget. When that didn't work, I let it consume me, drain me of all that I am until nothing but a husk was left. Now, I can talk about it, think about it without breaking down.

"You're fine, you're such a crybaby," Blain says through a scoff.

"You don't understand what it was like, how could you," I mutter, looking at the table, that monster's eyes flashing in my mind before I push them away.

"Sorry to disappoint, Harpy, but my life hasn't been all hugs and roses," he growls making me look up sharply.

"No? Then why don't you enlighten me, I bet it was *so* hard for little Blainy growing up!" I shout sarcastically, done with being nice. We are going to hash this out, once and for all.

He growls and smashes his fists down on the table making me jump.

"You have no idea! You think it was easy growing up on the streets? Moving from settlement to settlement as a child by yourself? Trying to find anywhere, or anyone to live with. People will always take in girls, not so much with boys," he yells, his nostrils flaring with his anger, but pain flirts around the edges as does a quiet desperation. Maybe Blain isn't as much of an asshole as I thought, maybe he is broken too?

"What did you do?" I ask quietly, my anger gone at the pain and suffering in his voice.

"What I had to," he says coldly, or he tries to but his voice breaks at the end.

"Blain-" I reach across and cup his fist. "I'm sorry, I shouldn't have judged you. I know better than anyone the suffering a person can endure."

He looks at my hand for a while, before his voice comes out. No snark, or attitude, just a little boy revealing his monsters.

"I stole, I joined a couple of kids on the street who stole from travellers. We sold it to a man named Cor. A cruel bastard, he used us street kids as he wished. Sex, food, money making, you name it." Horror washes through me and he must see it.

"That's right Harpy, it's not just girls those pigs out there rape." My hand clenches around his, anger so fierce I fear I might implode races through me. God, I wish I could go back and protect him but all I can do is listen to his story and pray I can make his future better.

"As I got older, his demands got bigger until I was stealing from rich people's houses. If I did not deliver, the punishment... Well, let's just say I saw him murder kids in cold blood for disappointing him."

"How did you wind up here?" I whisper.

He laughs bitterly, and raises his head, in his eyes, I see how lost he is.

"Alcide saved me. I was caught breaking into a house and dragged to the square for execution. I was so scared but angry too. I only wanted to avoid Cor's hands and it was going to cost me my life. Alcide was passing through and saw me, he managed to bargain with the man. I was already half-way dead at this point."

He takes a deep breath, "Alcide brought me back, nursed me back to health and then promised me they wouldn't touch me again, that I would always have a place here. A family. So, you see Harpy, why I'm so protective of them, I owe them everything. Without them I'm nothing, that's why I pushed you away. That's why I am like this, I am broken, nothing, useless. Yet I have all this anger burning inside of me, I don't mean to, but I lash out sometimes." He chokes the last out, his eyes swimming with his insecurities and utter belief that everything he is saying is true. "I'm nothing," he whispers.

"Blainy, that's not true." When I say his nickname this time, it's not filled with its usual anger, more understanding and caring for the asshole. "You're strong, so much so, I was in envy of you when I met you and even more now. You didn't let your past break you, you let it shape you but not define you. You're caring and kind and so protective of your family. You're unbelievably talented and risked your life for some silly girl who you don't even like." I smile at him and his lips quirk.

"Why are you being nice to me, when I've been nothing but a prick to you?" he asks, his face open and curious.

"Not all the time. Plus, I've kinda gotten used to your brand of truth." I smile at him again and twine our hands. "You're my family Blain, asshole tendencies and all. If I could change your past for you, I would, but I promise you that I will protect you for as long as I am alive. No one will hurt you again, any of you," I vow it, with all the strength in my bones. My power pulses as if in agreement.

"You really mean that, don't you?" he says searching my eyes. He blows out a breath, his face going back to normal, minus his usual scowl. "Fuck, Harpy – shit, I mean Rhea." He rubs his hair with his hand, the one not in mine.

"I've kinda gotten used to Harpy," I admit, my cheeks heating.

He grins at me, making my breath catch at how handsome he is. "Harpy it is. Especially after I heard you grew wings and feathers, just like a real one."

I groan and drop my head forward, of course, someone told him.

"Well, isn't this cute." Comes Esme's snarky voice. I expect Blain to let go of my hand but instead, he squeezes it.

"What do you want?" he says harshly, directing a scowl at her.

She throws me a dirty look and rounds the table, trailing her hand over the wood until she reaches him. Then she trails it along his shoulders and back before sitting next to him, so close they almost touch. He doesn't move away, but he does glare at her.

"I will only ask one more time, what do you want Esme?" he snarls at her, gripping my hand tighter. I see his shoulder shake and the revulsion on his face from her touching him and I have to reign in my anger. Especially after his story, he might not want to admit it, but he is vulnerable. His past, the feelings of being helpless of being used still affect him and I know better than anyone what that is like. So, her touching him when he clearly doesn't want it has me nearly lighting the bitch on fire.

She lays her hand on his arm, the one I am holding. I tug on my hand, to do what I don't know, but he grips my hand tighter, refusing to let me go.

"Get your fucking hand off me," he growls, the warning in his voice clear. His eyes are pitch black at this point and focused on the woman with deadly intent.

"Blain," She purrs. "Why don't we send the kid away, the adults need to talk." She adds a pout at the end for extra effect. I stiffen at the kid comment, so sick of her now.

"No," he says slowly, his free hand clenching as if to stop his power from emerging again.

"Blain, why are you being like this? I have been nothing but patient with you, waiting for when you were ready to move on with our relationship," she pouts, actually stomping her foot.

My eyes widen, relationship? He- she- I swing my eyes to him. My stomach drops, and my heart hurts. Which is stupid, I haven't known him that long, and all our encounters have been... Eventful to say the least.

"Listen, you old cow, I don't know where the fuck you got it in your demented head that me and you are in a relationship, or why you insist on hitting on my family continually." She flinches back, and he lets go of my hand to remove hers from his arm. "You think I didn't notice how desperate you were, trying to get us all in your bed?"

Blain's words from when he met me about looking at all of them makes sense now. He was probably thinking I was going to be another Esme. I watch as he twists her arm, making her face scrunch unattractively in pain. I thought he was an asshole to me when he first met me, that is nothing compared to now.

"I don't know what you're talking about," she gasps, tugging on her arm.

"Shut up, I'm not done. I don't know what your issue with Harpy is, but you need to leave it alone." He flings her arm at her and she clutches it protectively to her chest.

"You don't even like her!" She yells. "What the fuck is so special about the little bitch that has all of you acting like pussies?"

He goes to answer when a scream rips through the camp. Jumping up, I look around for the source. Blain grabs my hand, making me jump again, I didn't even hear him move but he is at my side now. Looking around, searching for the sound like I am. His body tense and ready to fight if need be.

"Stay behind me," he growls, before tugging me after him. We round a tent to find Rex fighting two men. One of the camp hands is laying on the ground, his unseeing eyes staring at the sky as blood pools around him.

"Fuck." Blain mutters, looking from me to Rex.

"Go!" I shout, pushing him towards them. He spins to me and grabs my face.

"Do not move, do not interfere," he demands before smashing his lips to mine in a soul-searing kiss. When my eyes open, I see him running towards the men.

They must sense they are soon to be outnumbered as they start to back away. A panting Rex matching them step for step.

"This is just a message, we will always keep hunting you freaks!"

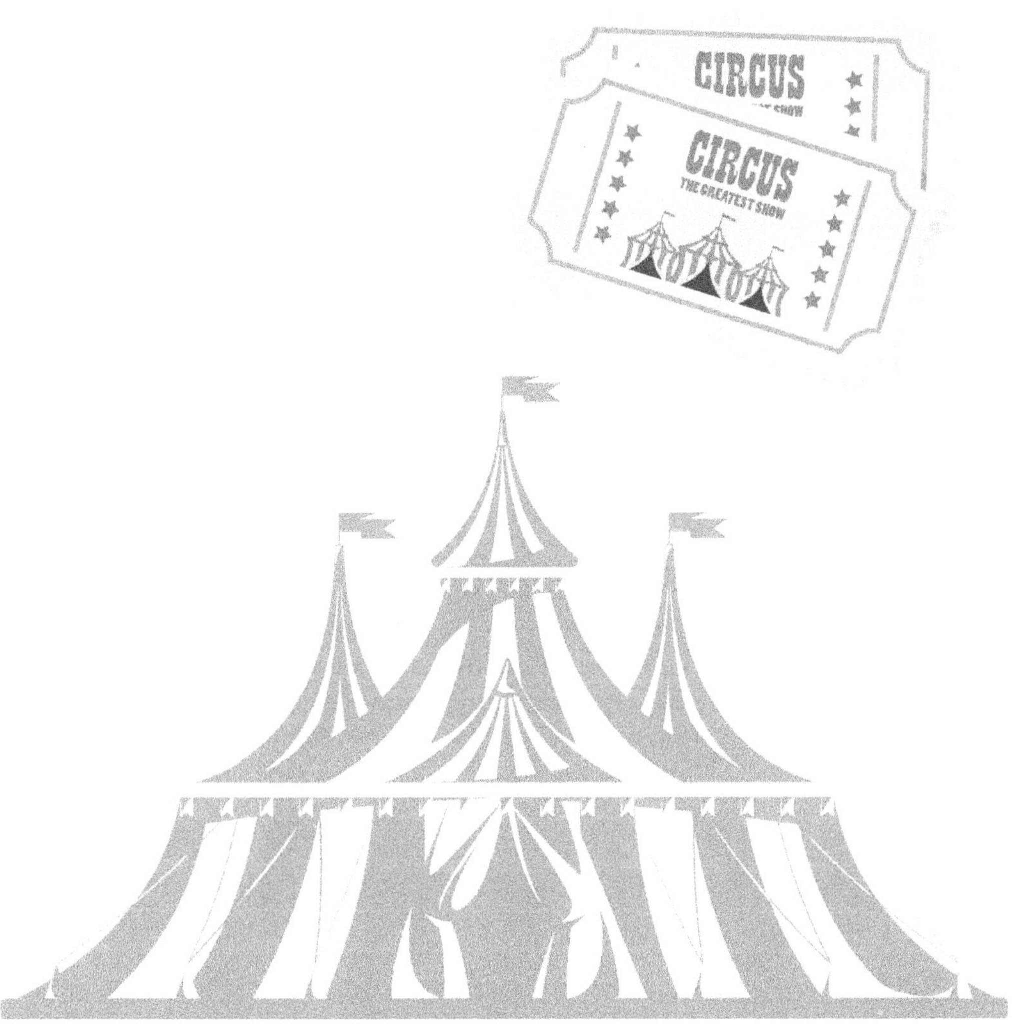
CIRCUS
SHOW
CIRCUS
THE GREATEST SHOW

A roar sounds and my eyes flicker to Rex in shock. His eyes are orange, like when he uses his powers, yet there are no animals in sight. My eyes drop to his hands to see them change into Fluffy's claws. His mouth drops open slightly as two large fangs descend. Even the attackers stumble in shock before turning and fleeing. Blain tries to stop Rex from chasing after them, but Rex pushes him to the ground. I curl my hands into fists to stop the shaking and ignoring Blain's advice, I get involved.

"Rex?" I ask, before clearing my throat and repeating his name louder.

He turns to me, his chest heaving, his eyes strange and more animal than man at the moment, but I know somewhere inside is still Rex and he would never hurt me.

I approach him like I would a scared, wild animal. Softly and not making too much eye contact.

"Hey, it's okay. They're gone, we are safe," I offer reassurance until I stand before him. Those strange eyes locked on mine. Blowing out a breath, I raise my hand.

"Harpy, don't-" Blain warns.

I ignore him and rest my hands on Rex's chest, showing him how unafraid I am of this change. His eyes start to shift back to normal as his breathing slows, but then he falls into me with a pained roar. His eyes flicking from normal to orange as he pushes me to the ground gently and spins, his claws outstretched. I gasp and cover my mouth in horror at the arrow sticking out of his shoulder.

Blain runs over and flings himself over my body, blocking my view. All I can hear is animalistic noises and running feet.

"Blain. Let me up, Rex needs me," I cry, pushing at his chest, his weight pinning me down to the ground.

"Wait," he growls, his body protecting me. It goes quiet and eventually, Blain sits up. He looks around before offering me his hand. I accept it and get to my feet, looking around frantically. Rex sits on the ground, his back to me as Jesse looks at the wound.

"Is everyone okay?" I ask, running to Rex's side, my hands fluttering over him helplessly. I look at Jesse, his face locked in concentration. I have never seen him this serious.

I wait nervously as he patches Rex up. Nixon and Alcide go around the camp checking on everyone as Jesse, Blain, and I help Rex to his tent and get him to rest.

Once he is laying on his front, I lean down and run a gentle kiss over his forehead. His eyes close peacefully as a hand lands on my shoulder.

"Come on, Firecracker, you can stay with me tonight. Nixon is coming to watch Rex," Jesse murmurs.

I nod and stand up. Blain has disappeared but that doesn't surprise me. Jesse and I make our way through the camp, more alert than before. It's not until we are in his tent that I start to relax.

Jesse is quiet as we get ready for bed and when he slumps on the edge and puts his head in his hands, I start to get worried.

"Jess?" I call, I see him twitch but he doesn't look at me. Stepping closer, I stop myself from touching him in case he doesn't want that. "Jess?" I try softer.

"I was useless, god, how can I protect you when I couldn't even protect my brother?" He yells, gripping his hair and yanking. I've never seen him like this and I bite my lip before deciding to just go with it.

Kneeling before him, I uncurl his fingers from where they abuse his hair and take his face in my hands.

"You are not responsible for what those nut jobs did. You did your best to help everyone and I have never doubted that you could protect me. Plus, I can protect myself."

His eyes beg me to tell him the truth, right now he looks like a scared child or someone who just got the rug ripped out from under them. I know the look all too well. He needs someone - he needs me. Standing, I straddle his lap, facing him, making sure he can't try to escape my truth.

"I was so scared, I didn't know what was happening. I thought I could lose you all." I cup his face again and make him meet my eyes, "You were amazing Jesse, the way you took charge. The way you helped Rex. You're amazing," I finish breathlessly. When I realise how close we are, my cheeks heat. Before I can move away, he grips my hips to hold me on his lap.

We stare at each other and I throw caution out of the window, he needs me right now and he was there when I needed him. That's what family means, so if I have to overcome my shyness and take charge, I will.

I bring my lips to his and softly kiss him, showing him how much he means to us - to me. I worship him the only way I know how.

He doesn't respond at first, frozen in shock in my arms, before finally his hand drifts up and grips the back of my head and he deepens the kiss.

He stands up and I wrap my legs around him automatically.

He turns us around, our lips still locked, and lays me on the bed. He follows me down, his body pressing into mine as we breathe each other in.

"I need you," he whispers, searching my eyes. I cup his cheek and bring his face to mine.

"I'm yours," I whisper back before kissing him again.

We take our time, making sure it's perfect. Now that we both have agreed, there is no hesitation. Just our lust and need for each other.

His hands trace down my sides, making me shiver before they slowly push my top up. We only break the kiss to pull it over my head and I lay bare before him, not even a bra on. My cheeks heat and I try to fight the need to cross my arms and cover my breasts. The only thing stopping me is the adoration in his eyes and the fire raging there.

"You're so beautiful. No, that's not enough. You are perfect." I grin as he bumbles, the usually smooth charmer lost at the sight of my bare skin.

"Your turn," I pant.

He sits up and quickly drags his shirt over his head, baring his chiselled chest to me. He is smaller than Rex and Nixon but no less defined and my eyes are drawn to his abs. I have the strangest urge to lick them, and then I think, what the hell. Leaning forward, I trace a path with my tongue along the lines of his abs.

"Rhea," he moans as I lay back, propping myself up on my arms and watch his reaction. As he drinks me in my nipples pebble for him, similar to when I am in my diamond form.

He grins before leaning into me and licking a path up my stomach and between my breasts. He blows air on where he just licked making me shiver again.

"You are wearing too many clothes," he murmurs before reaching down and tugging at my pants. I freeze for a second, the move so similar to the attack the other night.

"Rhea, you okay? We don't have to do this? Did I do something wrong?" He asks nervously.

I breathe out and let myself go pliant, reminding myself it's Jesse and he would never hurt me.

"I'm fine, honestly."

He looks at me like he is thinking of moving away, so I wrap my legs around his waist, making him bite his lower lip.

"Please Jesse, I need you." And it's not a lie. My stomach is clenching, and my pussy is throbbing. The lust running through my body. He obviously makes up his mind, reaching down and flicking open his pants. I drop my legs and let him stand. He drops them to the floor, completely naked. I swallow hard as I look at him. He called me perfect, but it is definitely the other way around. There isn't an inch of fat on his body and he looks like he was made from stone. Even his cock, which stands at attention between his legs, has me licking my lips and clenching my thighs together.

I can sense his nervousness and I decide to try and ease it, I lift my butt and shimmy out of my trousers and panties, leaving me bare.

I hear him inhale before he comes to stand over me.

His nervousness seems to fall away as he drops to his knees on the bed, his curls falling into his face as he kneels above me.

"I want to touch you everywhere, taste you." He groans, his hand trailing along my rib and circling my breast.

He leans down and blows on my nipple before licking around it. Biting my lip, I arch my chest, needing more. He grins against me before sucking the nub into his mouth, making me cry out. I raise my hand and grip his hair as he nips and sucks before turning to my other nipple, giving it the same treatment.

"Jesse, please," I cry, making him lift his head.

"I want to taste you," he murmurs before dropping tiny kisses down my stomach and swirling his tongue around my belly button. When he reaches my pussy, he doesn't hesitate, but I have my thighs clamped shut in embarrassment.

"Let me see you, Firecracker." He says before prying them open. My cheeks heat as he stares at me, his tongue running along his plump bottom lip.

I let out a whimper as he runs the back of his knuckles along my seam before spreading me open to his gaze. He looks back up at me. "I bet you taste sweet." I can't even reply as he lowers his head and licks the path his hand just took, tasting me, driving me wild.

My thighs fall further open as he tongues my pussy like he did my mouth. All hints of reservation fall away as I reach down and grip his hair, my head thrown back in ecstasy.

He licks around my nub as his fingers play at my entrance, fire races through my veins. I've never felt so alive, so in control and sexy at the same time. He worships between my legs and has me crying out as my stomach clenches in a powerful orgasm. It's not my first, but it is my first with someone else. He looks up from between my thighs, a wicked smile on his lips as my juices coat his chin. Without hesitation, I grab his face and pull him up my body, he surrenders to me and crawls up until we are face to face.

He searches my eyes, his lighting with lust and tenderness.

"I'm crazy about you, Firecracker, I'm so glad we are going to be each other's firsts. I can't imagine doing this with anyone else."

"Me either," I whisper, and it's the truth. As much as I like the other guys and want them as well, there has always been a connection with Jesse. Maybe it's because he was the first one I met, the first to see me as I am. Maybe it's because no matter what, he is always there, or maybe it's just because I know he wants me as much as I want him.

He leans down and kisses me gently as he lines up his cock at my entrance. I tense but he washes it away with his gentle persuasive kiss until I am putty in his hands again, panting from need. He pushes in, inch by agonizing inch until I feel a slight discomfort as finally he breaks through the last of my innocence. He stops then, staring at me in wonder as he shakes above me from the effort of staying still. Once the momentary pain is gone and I start to adjust to his size, my pleasure floods back and I need him to move. I wrap my legs around his waist and encourage him by thrusting slightly. We both gasp as he closes his eyes.

"Fuck, I'm not going to last long, Firecracker. I know that's not what you want to hear but with tasting you and feeling how tight you are for me..." He groans and drops his forehead to mine. We breathe each other in as he starts to move inside of me, slow purposeful strokes, driving us both higher and higher until we are moaning.

It's slow, loving, and perfect as the orgasm surges through me again and we cry out together, staring in each other's eyes.

When our breathing slows he moves off me so as not to crush me, I have to bite my lip to stop from crying out as he slips from me. He curls up next to me, watching me with a new softness to his expression.

"Are you okay? I didn't hurt you, did I?" He asks worriedly.

I grin before shaking my head. "No, it was perfect. Thank you."

He grins and kisses my shoulder before laying his head on me. We lay like that for a while, both lost in our own world.

Jesse's head is heavy on my chest but comforting in a new way. Our bodies are still sweaty and right now I am more relaxed than I have ever been. He mumbles in his sleep and kisses my shoulder before burying his head again. I smile at the cute gesture and finally close my eyes. I know tomorrow will be hard, Alcide will have a lot to say about what happened with those hunters, but maybe he was right. If we are to protect our family, we need to be more. We need to become the freaks they accuse us of being. We need to embrace our powers.

I wake up and languishly stretch across the bed, for a moment forgetting the events of the night before. I enjoy the feeling of the sheets on my bare skin as I roll onto my side, smiling as the heat of another body presses up against me. Wait. I don't usually sleep naked.

My eyes shoot open and I remember the night before. The fight, the dead stagehand, and Jesse afterwards. We had sex. I bite down on my lip, trying to stop the happy smile that is threatening to take over. It may not have been perfect, but it was our first time and I'm glad that we experienced it together. Besides, we have plenty of time to work on our, ahem, technique.

Jesse shifts his weight and pulls me closer to him, our bodies pressed together. Just thinking about last night has my cheeks heating and my arousal growing. I turn my head and look over my shoulder. Jesse is still sleeping, his soft hair curling around the pillow. He looks so peaceful, I almost don't want to wake him up. *Almost.* I don't just want to wake him up and ask for sex though, how would that make me look?

An idea forms in my mind and I find myself biting my lip again as I think through my plan, nerves butterflying through my stomach. I've heard that guys like this, and the guys in Cinders were always making lewd comments about girls doing it. Pulling on my metaphorical big girl pants, I press back into Jesse's body again. I can feel him against me, semi hard already as he sleepily grumbles. I gently pull from his arms and shuffle down the bed, being careful not to wake him in the process. I run my hand down his chest before it comes to rest on his cock. I run my hand up and down it experimentally, watching him shift in his sleep. Before I chicken out, I lower my lips and place them around his length, taking as much of him as I can into my mouth. Sucking slightly, I bring my mouth back up, before sliding back down, my teeth scraping gently along him as I take him a little further into my throat. Jesse groans and I immediately sit back, worried that I had hurt him.

"Jesse, I'm so sorry, did I hurt you? It was a stupid idea I just wanted to…" My rambling comes to a stop when I see how he is looking at me.

He is propped up on both elbows, so he can see me better and his hair falls in messy curls over his forehead, almost obscuring his view. His eyes are glued to me, and they are lit with a passion that I have never seen before. Looking at me like he is the luckiest man in the world he slowly shakes his head as a sexy smile crosses his lips.

"You weren't hurting me, Rhea." His voice low.

"Oh, well in that case…" I trail off before leaning back down to kiss up and down his cock.

I pump my hand around him a few times before placing the tip of him back in mouth. Swirling my tongue around the head I stop when I hear him hissing out a breath. I go to lift my head until I hear him call out.

"Don't stop! God Rhea, it feels so good."

Trying to stop the satisfied smile that crosses my lips, I sink deeper onto his cock.

I soon find a rhythm and realize that I like pleasing him in this way. I have all the power here, and there is something very arousing about that.

"Rhea, Firecracker, come here. If you keep going I am going to cum, and I want to be inside you when that happens," Jesse tells me, his voice tight as he tries to hold himself back.

I sit back on my heels and look at him laying back across the bed like one of those statues they used to have in the museums before the bombs dropped. With a smile, he beckons me forward and I straddle him so my core presses against his cock. We both groan at the contact and lean in to kiss each other at the same time.

This kiss is nothing like last night, last night was about love, this morning it's a frantic need to feel each other's bodies.

"Jesse, I need yo-" I begin, dragging my nails down his chest.

"Jesse, are you up? Have you seen Rhea this morning?" Rex's voice calls from outside the tent.

We still and my face heats with shame. I have been lusting after all of these men, hell, I've even kissed all of them and here I am sleeping with Jesse. What am I doing?! I struggle out of Jesse's arms and hurry for my clothing where it had been discarded around the tent.

"Rhea, wait-" Jesse begins, before cursing as he realises I'm not going to stop.

Tears fill my eyes and threaten to spill as I pull on my shoes and hurry out of the tent. I immediately bump into Rex who reaches out to steady me.

"Woah, Rhea, what's wrong? Is everything okay?" Rex asks, concern clearly written across his face.

I hear cursing and crashing behind me as Jesse tries to get dressed and follow after me. I need to get some space. I pull from Rex's arms and hurry away, my clothing sliding off one shoulder from where I've thrown them on haphazardly.

"Rhea!" I hear Jesse call after me, his voice catching with something that sounds like panic.

"What did you do to upset her?!" I hear Rex accuse Jesse as I run away.

I can't be near those guys at the moment, with my shame clearly written across my face. I need to clear my head, get my thoughts straight. How can I be sleeping in Jesse's arms when I clearly have feelings for the others?

Not just one guy, but five! My head is spinning. The other guys will be disgusted with me when they find out that I want all of them. Sure, I wanted Jesse to be my first, but I couldn't possibly choose between them, I love them all for different reasons. I pause at that word. *Love.* Is that what this is? I've never loved before, I've never ever really had friends, my life in Cinders didn't allow for that.

My breath is coming in pants as I continue my panicked run through the camp. Coming to a stop, I lean against one of the wagons and slide to the ground, resting my head against my knees. I'm just as bad as those women who whored themselves around Cinders.

When women became so scarce and viewed as a prize or possession, those who were left had two options: adapt or die. Of those who adapted there were some who decided to go with changes, deciding the only way to survive was to give the men what they wanted, their bodies.

Am I really any better than them? Maybe Esme was right, perhaps I am a little whore, sharing myself with all the guys in the circus? Will anyone respect me if I share my body around? I may have been little more than a slave back in Cinders, but I have always been firm that I would not debase myself by using my body in that way. I find that the idea of the guys losing their respect for me is what upsets me the most. Since when did their opinions of me matter so much?

My head rises as something soft brushes across my leg. I smile as I see Sid curled up by my feet. Running my hand through his fur, his purrs comfort me. We stay this way for a while until the sound of footsteps has me looking up again. I am calmer now, accepting of what has happened. I do not regret sleeping with Jesse and I won't let shame ruin that. If I am branded a whore for how I feel then I will deal with it, but I can't change the fact that I care for all five of them.

Alcide walks around the side of the wagon and stops when he sees me, his eyes running over my tearstained face and rumpled appearance. I can feel the anger radiating off him and I see his hands balled up into fists.

"I didn't want to believe it," he spits out and I flinch at his words.

"Alcide, I'm sorry-" I begin, scrambling to my feet, trying to pull my clothes into place to cover me fully.

"Don't you dare apologize!" He shouts and I close my eyes shut tight against the tears that threaten to fall again. I hadn't even considered this. Will Alcide make me leave?

"I couldn't believe that Jesse would hurt you-" The anger and disbelief in his tone has my eyes opening as I look at him.

"Wait. What?" I ask, confused. Jesse never hurt me, why would he think that?

"Jesse is beside himself. He says that you two had sex and then something happened, and you ran off. He said he hurt you, thought he set off one of your triggers." Alcide explains, although I can see he is confused at why I'm questioning him.

I want to laugh, but there is nothing funny about this situation.

"Alcide, he didn't hurt me. Yes, we had sex, but I wanted to, and he didn't cause a flashback." I pause and take a deep breath. "I have feelings for all of you-"

"Rhea!" Jesse's worried voice calls out.

Running around the corner Jesse stops when he sees me, Nixon, Blain, and Rex just behind him. I guess I am going to have to say this in front of them all. Jesse looks a mess; his eyes are red like he has been crying.

"I am so sorry-" he begins before I cut him off by walking up to him and placing a finger to his lips.

"Jesse, you didn't hurt me," I say as I take a small step back and look at all of them.

"I ran off because I care for all of you. I don't really know what love is, but I think this might be it. But I feel it for all of you, and I can't choose between you. I ran because I realised that, and I am scared of what you will think of me," I admit, looking at the range of shocked faces.

There is silence for a moment before Jesse pulls me into his arms and hugs me tightly. I feel the tension run off him as I hug him back and hear the sigh of relief that he lets loose. Alcide is looking at the other guys before looking back to me, his eyes soft.

"Cariñoa. Nothing could change our opinion of you. I had no idea when you joined the circus that you would have this effect on us. I'm sure it's not just me, but you have worked your way into our hearts." I see the others nod in agreement, except for Blain who is leaning against one of the wagons, arms crossed as he watches in silence.

"With how the world is, I don't think any of us ever thought that we would have someone like you care for us, which is why we are so close, like brothers. We created a family. If you had chosen one of us, then we would have accepted it, I would not deny my brothers that happiness." He looks at the others again, who once again are nodding in agreement.

"It's not always going to be easy, but don't fight your feelings Rhea, we can make this work," Alcide says before striding towards me and kissing me on the forehead before striding away.

I stand in shock as Jesse hugs me again, emotion shining in his eyes. Rex comes forward and wraps his arms around me.

"You know how I feel about you right?" he asks quietly as he presses his lips softly to mine.

I nod mutely, causing him to smile and pat Jesse on the shoulder.

"Come on Jess, I think you need a drink." He teases, tugging the younger man with him as they walk away.

I glance at Blain who hasn't said a word through this entire scene. He is staring at me, an expression I can't describe on his face. I have no idea what he is thinking. Nodding at me, he pushes away from the wagon and follows after the other guys, leaving me with Nixon.

I look up at the big man and walk slowly towards him. Of all of the guys, Nixon is the one I struggle to read the most. His past has taught him to stay silent, so he is a man of little words. I have learnt to pay attention when he speaks as there is usually a truth behind it. He suffers from triggers, just like I do, and I feel safe around him.

"Nixon," I say before he closes the gap between us.

He gives me that half smile that I love and takes my hand, walking back though the camp. I am still reeling over the conversation, so I follow him silently as we walk towards his tent. I keep stealing glances at him, trying to gauge his reaction to what just happened but he isn't giving anything away.

We reach his tent and he holds open the entrance for me before walking over to where he stores his clothes. Pulling out a large shirt he passes it to me along with a pair of training leggings. I gratefully take it, eager to change out of yesterday's clothes. Nixon turns his back so I can get changed. They are huge on me, the shirt is more like a dress, and I have to roll up the bottom of the leggings, but I feel more comfortable now. I will get changed into my own clothes later, but for now I am enjoying the feeling of Nixon's clothes against my skin with his scent surrounding me.

"So. About what I said," I begin, nervously playing with my hands as I watch him turn around.

I feel his approving gaze as he sees me wearing his clothing. He takes a step towards me before kneeling on the floor bringing his face level with mine and I can see the desire in his stare. He brings his head closer to mine and pauses just before my lips, giving me a chance to pull away. Warmth fills me, and I lean forward, pressing my lips gently to his. This kiss is different from kissing the others, this is soft and gentle, the complete opposite of Nixon's appearance. He moves so he is sitting on the end of the bed and placing his hands on my waist he gently tugs me closer to him, so I am straddling his lap. I can feel his erection pressing against me, but he doesn't hurry the kiss, just lovingly explores my mouth. Bringing one hand to cup my cheek he pulls away, staring into my eyes.

"I love you," he tells me solemnly.

A soft smile spreads across his face as he registers the shock on mine. This gentle giant who has suffered so much at the hands of others, who has suffered so much that he learnt that talking only brought him pain. The enormity of what he just said fills me, the warmth spreading through me. I am about to reply, to tell him what it means to me that he loves me, when he shakes his head softly, pressing a soft kiss to my lips.

"I know," he tells me before shifting my weight, so I am sitting on the bed as he walks towards the tent flap.

He turns back to look at me before exiting, love burning in his eyes and a smile I have never seen before on his lips.

I lay back on the bed, dumbstruck at the events of the day, happiness swirling through me making me feel like I am floating. Until a thought crosses my mind that has me crashing back into reality, we are being hunted. Whether we care to admit it or not. Someone is trying to kill us. I will not allow those bastards to kill the men that I love, or these people that I call family. I had thought it the night before, but it rings with clarity now. I need to protect those I care for. We need to fight, and I need to be a part of that. I need to be stronger, I refuse to hide behind them anymore.

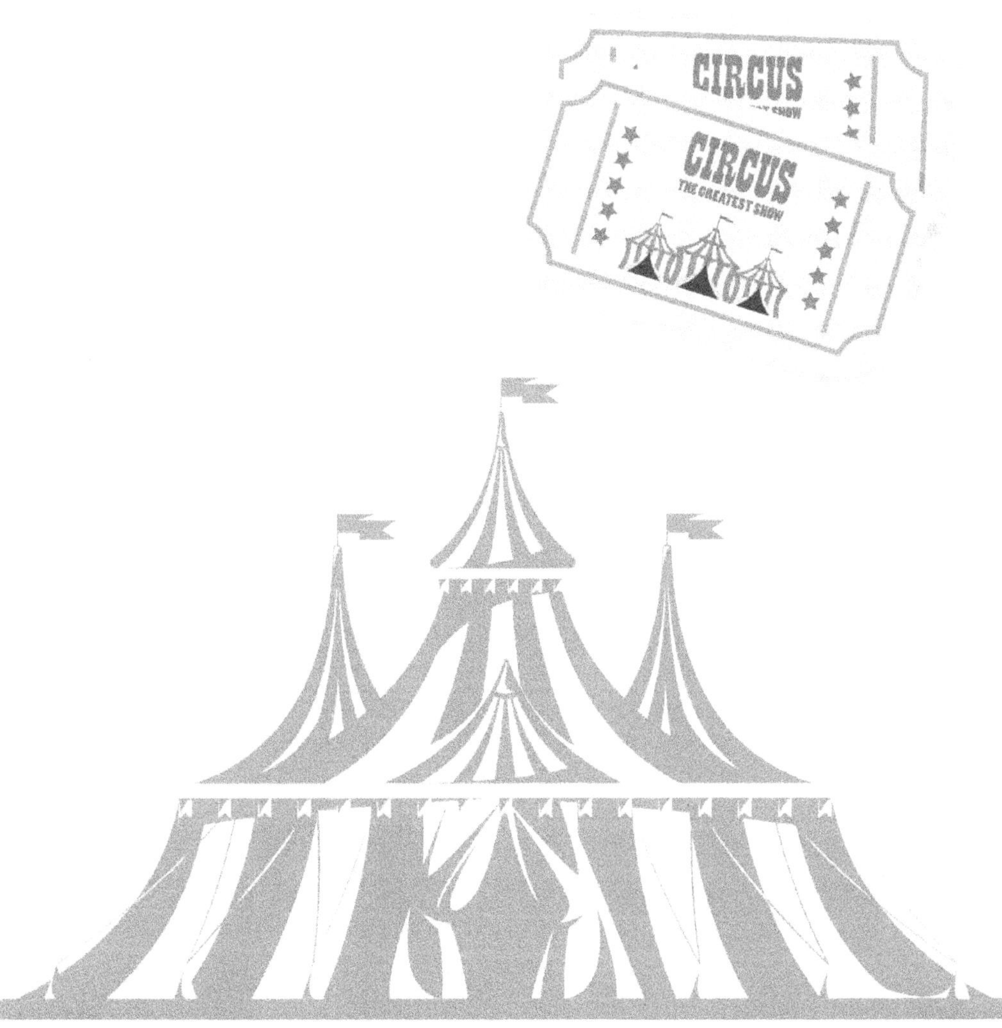
CIRCUS
CIRCUS
THE GREATEST SHOW

Chapter Fourteen

I need to protect them, the thought rings in my head again clearer than before. I can't keep relying on them to always save me, and what if Rex had been really hurt? Or if Blain wasn't there? No, Alcide was right. We need to push ourselves, we need to become who we were meant to be, and I need to do whatever it takes to make sure my family stays safe. I make a quick stop at my tent and change into something a bit more my size. A high necked backless top and some more loose trousers.

Determination lightening my steps as I stride into the big top. It's empty at this time. No more running, no more hiding, it's time I become the freak.

A few stage hands stop at the flap when they see me. I throw them a smile and they smile back before bustling around getting everything ready for the next show. Drawing in a deep breath, I straighten my shoulders and jump over the barrier and into the middle of the ring.

Closing my eyes, I draw on my power, the one that runs through my bones, lighting me up - fueling me. How I ever thought I could suppress this I will never know. With it coursing through me, ready to do my every bidding, I have never felt so powerful. Maybe I needed to see the dark and be weak to become strong and live in the light.

Alcide's words about being *more* run through my head, pushing me, making me want to do better. Snapping my eyes open, I walk slowly to the ladder that leads to the top of the tent. Climbing it, I don't bother looking down. I keep my gaze locked on my target. Once I am up there I look ahead, not wanting to chicken out when I see how far below the ground is. I need to do it myself this time, not be pushed or prodded.

Closing my eyes for a second, I send up a little prayer before embracing my power and stepping over the edge of the platform, plummeting to the ground below.

I let the air whiz past me before opening my eyes and swallowing my panic.

I can do this, I am a freak. I am Rhea the immortal.

I tug on my powers and they cry out at being let free, changing my body, I feel it run through me as I adapt to survive the fall.

I land on the sand, my knees bent, and my arms outstretched. Looking over my shoulder, I spot a pair of beautiful multi-coloured wings. Grinning, I turn and start climbing again. It's harder this time, with the added weight of the wings and halfway up, I have to stop and let the change course through me until I am human again, it was quicker than ever before and in a couple of seconds I am climbing again.

I throw myself off the top of the tent ten more times. Sometimes blindfolded, sometimes backwards until I know with certainty I can draw on my power. Like a muscle that I don't have to think about.

Now, I face Blain's weapons and board. I am guessing the hands must have laid it out ready for him to practise. An evil smile lights my lips, I was planning on practising flying, speed, and reacting to the environment but knowing how to use a weapon would be handy.

I palm one of the smaller knives and eye his target, surely I can reach that... right?

I cock my arm back and throw, it lands on the floor not meters away from me. Grimacing, I grab another, adamant that if Blain can do it - I can. I throw five more, each one no closer than the first, until I am angry at myself. How can I protect those I care about if I can't even throw a knife!

Picking up a bigger one, the anger coursing through me, I cock back my arm and my power bursts forth as I let the blade fly. I watch in shock as it embeds in the centre of the target. Blinking, I stare at it as I hear laughter from behind me.

"Fucking hell, thought I was going to be here all day, Harpy, before you hit that thing. Not bad, now do it again." Blain grins, the scowl nowhere to be seen as pride shines in his eyes. It seems we have come to some sort of understanding. I smile before turning around and selecting another blade. I throw it, but it falls with the others to the floor.

Hot breath fans over the back of my neck making me shiver, I go to turn again when his hands bracket my thighs and he whispers in my ear.

"No, you need to let your powers free. Get angry, get horny, whatever it takes for you to throw like before until it becomes second nature. You are going to throw it again and again until you can hit that bullseye without even looking."

I go to protest and his hands dig into my hips stopping my mouth from opening.

"Yes, Harpy you will. I will not have you weak, useless, and a danger to my family."

I freeze, my body hardening. I had let down my walls, and he's right back to being a dick. I clench my jaw and debate stabbing him with his own knives. He must feel my intent because he laughs before biting my neck, hard.

I gasp and stumble, but he holds me upright.

"I am not saying it to be an asshole, it's the truth. You might not like it, but I will never sugar coat things. Now throw the fucking knife Harpy."

"I can't!" I cry out, "Not with you right behind me."

"You will. You think those hunters are just going to stand still and wait for you to line up your aim?" He growls before pushing me into the table, hard enough to rattle the knives. "They won't go soft on you, they will attack you and they will kill you. So, I want to see that determination I saw when you flung yourself off the top platform ten minutes ago. Pick up the fucking knife and throw it."

Gritting my teeth, I do as he said, only for it to fall short.

"Again," he demands harshly.

I do, time and time again. Each time he gets angrier with me, and me with him until I can feel the tension between us. I don't know whether to stab him or kiss him.

"Maybe you are useless, maybe Esme was right about you," he drawls, and the blow hits me before fury ignites in my body.

Yelling, I pick up a knife and throw, it hits the board right next to my other one.

Blain laughs and brackets me with his arms on the table. "Good, I like that fire, Harpy." He runs his nose down my throat before pulling away and leaving me and my confused body wishing he would have carried on. "Again," he says sternly.

I don't moan or complain, I wanted this. I wanted to be able to protect them, if putting up with him shouting at me gets me there, then so be it.

An hour later my arm is like jelly when Blain declares me 'okay.' I did throw a knife at him this time. He caught it and winked at me, stupid cocky asshole. Why does my body seem to light up when he is like that?

Jesse and Rex wandered in halfway through. At first, they watched then they started practising themselves. I'm glad me and Jesse got a chance to talk, I would hate to have any distance between us, especially after last night. I catch him watching me a couple of times, and he also catches me watching him. I smile back at him and try to focus on Blain showing me how to hold the knives.

I'm now sitting watching Jesse and Rex when Blain slumps down next to me, his legs outstretched, his thigh touching mine.

"I said you wanted my brothers," he murmurs, his eyes on them in the ring.

Licking my lips, I try to think of a way to explain, I knew Blain would be the hard one. Hell, sometimes I don't even think he likes me! Plus, he didn't say anything earlier which has been bugging me, but I didn't want to push him. He and I are like fire and wind, when we come together we explode into chaos. It's not my fault I seem to love that chaos.

"I- erm," I stutter, and he laughs before turning those intense eyes on me.

"It's okay. I know you aren't like, well, what I accused you of being. I see you genuinely care for them."

Bolstering my bravery, I meet his eyes boldly. "I care for you too."

He searches my face before he softens, reaching out with one hand he cups my cheek.

"I know, I don't deserve it, but I know. Just don't hurt us, Harpy. I don't think we would survive."

My eyes close at the heat from his hand, when the pressure disappears they snap open to see he has left. I blink stupidly, being with Blain is like being tied to his board. You never know how close you will get, but the thrill, the fire he ignites in me makes it all worthwhile. But he's wrong, I don't think I would survive if they hurt me, not the other way around.

I get back to training, this time Rex helps me. He and Tiny take turns throwing things, jumping out and creating different environments until I am breathing heavy and collapse on the floor. Even my power seems tired and when I see boots stop next to me, I groan.

A hand reaches down, and I accept it, my eyes meet Alcide's as he pulls me up. I have to catch myself on his chest, not that he cares.

"Thank you," he says quietly, the rest of the tent disappearing like it always seems to when I am around him.

"What for?" I ask breathlessly, I would like to say it is from training but I would be lying.

"You showing them you are pushing yourself, seeing it helps them want to as well. It makes them finally listen to me," he admits.

"That's not why I did it, I wanted to be able to protect you all." My eyes drop to his chest and his finger lifts my chin.

"I know, I see it in your eyes, but look around, Cariñoa. You being in here, you training and letting them help you. It has lit a fire in them, made them want more. Made them not afraid to be more." My eyes flit around as he talks and I see he is right. "If one little girl can come from the dust and pain and still come out swinging, so can they. Thank you for helping my family realise who they can be."

My breathing stops and my heart stutters as right there in the middle of the tent as he leans down and gently ghosts his lips over mine.

"You are our reason to fight, Cariñoa." He pulls back and smiles that breathtaking one at me, making my cheeks heat as he steps back and turns to the others.

"Okay, you have been at this for hours. Let's take a break before we come back and go again."

"What, you going to join in?" Blain scoffs, throwing a knife at Rex, who dodges it. His eyes bright orange, and his hand nowhere near Fluffy, who is watching. They are learning, they are changing, and I can't help but smile at that.

"Yes, I am part of this family. It's time I realised what I can do as well." He throws me a smile before striding out of the tent.

"Well shit, looks like Firecracker can teach an old dog new tricks," Jesse says with a laugh as we all follow after our ringmaster.

We decide to go to town for dinner, seeing as though we are nearly out of food and deserve a break from everything. Everyone is in high spirits and even Blain joins in with us, laughing and joking.

We decide to eat at the pub on the outskirts of town. We take up a big table in the corner, still laughing and teasing between ourselves. We get a few dirty looks but everyone else seems to be unbothered by us and the pub isn't full during the day.

I'm sitting between Jesse and Blain and when a girl, yes girl, just a bit older than me, walks to our table and I see her mouth drop open as she takes in all the guys. I narrow mine on her as she licks her lips and her eyes light up with appreciation. She's pretty, annoyingly so. Her eyes are bright emerald green and her hair a beautiful shade of blonde that hangs around her shoulders in loose waves. Her lips are pink and plump and her body is curvaceous. She has a small scar running through her eyebrow and one along her jawline, but it only adds to her beauty.

"What can I get you, gentlemen?" She purrs, and I can tell that is her natural voice which makes me hate her that much more, her eyes locked on Jesse.

Jesse smiles at her, but it's not as amazing as the one he directs at me. Even so, jealousy rears its ugly head.

He turns to me, his smile turning wicked when he sees my narrowed eyes. "What do you want, Firecracker?"

I sit stiffly in my chair as her gaze moves to me, eyes widening in shock. I can understand why she didn't see me before. Hell, I don't even blame her with all the hotness at this table.

"Ree-ree?" She gasps, her pen and paper dropping to the floor.

I stop breathing as I stare at her. No one calls me that, not since-

"Lily, Liliana?"

Tears fill her eyes as she wraps her arms around herself. "It's you, it's really you."

I can see the others looking confused at me, but I ignore them as I push my chair back and rush to her side. With a cry, we fling ourselves in each other's arms. Talking over each other as we laugh and cry.

"I thought you were dead!" I shout.

"I nearly was, god they wouldn't let me come back for you."

"You-

"-okay?"

We both laugh and pull back.

"Lils, everything okay baby girl?" A big burly man calls from behind the bar. His beard is long and brown and his brown hair fades into it. His eyes are a piercing blue and he's as big as Nixon. He looks like a bear.

"Yes, everything is perfect. Yavin, this is Ree-ree," she calls, swiping at the tears falling down her face. I watch his eyes fill with shock before they swivel to me. Another tall man rounds the bar, his long blonde hair tied back, and brown eyes filled with mischief.

"Yav, I was…" He cocks his eyebrow before looking at Lils. His eyes round in horror as he stumbles back pointing a finger dramatically at her.

"No, nope. Not dealing with your tears again. Last time I ended up naked in a forest with my dick swinging in the wind trying to avoid Yavin's bear hands. Nope, not today." He spins on his heel and marches back through the door.

Yavin smiles as Liliana laughs. She looks back at me.

"Let me get you all some drinks and then we can catch up." I nod as she walks to the man behind the bar, their heads bent together.

She is exactly as I remembered her, a beautiful whirlwind of trouble.

"Wildcat?" Rex calls, my future calling me as my past looks back at me with a smile.

I turn to my family and sit back down in my spot in shock.

"Cariñoa, who is that?" Alcide asks.

"A girl, she- I." I blow out a breath and try again. "We were together in my first house. We went through everything together until one night she didn't come back to the slave quarters after serving the master. I looked for her, but she was nowhere to be found. The next day he told me she was dead. I- Frederick bought me that day and I never saw her again. I guess she got out somehow…" Jesse grabs my hand and squeezes and I throw him a watery smile in thanks.

The pub door slams open as two identical men fill the doorway, both large and wide and they look like Frederick's henchmen in the way they carry themselves. Confident and strong, men who know how to kill someone. They have cold, dark eyes almost black and their hair is cut short. They are handsome but in a terrifying way. They don't bother looking around before striding across the pub, like they own the place, and going straight to Yavin and Liliana. When they look at her, their faces soften and they turn from terrifying to downright stunning.

"Ahem." Alcide coughs, making me blush and turn back to my men who are all watching me with varying degrees of amusement.

"Rhea! You have to leave now!" Liliana shouts as she hurries to my side. She grabs my arm and yanks me up. My men all burst into action. Growling and coming to their feet they try to protect me. She throws them a exasperated look before turning to me with panic in her eyes.

"Hunters are in town." She throws me a meaningful look and I swallow the lump in my throat. Liliana is the only other person besides my men I told about my powers, and only because she saw me use them once.

"We don't know if we can trust her, she could be leading us into a trap," Blain adds casually. I throw him a glare.

"I trust her with my life, if she says there are hunters then there are," I turn back to her as she smiles at me.

She tugs on my hand. "Come on, Yav will take you out the back way and get you out of town." I nod and follow after her, my men right on my heels. She leads us through the bar to the kitchen. I don't get a chance to look around as she drags me to a back door where Yavin waits impatiently. Once there she turns to me, tears in her eyes again.

"Be safe, okay? I will find you again." She smiles sadly as I nod and steps back into the awaiting arms of one of the twins. I square my shoulders and look at Yavin.

"Let's go," I declare with a nod at him. He smiles at me before looking at Liliana.

"I see why you like her, be safe, I will be back," his voice is deep and gruff and matches his exterior but the love in his eyes for my friend softens him.

He hurries us outside and through twisting alleyways until we are at the edge of town, back on the road to lead us to the camp.

"I have to get back to my woman, this road will get you away. Stay to the edge, Lils would be sad if you died." With that, he turns and slips away.

"Come on, let's get back to the camp," Alcide says before coming towards me and wrapping his arm around my shoulders.

We follow Yavin's advice and stick to the side of the road but a twig snaps to our right and before we know it, we are surrounded.

The attack is fast and brutal, and I find myself facing off with two men. There are more than ever before, at least fifteen large skilled hunters attacking my men.

Rex throws me a worried look and tries to get to my side to protect me but gets cut off by a large man who throws a punch at him. I don't have time to panic as the two men advance on me.

I refuse to run, I straighten my shoulders and wait for them to get closer. The one on the right rushes forward and I just manage to duck under his punch. Using the movement, I lean down and grab my dagger from my boot. I spring back up and slash at the man who stumbles back with a cut across his chest. He fingers it before scowling at me. They both start to circle me, and I spin trying to keep them in my eyesight. One starts to advance, and I dart forward and stab my knife towards him. He cries as he falls to the ground, blood spreading through his shirt and dripping off him. Another hunter takes his place and I prepare to carry on fighting.

Nixon barrels into them, throwing them both across the road. His back to me as he heaves a breath. I keep my dagger out as I watch the others slip past the attackers and run to us.

"Let's go! There's too many!" Blain shouts as he runs to my side.

The distraction is all it takes for two men to fling themselves at Nixon. He roars as he tries to fight them off.

"Nixon!" I scream as more men pile onto the furious giant, to the man who holds my heart. His eyes meet mine, filled with determination and acceptance as Blain picks me up and throws me over his shoulder. Tears stream down my face, but I keep my eyes locked on his. I watch them soften for an instant before he cries out and falls to the floor and we turn a corner, so I can't see him anymore.

I fight against Blain's hold, desperate to go and help Nixon but his grip is too strong.

"Harpy, will you quit it!" He shouts at me as he hurries after the others.

"Blain, put me down! We have to help Nixon, he is hurt!" I cry out, my voice breaking at the thought of my gentle Nix getting hurt.

The panic at losing him is beginning to rise in the back of my throat and I am struggling to keep my thoughts rational.

"Blain, if you don't put me down I will make you let me go. I don't want to hurt you, but we *need* to help him," I implore, not understanding why they aren't helping their brother.

Stopping, he pulls me roughly off his shoulder and grabs both my shoulders, making me look at him.

"Rhea, we have to get you out of here. Any one of us would die if it meant that you would be safe," he tells me harshly and pain flashes through me at the thought.

"But he doesn't have to die! We can help him!" I insist, my voice getting hysterical as my worry increases.

Blain roars in frustration and shakes me, the worry for his brother clear in his eyes.

"You think I want to leave him? It is killing me that we are leaving without him. It would be suicide to go back right now. We need to go back to the circus. We will come back for him, we look after our own, do you hear me, Harpy?" His stare is burning, and I am forced to nod.

Taking my hand again he turns and runs back towards the circus, me stumbling along behind him, my heart breaking a little more with each step we take away from Nixon. I can't help but feel we are giving up on him.

We sit in the silent ring of the big top, the atmosphere heavy with worry. Alcide had done a roll-call when we got back to check everyone was accounted for. There was a noticeable pause when he called Nixon's name, but thankfully he is the only one missing. The rest of the performers and crew have retired for the night but Alcide has asked us to stay. We have waited, hoping that Nixon would stumble in through the entrance. This was Nixon after all, our strong man, surely nothing could beat him? But as the hours passed by and there was still no sign of him, the mood descended further.

"We need to go back," I say, my voice scratchy.

I am not ashamed to say that I've been crying. Some might say it makes me look weak, but I don't think that's the case, even Blain didn't make a comment.

"She is right," Blain agrees, shocking me.

The others are nodding and Alcide walks closer, a gleam in his eyes that usually signals he has an idea.

"Okay, let's get our brother back," Alcide states.

A shout interrupts what he was going to say next and has us all jumping to our feet. I run towards the sound, the guys close on my heels.

There is a crowd around one of the wagons and I see Esme amongst them. Even she looks upset which worries me. She has seemed quite calm throughout the issues with the hunters, so the fact that she is upset now has fear lining my stomach. I push towards the front of the group, wishing I hadn't when I see what everyone is looking at.

Dropping to my knees with a cry, I can't pull my eyes from the side of the wagon. Written on the side in what looks like blood is a message, along with a human hand nailed to the wall of the wagon.

WE KILLED THE GIANT. WHO IS NEXT?

Chapter Fifteen

'm ashamed to say I don't remember much after that. Someone's warm arms picked me up and carried me through the camp until we were in a tent. I can't find it in myself to care where we are or who holds me. I'm on someone's lap, being rocked back and forth but when I feel something drip into my hair and dampen my face, that I start to come back to myself. Shame fills me. How selfish can I be? They are just as, if not more, upset than me, this was their brother and here I am taking all the attention. I lift my head, but it seems to take forever until I spot Blain's face. To say I'm shocked is an understatement. I thought it would have been Jesse or Rex, not the surly asshole. When he sees me looking, he wipes his tears and looks at me with red rimmed eyes.

"I'm sorry," I croak. He frowns at me, a hint of the scowl I am so used to seeing flirting with his lips.

"Why the fuck are you sorry, Harpy?" he demands.

I duck my head, burying it in his shoulder.

"It's my fault, if I hadn't been with the circus, if I hadn't come along…" I hiccup, my tears starting again. Nixon's face flashes in my mind making me cry harder. What we had was new and different, but strong nonetheless. A part of me recognised Nixon and he understood me and my scars like no one else. And now he is gone…

I'll never get to kiss his lips again. I'll never feel the safety of his arms or see that little smile.

I grip onto Blain's shirt as he wraps his arms around me.

"Listen up and listen good Harpy. It is not your fault, it was the hunters who attacked *us*, and Nixon knew exactly what he was doing. Sitting around here crying isn't going to change anything," he growls the last part, but I can hear the pain and suffering in his voice.

I raise my head again, uncaring I look like a mess. "Then what will?"

"We make them pay," he growls.

The tent flap opens behind me as I watch darkness bloom and overtake Blain's eyes until they are black and menace vibrates from his body.

"I can't lose you too," I whisper. He clenches his jaw before leaning forward and kissing me softly.

Without speaking, he gently places me on the bed and I watch with my broken heart scattered around me as he leaves me. Alcide watches me from just inside the tent. His face empty of emotion. He looks numb, but that's okay, I am feeling enough for the two of us. Guilt is wrapping around my body with regret, Blain might not blame me yet, but he will.

Without speaking, Alcide comes and sits next to me on the bed, his elbows on his knees as he looks at the floor. He is silent for a moment and I wonder if he is going to say anything.

"He-he can't be *gone*," he whispers, my usual confident and charming ringmaster gone in the flash of an eye.

"Alcide - I'm sorry." It's not nearly enough but it keeps slipping from my lips, not that he seems to hear me.

"Did you know he saved me?" he says around a bitter laugh, it soon turns to sobs before he grips his thighs and staunches his crying.

"When?" I ask curiously.

"When I was younger. I was a poor kid, turning tricks. I had just started at the circus when it was owned by Nixon's old man. Back then it was more of a place of torture. I always had this dream in my head of it being about family, not exhibitions. Not somewhere for people to gawk at us, but a place to belong. Nixon's father was a bastard, a stone-cold bastard. I had strung up the lights 'wrong'." He lets out another bitter laugh. "It was an excuse to beat me. It was bad. I remember laying on the grass drenched in my own blood when Nixon came charging in. He protected me from him."

"What was Nixon like back then?" I ask curiously. I watch a beautiful smile grace his face as he thinks about his brother.

"Quiet, even then. I never understood why but he was always there when you needed him. He just knew… He knew I was like him and he decided to stick with me. He protected me quite a lot, and in turn I promised him I would free him from his father's abusive hands…" He looks at me, the tears trailing down his cheeks. "Have you ever seen his back?" He asks.

I hesitantly nod, and he frowns in pain.

"Back then, he had less scars, but I failed to protect him and instead he got between me and his father. His father tried to kill him for that, and almost succeeded until my power decided to reveal itself. I charmed his father into walking off a cliff. Some of the older circus performers didn't agree with the torture either, and together we chased off his father's friends and I nursed Nixon back to health. When he woke up he was different, more withdrawn. He hardly ever smiled, until you."

I wipe at the tears streaming down my face and stare at him again. I know I should feel cold at Alcide's causal mention of killing Nixon's dad, I always knew there was something darker about Alcide. But, I can't find it in me to care, a part of me is pleased that he killed Nixon's abusive father.

"What happened to the other performers?" I ask quietly.

"Some stayed, some chose to leave now that they weren't slaves. Those who stayed helped me build this, build my dream for a safe place for us freaks. But Nixon? He was the start of it all, he pushed me to dream, pushed me to be me and then protected me. He can't be gone." His voice breaks on the last word, spreading agony through my chest. I don't know how to make this better.

Slowly, the others trickle in as if they need to be with each other, like they sense their ringmaster's pain. Alcide looks like a broken shell of himself and so do the others. All of their eyes are red rimmed, and their shoulders slumped.

"Thank you for telling me that," I whisper and grip his hand. He nods, and we fade to silence, all fighting our own demons and broken hearts. It feels wrong, it feels so empty in here without my gentle giant taking up space. The message on the wagon flashes through my head again and I cringe before thinking it through. It's a slow process, my head hurting from all the crying and my heart still painful.

"Do we know for sure it was his hand?" I feel Alcide freeze next to me as he thinks through my question. "Or that they are telling the truth? What if he is still alive?" I ask softly.

"We need to be sure," Alcide confirms, rebuilding his usual confidence as he stands. He nods, and the others' faces fill with purpose even as their eyes hold pain.

"I'm coming with you," I say, standing up from the bed to face them.

"It's not safe for you. You will stay behind and that is final. Come on," he says to the others, ignoring the fury radiating from me. Behind it all is sadness. They think I am weak, and I haven't exactly proved them wrong today. It's my fault Nixon is gone, although I refuse to believe he is dead, especially now that the shock has worn off. I would know if he was, my heart wouldn't be able to keep beating. Blain throws me a look before following Alcide, and Jesse drops his head before following after them. Only Rex hesitates.

"Stay safe, Wildcat." His voice is empty, and I can see the darkness in his eyes as he turns and follows his brothers, leaving me all alone in the tent, my heart shattering at the idea of losing them too.

I am pacing around the ring of the big top, my emotions warring for a place within me. Anger surges through me at being left behind, that they think I am weak. It's like I am a slave again, a possession rather than a person with feelings and opinions. Alcide spouts that I am equal here, like family, but when things get tough, *he* has decided what is best for me without considering my opinion. Part of me knows that he is doing this to keep me safe, that he can't bear to lose me too. No, we haven't lost Nixon, I won't think that way. I try to rationalise that Alcide is so used to being in charge, and people following his orders that he does it without thinking. The fact that the guys went along with it too fuels my blood with a rage that I hadn't known I possessed.

Worry for the guys also fills me, I can't lose them either. It was so easy for them to leave me behind for my own good, for their peace of mind, but what about mine? I am just as worried about them, but it is fine for them to march off into danger. As a slave, I've never had my own free will. Always owned, my mind was invariably made up for me. The abhorrent treatment of women has consistently felt unjust, unfair. It was not until I experienced the freedom of being treated as an equal, that I realise how important it really is. Now that has been taken away from me again, I'm not going to take it lying down. They have taught me how to have a mind of my own, encouraged it, but they feel free to shut that down when it benefits them..

I'm going to follow them. Why should I stay behind? I care for Nixon just as much as they do. He is probably injured. I know that I'm not the best fighter, but I can help bring him back and protect him if I need to. They have already been gone an hour or so, they should be back by now. What if they are in trouble? Mind made up, I stalk towards the exit, freezing in place when I see several menacing looking guys staring at me from the tent flaps.

I don't recognise them, and from their expressions they mean me harm. Their next comments confirm it.

"They left one of their women behind… Unprotected." He sneers, his sick gaze running over me.

Fury fills me.

"Why is it you men always assume because I am a woman I can't protect myself?" I demand, fire fueling my voice.

The man looks at his friends and sniggers before taking a step towards me, a couple of his thug buddies following him.

"Okay sweetheart, you want a piece of me? Help yourself." He leers, clearly underestimating me.

Right, enough is enough. I need to prove to everyone, even to my guys, that I can protect myself. They are never going to treat me equally if they think they have to look after me and wrap me in bubble wrap every time a difficult situation appears.

The first guy rushes towards me and I run forward to meet him. That throws him off guard, he expected me to run in the opposite direction. Channeling what Jesse taught me, I place my hands on his shoulders and jump, using my momentum to flip over the top of his head. I focus on the fact that these bastards are here to hurt me and the guys to fuel my actions. Spinning so I am facing his back, I place my hands where Nixon and Blain have shown me and twist his neck sharply as I was taught. I try to ignore the sickening crack of his neck as he drops to the floor before he can even realise what is going on. I know this moment will haunt my dreams, but I can't focus on that right now. These guys hurt Nixon and now they've come for me.

The other guys have stopped and watch in shock as their buddy dies at my hands. Their faces twist in fury as they advance towards me. I close my eyes briefly and call on the power running through my veins to toughen my skin. I look around the tent to see if there is anything I can use as a weapon, as these guys clearly have knives. There is nothing here, I guess I must become the weapon. I don't have time to think any further other than to trust my body as I am surrounded, more unknown men filling the tent.

Everything blurs around me as I focus on protecting myself from the advancing men, my skin tingles and I know my powers are helping me. It doesn't help that I don't have a weapon. Almost as I think those words my hands tingle and my nails have grown into what look like razor sharp talons. I spin like a tornado, my body faster than usual as I throw out my arms, slashing and hitting at anything that comes close to me. Finally, there is just me and one more guy, who is looking nervous now that his buddies are laying on the ground. I punch the last guy in the face, catching him off guard and knocking him out when I hear running footsteps.

Cursing, I spin around, covered in other people's blood and panting from exertion. There in the entrance is Rex, Jesse, and Alcide watching me with their mouths open wide in shock. Blain walks in clapping, his usual smirk in place but I can see that he is proud of me.

"See Alcide, I told you she would be fine," he goads as he walks towards me, his eyes running over my body.

His words may sound tough, but I can see him checking me for injuries as he gets closer. Picking up one of my hands he runs a finger along one of my talons, shaking his head as it slices his finger. Placing the finger in his mouth he looks at me with lust in his eyes, as if all the danger and bloodshed has turned him on. *Strange man.*

"Talons. Why am I not surprised Harpy?" he teases.

Jesse and Rex rush towards me and I can't help but to breathe a sigh of relief as I see they are uninjured, even though I am still mad at them.

"Rhea! Are you okay?" Rex asks, eyeing the blood covering me.

"I'm fine. I protected myself," I say shortly, turning to look at Alcide who hasn't moved from the tent entrance. "You left me," I accuse.

He nods at me, taking slow steps forwards.

"I did. I thought you'd be safe here. I see I was wrong. I just wanted to keep you safe. I'm sorry Rhea."

The fact that he has admitted that cools my anger, and I think back to what he said before. This isn't always going to be easy, this is as new to them as it is to me. We were going to have to learn to trust and rely on each other, and that included them relying on me.

"Rhea," Jesse calls and I turn to the youngest member of the circus.

He is practically bouncing up and down on his feet. I turn to the others and see that whilst they are not acting like they usually do, they seem more positive, their eyes gleaming.

"What? What happened?" I ask, nerves filling me at their expressions.

"We found him Rhea. Nixon is alive."

Chapter Sixteen

As soon as they tell me about Nixon, I want to go and get him, but they refuse. They say we need to re-group, to plan. I disagree. I am sitting with the guys, a bowl full of broth in front of me, which I am stirring aimlessly. I don't have an appetite, in fact, I feel sick after the events of the day play through my mind. I take a spoonful of the food to please the guys, all of them watching me nervously, although they are pretending not to. I stir the broth again before sighing and placing down my spoon.

"Tell me again, what happened?" My voice is weary.

I have heard this before, but I need to hear it again. Jesse looks up, his eyes are sad. He hates that I was left behind for my own safety but was attacked anyway.

"We went back to where we were attacked and followed their tracks back to their camp, it wasn't far from the town." He explains again in a low voice.

Rex walks over from his place by the cooking pot and sits next to me, placing his hand on my knee. Usually, the gesture would comfort me, but my emotions are all over the place right now.

"When we got to the camp, we could hear loud cheering noises, so we followed them and we saw Nixon." Rex takes over the story, but as he stops I know there is more that they didn't tell me the first time.

"Tell me," I demand quietly, I will not be coddled.

Rex and Jesse look at each other like they are deciding if I can handle hearing what comes next.

"Tell me!" I cry out, needing to know.

I am overjoyed that Nixon is still alive, but I need to know if he is okay.

Blain throws his spoon down into his broth and looks up at me, fury in his eyes but I don't think it's directed at me.

"He was tied to a whipping post, Harpy. Is that what you want to hear?" He spits out, his anger making his words harsh. "He was being whipped in front of them all, and they were cheering as if it was some kind of sport." He stands up from the table and looks at the others. "And we did nothing."

"Blain. We spoke about this. We couldn't attack then, not in the state Nixon was in, we wouldn't have made it back," Alcide pipes up, his expression tired like he has the weight of the world on his shoulders.

"I know," he mutters, and it's self-loathing I can hear in his voice. "But we just left him. Again."

The others fall silent and look at their half-finished meals, seems I'm not the only one who isn't hungry.

"There is nothing we can do to help him tonight. Get some sleep and we will come up with a plan to get him tomorrow." Alcide stands and I can see what it cost him to say this. I know that Alcide and Nixon go back a long way, that he is his oldest friend. The others nod, and I feel my anger start to rise. Not at them, but the situation. They would want to leave me behind again, even though I have proven myself. I still haven't fully forgiven them for that, and I can't take the risk that they will leave me behind again.

I stand up and push away from the table, all eyes falling on me as I do this.

"I'm heading to bed," I inform them, and I know the grey bags under my eyes show how tired I am.

Rex nods and stands up, moving towards me.

"I'll come with you," he softly tells me, and we walk towards his tent.

Stepping inside, I start to pace the small space, my emotions needing an outlet. Nixon is alive. My heart soars, only to crash a second later. He may be alive, but the hunters are hurting him. They told us he was dead, so they aren't using him as bait or ransom. Which means they are probably going to kill him. Why haven't they then? A dark part of me thinks it's because they want to stretch out his pain for as long as possible.

"Rhea." Rex's soft voice pulls me out of my anxious pacing.

I look over at him and from his troubled expression, I can tell he is struggling with leaving his brother behind just as much as I am. I hurry over to him and hold back tears as he wraps his arms around me.

"We have to get him back," I mutter into his chest.

"I know." Is his only reply as he runs his hands up and down my back in comfort.

I look up at him again to see he is gazing at me. Our eyes lock and our despair turns to something else, something carnal. A need I've never experienced before runs through me and I see it reflected in Rex's eyes. My mouth crashes into his and I moan as he kisses me back, enjoying the feel of him exploring my mouth. My hands run up his back, pulling his shirt up as I go.

"Rhea…" He gasps out around my kisses, stopping as I pull his shirt over his head.

I should be taking this slower, I've never gone this far with anyone other than Jesse, but right now I need this comfort. Looking at Rex and seeing the mixture of desire and despair across his face, I can tell he needs it too.

"Shhh…" I murmur into his mouth, returning his kisses.

I feel the moment he gives over to his desire as his hands start to roam my body. He feels unsure until I moan into his mouth as his hand runs over my breast. The uncertainty disappears as he pulls me closer to him, his cock pressed against my body, his arousal clear. I drag my nails down his back which seems to spur him on more. I let out a little shriek as he lifts me up and carries me to the bed. Gently placing me on it he stares down at me, his eyes alight with desire. I bite down on my lip as I look back at him, suddenly remembering that I'm still a novice at this.

I forget this as he kneels down and climbs up onto the bed, and like one of the animals he loves, starts crawling towards me, the gleam of a predator clear to see. I lay back as he climbs over me, his hand skimming up my stomach and coming to rest on my breast. My back arches off the bed as he squeezes my nipple through the fabric. I reach down and pull at my top, desperate to get rid of the layer between us. He chuckles deeply as he watches me before leaning forward to capture my mouth, his hand working its way back to my breast.

I am desperate to feel him, and I reach towards him, fighting past his waistband until I feel his hard, velvety cock in my hand. I start to stroke the length of him, surprised at how big he feels, pausing when he groans and closes his eyes, pressing his forehead to mine. Worried I've hurt him, I start to pull away.

"Don't stop Rhea, it feels so good," his breathy comment brings a smile to my lips as I carry on the delicious torture.

He decides to get me back and slides his hand down the front of my leggings, cupping me. I gasp into his mouth as he gently strokes my folds before pushing a single finger inside me. I gasp again, still a little sore from my night with Jesse. Rex must feel me stiffen as he pulls away to look at me.

"Sorry, I forgot you're new to all this. I'm too eager, I've wanted to do this for weeks," he tells me before kissing me deeply again.

I relax into the kisses and resume stroking up and down his cock. His fingers move up to my clit and he starts moving around it in small circles. My breath starts coming out in pants as he winds me higher and higher with his talented hands. His fingers dip back down into my folds and he groans at the wetness he feels there.

"You're so wet. Are you ready?" He asks, his own breath coming out fast.

I nod in reply and try to wiggle out of my leggings, but my legs are tangled in his and I can't get them off. Laughing he moves away from me, removing his own trousers as I struggle out of mine. My eyes widen as I see Rex in all his naked glory and I wonder how he is going to fit. Crawling back on the bed, Rex settles over me, his cock teasing my entrance before he groans and pulls away slightly.

"Rhea, we should stop. I don't have any protection on me," he grits out, and my heart swells that he would think about something like that. Many men in this world wouldn't stop to think about that.

"It's okay. I can't get pregnant," I admit quietly. "When I never got my period, Frederick sent me to a doctor, I can't conceive." I expect Rex to be pleased about this, but I see something sad flash across his eyes before he leans in to kiss me again.

His cock presses against my entrance again and he slowly eases inside me. I gasp, he is so big, and I am still a little tender but slowly he fills me and stills to let my body adjust. He moves slightly, sending desire straight through me and I start to rock underneath him. Laughing, Rex mutters something about me being impatient before claiming my mouth once again as he pulls out almost all the way, before sliding back in again. I urge him on, needing it harder, needing all of him. A pressure builds up and we begin to lose rhythm as we come closer to our climax. Rex slides his hand between us and presses his thumb against my clit, pushing me over the edge. Rex joins me shortly after as I clench around him, his breathy groan filling the tent.

Now that we are both sated, he pulls out and collapses next to me. A happy smile fills his face, until he remembers what we have to deal with tomorrow. I place my hand on his cheek, this man has come to mean so much to me, all of them have and tomorrow I could lose them all. I close my eyes and curl up into his side, the afterglow of sex not enough to chase away my fears. There is only one thing that will do that, I know what I have to do.

Rex's arms slacken around me as he falls asleep and I start to plan. I can't let these guys get hurt, I know now that losing any of them is going to break me in a way I know I can't heal. I also can't risk them leaving me behind again. There is only one option, I need to go and rescue Nixon on my own.

The air is cold and misty, and I shiver as I hurry through the barren land. I know I am being rash, but I have this *feeling*, call it an instinct, I know I *have* to go tonight. My escape from the circus was uneventful and surprisingly easy. I feel bad, leaving them behind, but they will understand...I hope.

I follow my gut feeling that has never let me down, until I see a light in the distance. The camp has been built around some derelict buildings out in the wastelands. Not too far from the town but no one dares come out this way usually, as the threat from mutated predators and gangs makes this land dangerous. Adrenaline, fear, and the misty weather is playing on my overactive imagination and I am jumping at shadows. Maybe Alcide and the others were right, perhaps I should go back, and we can do this together. No. I can't risk that, they might hurt Nixon more.

I crouch down, using the shrubbery and long grass for cover as I scuttle closer to what I discover is a campsite. This must be where the guys had come. In the middle of a cluster of buildings is a campfire and inside some of the doorways I can see discarded bottles and blankets. Someone has definitely been staying here, but it seems too quiet and I can't see anyone around. But I don't dare go any closer until I have a better plan, there could be anyone inside those buildings and I need to know where Nixon is being kept.

A noise in the distance has me ducking down again and a feeling of horror fills me as I see a shape lumbering towards me. I've been spotted! I stand, prepared to fight, I will not go down without one.

"Rhea." A deep whispered voice reaches me, and I have to fight against crying out.

"Nixon!" My voice breaks as I run to my protector.

Flinging my arms around him, I pull back as he grunts in pain. I am horrified by what I see. His face has been beaten so badly I hardly recognise him. There isn't an inch of skin that isn't bruised or bleeding. My eyes well up with tears, but I fight against them as a dark anger fills me.

"Rhea, you need to go," he tells me, his voice broken. "The hunters...they are going to attack the circus...you have to go warn them," he pleads, his breath coming in big pants.

I had wondered why getting this close was so easy. I must have passed them on the way and not even realised. I had left to save Nixon when the others were in danger.

"We have to go!" The urgency in my voice has Nixon shaking his head at me.

"I can't. I would just hold you back. You have to go without me." His voice is dark and I know it's costing him a lot to say this, to admit he isn't strong enough.

I hate the thought of leaving him when I've just found him again, but he is right, I have to warn the others. I take a deep breath.

"I'm not leaving you, not again. But I agree you can't fight. Come back with me and wait outside the camp. If you run into trouble go back to the pub and find Lilly, she will help you. I will come back for you when it's over."

Nixon doesn't look happy but he nods in agreement, knowing that I won't take no for an answer. I look him over again and relief fills me as I see that although he is badly injured, he still has both hands. I don't want to know what poor soul lost their hand for the message left for us. I pull his arm around me and we start the walk back towards the circus.

We walk in silence, but we don't need to talk to know how the other feels. We come to a stop when we can see the bright lights of the circus in the distance. I turn to look at Nixon, leaning forward I press a soft kiss to his lips, my heart filling with bittersweet happiness as he returns the kiss. Placing my hand gently on his cheek, I try to memorise his face in case I didn't see it again.

No, I won't think like that. We will see each other again.

I squeeze his hand and help him sit in the tall grass behind the shelter of a large rock. I start to walk away but stop and glance over my shoulder and see he is still watching me. A thought occurs to me.

"How did you get out?"

He just gives me that half smile I love and a half-hearted shrug of his shoulders.

"I knew you were coming for me." Is his only answer.

I smile back at him, my heart breaking as I take a step away from him. Time to go warn my family.

CIRCUS
THE GREATEST SHOW
CIRCUS
THE GREATEST SHOW

Chapter Seventeen

he moon shines around the camp, and the fog has rolled in, turning my home, the place I sought sanctuary, into a nightmare. It doesn't help that I know somewhere hiding between the tents are hunters just waiting to kill me and my family.

Shadows are thrown everywhere by the moon's rays making me extra jumpy as I slowly make my way through, ignoring the bad feeling blooming in my gut.

I start at the outskirts, slowly checking every tent. I don't want any hunters to jump out behind me. It's slow going and with each minute, I can feel my panic building. That I will be too late, that they will already be dead.

I shake my head, I refuse to think that. Other than two hunters at the camp border that I hit over the head with my hands that hardened into rock, I haven't seen any more. Maybe they are all waiting in the middle, or maybe they think I have run off never to come back. It doesn't look like they care. They are underestimating me, thinking that they have everyone that could possibly hurt them or stop them. I am going to prove them wrong.

After searching all the tents but the big top and animal tent I groan, I knew they would be in there. A scream has me spinning around and moving behind the tent I was just searching. Just in time as Esme runs into view between the tents before falling with a cry. I spot an arrow peeking out of her leg and freeze. A big guy, obviously a hunter strolls into view whistling to himself as he watches her. He grins before leaning down and pulling out the arrow. She wails and turns pale but manages to stay conscious.

"So, you want to run?" he sneers, his wide face breaking with it. He's dressed in all black, like the others, and his hair is cut short. He has weapons strapped to nearly every inch of his body - a few covered in blood. I don't think about who it belongs to as my eyes drop back to Esme.

"Fine, let's play." He laughs.

Esme crawls along the ground, tears streaming down her distraught face as the hunter stands tall above her, sneering at her attempts to escape. He stomps on her leg, her scream cuts through the night and makes me shake in fear.

"Did you really think we would let you live? That just because you told us a few bits of information, you would be spared?" He shouts, spittle flying from his mouth.

He leans down and flips her over and she cries out. Dragging her up by her ripped shirt he backhands her before grabbing her cheeks and forcing her to look at him.

"You are nothing, you are a freak. A mistake, a fucking mutation."

He backhands her again and lets her fall to the ground in a sobbing heap. She tries to crawl again, her fingers grabbing onto the grass and pulling as he taunts her.

"You betrayed your family, and for what? You are going to die alone!" He shouts before laughing.

She raises her face and her eyes round when they spot me hiding behind the tent. I freeze, sure she is going to call out, sure she will betray me. I always thought there was something off about her but how could she betray the guys? They took her in, gave her a home, a place to belong.

Her eyes close before opening, new determination in their depths.

"Run." She mouths at me before turning over, stopping her slow crawl towards where I am.

"I made a mistake. I was angry, I thought I was being tossed aside. That they were replacing me with that girl." No real hate warms her voice and it stops me from turning and doing what she instructed. She has accepted her fate, stopped running to try and give me time to get away.

"Your man was slimy, he convinced me it was for the best. That they wouldn't hurt my family, that they would just take care of the girl. Get rid of her."

"And you didn't care what happened to her, you are no better than the devils you claim we are." He kneels over her, running a knife through his hands. Blowing out a breath I hesitate, I need to get to my guys but I can't leave her to be tortured. She might have betrayed us, trusted someone for the wrong reason, but I can't condemn her to death.

The guys are going to be so pissed.

The thought makes me smile as I step out from behind the tent and into the light. He doesn't see me at first, intent on cutting slow shallow strokes with his knife into a screaming Esme.

Palming my knife, I remember everything Blain taught me.

"Hey, asshole?" I wait for him to look up before letting the knife fly. It embeds in his eye and I watch the horror bloom over his face before his eyes become vacant. He slumps to the side, partially covering Esme and I jog over and help her move the body. I ignore him and grab the knife, nearly vomiting at the noise it makes leaving his skull.

"Thank you," she cries. I just nod and turn to the last tent I haven't searched - the big top.

"Where are you going?" She gasps, grabbing my arm and pulling herself to her feet. I glare at her hand then her.

"I might have saved you, but I don't forgive you. You betrayed us, you nearly got us all killed all because you were jealous?" I whisper shout in her face. She hangs her head in shame before looking at me.

"Yes. Yes, I did. I can't change the past, but please… let me help you save our family. Let me earn my redemption. It's my fault we are here, let me make it right."

I search her eyes and see the truth of her words, her usual pride and attitude lays in tatters like her shirt and I can see the horror in her eyes at the knowledge she caused this.

She might not be a good person, she might have betrayed us all, but everyone deserves a second chance.

"Fine. Stay behind me and get ready to use your powers, we are going to need them." I face the tent again.

"What's the plan?" She asks, and I am glad to see her straighten with new purpose, even as pain flickers over her face.

"We show them how the freaks protect what is theirs."

We share a grin as we fade into the night, ready to fight for our circus, and our family.

Chapter Eighteen

"What if we get the animals to help?" I whisper to Esme as we near the big top. She throws me a look but closes her mouth on whatever sarcastic comment she was going to make. To me the animals are like family, they would want to help, and Esme doesn't get that, she never has. Wisely she doesn't voice her opinion.

"That… might work," she concedes.

Her comment surprises me, maybe she has changed? Or at least working towards changing and being more accepting. I don't have time to comment though, but perhaps she can redeem herself? Not that I trust her.

We head to the tent next to the big top and slip inside. The inside is darkened and it's obvious all the lights have been turned out. I pray that the hunters have left the animals alone, although the quiet from the tent makes me wonder if they are still here. We have never caged the animals, they are free to come and go as they please, so I wouldn't blame them if they escaped when the fighting started.

"Fluffy? Tiny? Rumple?" I call hesitantly.

I manage to hold in my scream as I am thrown to the floor, Fluffy landing on my chest and licking my cheek.

"Hey buddy, I need your help," I coo. He tilts his head then slinks off my body and waits beside me. Soon I am surrounded by animals, even Rodger slips out of the darkness and to our side. Sid bounds out of the darkness and plops down to the ground next to me. I can sense Esme's fear of them, but I feel better with them near me. I crouch to the floor and face them all, talking to them like they understand me, which I know they can.

"Okay, the hunters have the guys in the big top. I don't know how many hunters, or where they are. I need you guys to slip in from every possible direction and work together to distract them and if you can, take them down. Tiny, I need you to get to the guys and try and get them out of whatever chains they are in."

"How do you know they are chained?" Esme hisses. I throw her a cocky look.

"If they weren't chained, they would have already escaped and killed the hunters." I turn back to the animals.

"Do what you do best. Rumple and Bubbles I want you to go with Tiny to the guys."

Tiny nods so does Rumple while Bubbles blinks at me.

"Okay, let's do this then," I say nervously, I try to hide it, but it would be no use. I don't know what we are walking into, I don't even know if they are alive...but I am about to find out. No, I would know if they were dead, I am sure of it. Something deep inside me told me not to give up on Nixon, and that was true, it guided me to him. That same part of me is telling me the guys are still alive, and I am going to trust in it. Time to face the music.

I turn back to Esme and she nods at me, slipping out of the animal tent, we go around the back of the big top. I'm not stupid enough to go in guns blazing in the front entrance. That's what they would be expecting. I have to remember that they always underestimate me, so I am going to use that to my advantage.

When we are outside the flap, I let the change run through me, hardening my skin in preparation for anything. I turn back to Esme.

"Stay behind me, my skin is indestructible. Use your powers when you can, try and get the weapons out of their hands," I whisper, she nods but looks terrified, so I give her a smile. She cocks her eyebrow at my failed attempt and I shrug and turn back to face the tent.

I poke my head around the tent flap, trying to get a glimpse of the guys without being seen, the need to know if they are alright burning through me. The guys are all there and alive, but this is going to be tricky. Alcide has a gag tied tightly around his mouth so he can't use his powers. I can't see Blain properly, but he is slumped forward, so something must be stopping him from using his powers. Rex's powers have only worked without animals when he was protecting me. No matter how much we practised, they only manifested on their own if I was in danger. Jesse's fire was a bit of a liability, especially when they were so close together, and his twisting and tumbling wouldn't help them whilst they were chained up. The stagehands and other performers are scattered around, and I can see some bodies lying on the floor. I have no idea if they are dead or alive.

Pulling my head back out quickly, I try to think of a plan that won't get us killed.

"What?" Esme hisses.

"It's worse than we thought, we-" I am cut off as a scream rattles through the tent and without waiting or planning our next move, we both rush through and stare in amazement at the sight before us.

All of the animals are sliding through the tent, attacking hunters left, right, and centre. I meet the panicked eyes of my guys and smile shyly. A hunter flying through the air has me looking back at Esme with a grin. Her face is set in concentration and her hand is raised as she flings him around like a rag doll until he hits the floor with a horrible squelch and doesn't get back up. Her anger at placing her trust in the wrong people coming to light, fueling her until she stands like the powerful woman she is, her eyes alight with hatred and deter-mination.

I walk further into the tent, keeping my eyes open for anyone who may be hiding, although most of the men seem to be busy trying to fend off the animals. I grin, and I know it must look feral, proud of the animals for protecting their own. Fluffy bounds past, an arm in his mouth as he aims for another hunter who is desperately trying to get a shot loaded in his crossbow.

I hurry towards the guys, worried about Blain who is slumped forwards and not moving other than his soft breathing. My heart clenches and I stumble before sprinting across the ring. As I reach them, I fall to my knees and grip his cheeks, pulling his head up gently. His eyes flicker open, which is a feat seeing as one of them is swollen, clearly from a heavy beating. I look around and see pride filling the eyes of Alcide and the others.

"You came for us," Jesse says quietly, a small smile on his face.

"Of course I did. I had someone I had to get first," I reply with a smile as I start trying to get them out of their chains. The others don't seem as bad off as Blain, who probably mouthed off and caused problems. He may act all tough, but I bet it was to take away some of the beating from the others.

His eyes are filled with pain and then a dawning horror.

"Be-behind you," he croaks, I spin to see a hunter approaching.

"You want to play with the men, little girl?" he sneers, his gun pointed at me.

"Funny, the only men I see are those behind me. You are just a bully trying to destroy what you don't understand. The real question is, are you ready to play with the freaks?" I laugh as he narrows his eyes.

All of a sudden, he grins before pulling the trigger, the bullet racing towards me. I don't even budge as the bullet bounces off me, the sound ricocheting into the ring. He fires again, his expression changing from a grin to a frown as I slowly walk towards him. He empties his magazine by the time I am right in front of him.

"I'm immortal motherfucker, but you aren't." Pushing my power into my arm, I punch like Rex taught me, with all my strength behind it. His mouth flops open and his eyes twitch as my hand pierces his chest, cracking open his ribs. Feeling a little sick, I grab his heart and pull back. He falls to the floor at my feet, the shock on his face is burned into my memory for life. I push all the guilt to the back of my mind, knowing he hurt my men. I will deal with the emotional backlash once my guys are safe, but for now I need to focus. I let the heart tumble to the floor, my hand dripping with blood.

I turn back to my men who are all watching me with shock, their faces in various states of bruises and covered in blood. A roar fills the tent and I see Nixon as he stumbles in like a drunk, throwing the dead man at my feet a dirty look before winking at me. I shake my head, bloody men. I don't have time to chide him now though, we need to get the others safe first.

"You get them free, I'll watch your back," I yell, turning back to the fight. With Nixon's strength, he will be able to break their chains in no time.

Esme cries out and I see a man tower above her, the same man who followed her around like a faithful sidekick. Only now he is dressed like a hunter.

She holds out her hand, but he bats it away. I start to run but I know I am going to be too late as he loads his crossbow and starts to take aim. I put on a burst of speed as her eyes meet mine, filled with acceptance. I cry out and try to fling myself in front of her, but I see her body jerk with the impact of the arrow. I land on the floor in front of her as she looks at her chest in shock. Stumbling she falls to her knees in front of me, the arrow sticking out of her chest like a declaration of war. Her eyes meet mine as tears spill down her cheeks. I jerk forward and catch her as she starts to fall backwards, gritting my teeth as hot scalding tears fall from my eyes, I lower her dying body to the floor.

I might not have always liked Esme, but she is family and made the mistake of trusting the wrong person. Her lips part as she coughs, blood bubbling between her teeth and staining her mouth. Her eyelashes flutter as she struggles to stay awake. Panic unfurls as I try to think of anything I can do to stop this, even though I know it is unavoidable. Her hand raises shakily into the air like it takes all her effort, I drag my eyes away from it and back to hers as she pleads with me. It's obvious she can't speak, but her eyes say everything for her. All the regret, pain, and downright fear reflecting there. Grabbing her hand, I twine our fingers, offering her comfort as she starts to fade, her face paling and her eyes starting to dim as blood pools underneath her in the sand. Staining it forever with her death and life.

"Tell them I'm sorry, they are your family now. Protect them…" She mouths, trying to say more but her mouth doesn't seem to work properly. I look at the arrow sticking out of her chest and put pressure on the wound, but there is so much blood I know it's useless. I feel a pang of guilt that she died trying to save us, but I know that she made that decision herself.

"Rhea!" Nixon's yell has me turning as I jerk with pain, I look at my shoulder in shock to see an arrow sticking out of it. I must have pulled my power back unintentionally in my shock at Esme's attack. Using the last of my strength I yank the arrow out, my arm starting to go numb. The hunter cocks another arrow as I push the change through my body, but it seems to stutter, unsure how to react to my arm. Gritting my teeth, I push to my feet, unwilling to die on my knees.

He raises the crossbow, the bolt aimed at my head when suddenly he screams. Looking down, I notice Rodger has snapped his impressive teeth around his leg and is gnawing on it. The hunter cries out as he falls to his knees. Even though he is in agony, he manages to bring the crossbow down, aiming it at the crocodile, and before I can move, lets the bolt loose. It spears through Rodger's eye and he falls to the side. His one eye unfocused and unseeing.

Screaming, I rush forward and using the bolt from my arm, I stab it into the hunter, the force of it pushing us both to the ground. I know that I probably look savage, covered in blood and screaming as I kneel in the sand. I ignore the dying hunter and rush to Rodger's side. I can't do this, this is all my fault. First Esme, now Rodger. How much blood and death will be spilt tonight to fulfill their need to harm what they don't understand? How many of my family will suffer for simply being born… and can I live with the aftermath?

"I'm sorry," I cry as my hands flutter uselessly over his body. I know he's dead, but I can't seem to move away.

A roar has my head snapping up as three hunters corner Fluffy. I stumble to my feet, and watch as Rex tries to hurry towards him, unchained and furious, his eyes flashing orange as his feet begin to move faster as his power fills him. But he won't get there in time, he is too far away. Everything seems like it is falling apart, but I have to keep myself together. I can't sit and cry, or let the horror run through me. My family is still in danger, I can mourn later.

I race to Fluffy's side, jumping on one of the hunter's back and screaming wordlessly as Fluffy cries, the pained noise wrenching at my heart. I watch in horror as a bolt pierces his side. He stumbles before falling to the floor. He lifts his head, trying to get back up but his legs don't seem to work. The hunter flings me off him and I land on the floor before Fluffy. I cover his body, just like I did when I first met him and wait for death - death that never comes.

Rex, Alcide, and Jesse are finally free and work as a team to dispatch the hunters before me. All three like avenging angels. Alcide is ordering hunters to kill themselves and I watch in horror as the hunters turn their weapons on themselves. Jesse is throwing flames, although I can see he is struggling, his fire powers have always taken their toll on him. Rex is slashing at the hunters with claws that have emerged from his knuckles. He is the closest to me and I hear him shouting our names. The hunters don't stand a chance now that they are all free and working together.

Pulling myself to my knees, I look into Fluffy's eyes, he whines, and tears fill my eyes. He might only be an animal to some people, but he has a piece of my heart just like my men. I can't lose him, a piece of me would die with him.

"I know, baby, I know it hurts. You are going to be okay, just stay with me. Please," I beg as the sound of fighting dies behind me, the last of the hunters taken care of. Rex falls to his knees and I crawl backwards to make room as Jesse takes my spot. My soul rages at moving away, as if I can do something, even though Rex and Jesse are better at this sort of thing. But it feels like if I look away, he will leave us. Fury and terror battle inside me, leaving me frozen in the sand watching my men fight for the life of a member of our family.

My heart stutters as tears race down my cheeks watching Rex sob over Fluffy as Jesse tries to work his magic. Alcide works his way toward them, his usual confident stride is more of a stumble. I spot Nixon suffering as well and know my family needs me. Pulling myself together as much as I can, I stumble to my feet. Knowing he needs me right now, they all do. I have to be strong still. I pull Alcide aside, placing my hand on his shoulder, looking him in the eyes. The comforting words die on my tongue and instead what tumbles out is a mixture of all the pain and anger. Even though the words are true.

"Never doubt me again," I tell him, before pulling him towards me, pressing my lips against his. I release him and walk towards Nixon who is collapsed on the floor, trying to rip the arm off a dead hunter.

"Nix, honey, he is dead. You got him," I call softly, knowing he is deep in a flashback right now. I kneel next to him, careful not to touch him until I see some of the Nixon I know come back into his eyes. He drops the mangled arm to the floor and stares at the body, panting. Placing my hand softly on his arm, he turns suddenly towards me. He looks fierce, but his eyes soften as he realises who is touching him.

"Rhea," he says, his voice raw.

"It's me. We are safe," I say, keeping my voice calm. I need to see to his injuries, and check that the others are okay, not to mention Fluffy. Even now, my neck is stiff and aching from the effort of not turning around to check on him. Sitting down in the sand, I take Nixon's hand in mine. Blain stumbles to my side and flops onto the sand next to me. I should get up, I should go around and check all the animals and staff but the numbness is wearing off and my body is exhausted and filled with pain. The silence stretches and I grasp at anything to try and make it stop, to drag my eyes away from Fluffy and stop my brain from overthinking everything.

"What a crazy few months," I say, not to anyone in particular, hoping to try and get them talking. More for my sanity then theirs.

"You thought this was crazy, the year is only just starting Harpy. Wait until we get to the big cities." Blain snorts and then scrunches his face adorably in pain.

My heart races at his words as his hand finds my blood covered one in the sand. It might have been a crazy year, but I have found my family and I will do anything to keep them. Rumple/Bubbles slithers in front of me and curls around my back, laying his heads on my shoulders. Tiny lays on the floor at my feet, and Sid curls up in my lap. I sit with my animals and men and know that Esme and Rodger won't be the last lives lost in this war. I hope Fluffy isn't on that list. But what can I expect? After all, I did run away with the freaks.

Acknowledgments

First and foremost, thank you to our wonderful team of beta readers, we literally wouldn't be able to do this without you. Thank you to our lovely editor who makes our words actually make sense.

To our families who put up with us whilst we were writing this and acted as sounding boards for all our ideas.

And without adue; thank you to all our amazing readers who have taken time to read our book. Our blood, sweat and tears have gone into this, so we really appreciate all the comments and support.

ABOUT ERIN O'KANE

Erin lives in the UK with her cat and works full time as an independent author. Now a *USA Today* bestselling author, she began writing in 2018 when she published her first book, *Hunted by Shadows*. She specialises in writing fantasy and reverse harem paranormal romance.
Previously to writing, she worked as an intensive care nurse. Despite having to now use a wheelchair, she doesn't let it stop her and loves to travel the world.
She met K.A Knight in 2018 when they became partners in crime and began writing together. In 2019, she became co-authors with Loxley Savage, writing fantasy reverse harem.
She's Disney obsessed, loves to read, craft and snack, and is always planning her next story.

Make sure to follow her on her social media pages for updates on what she's currently working on:
Facebook group: https://www.facebook.com/groups/ErinOKanesShadowRealm
Facebook author Page: https://www.facebook.com/ErinOKaneAuthor
Newsletter: http://eepurl.com/gJhSd9
Instagram: https://www.instagram.com/erin.okane.author

ABOUT K.A. KNIGHT

K.A Knight is an USA Today bestselling indie author trying to get all of the stories and characters out of her head, writing the monsters that you love to hate. She loves reading and devours every book she can get her hands on, and she also has a worrying caffeine addiction.

She leads her double life in a sleepy English town, where she spends her days writing like a crazy person.

Read more at K.A Knight's website or join her Facebook Reader Group.
Sign up for exclusive content and my newsletter here
http://eepurl.com/drLLoj

OTHER BOOKS BY ERIN O'KANE

Midnight Deception

Midnight Conviction

Midnight Ascension

The Complete Bloodlines Series – omnibus

The Brides of Darkness – interconnected standalones

A Kingdom of Broken Bonds

A City of Embers and Brimstone – coming soon

Standalones:

Second Chance

Love Bites

CO-WRITES

By Erin O'Kane and K.A Knight

Her Freaks Series:

Circus Save Me

Taming the Ringmaster

Walking the Tightrope

The Wild Boys:

The Wild Interview

The Wild Tour

The Wild Finale

The Wild Boys Series- The boxset

Standalones:

Hero Complex

Dark Temptations

By Erin O'Kane and Loxley Savage

Wicked Waves duet:

Twisted Tides

Tides that Bind

OTHER BOOKS BY K.A. KNIGHT

DYSTOPIAN

THEIR CHAMPION SERIES *Dystopian RH*

The Wasteland

The Summit

The Cities

The Nations

Their Champion Coloring Book

Their Champion - the omnibus

The Forgotten

The Lost

The Damned

Their Champion Companion - the omnibus

PARANORMAL

THE LOST COVEN SERIES *PNR RH*

Aurora's Coven

Aurora's Betrayal

HER MONSTERS SERIES *PNR RH*

Rage

Hate

Book 3 - *coming soon..*

COURTS AND KINGS *PNR RH*

Court of Nightmares

Court of Death

Court of Beasts

Court of Heathens - coming soon..

THE FALLEN GODS SERIES ^{PNR}

Pretty Painful

Pretty Bloody

Pretty Stormy

Pretty Wild

Pretty Hot

Pretty Faces

Pretty Spelled

Fallen Gods - the omnibus 1

Fallen Gods - the omnibus 2

FORGOTTEN CITY ^{PNR}

Monstrous Lies

Monstrous Truths

Monstrous Ends

SCIENCE FICTION

DAWNBREAKER SERIES ^{SCI FI RH}

Voyage to Ayama

Dreaming of Ayama

STANDALONES

Crown of Stars ^{SCI FI RH}

SHARED WORLD PROJECTS

Blade of Iris - Mafia Wars *CONTEMPORARY RH*

CO-WRITES

CO-AUTHOR PROJECTS - *Erin O'Kane*

HER FREAKS SERIES *PNR Dystopian RH*

Circus Save Me

Taming The Ringmaster

Walking the Tightrope

Her Freaks Series - the omnibus

STANDALONES

The Hero Complex *PNR RH*

Dark Temptations *Collection of Short Stories, ft. One Night Only & Circus Saves Christmas*

THE WILD BOYS SERIES *CONTEMPORARY RH*

The Wild Interview

The Wild Tour

The Wild Finale

The Wild Boys - the omnibus

CO-AUTHOR PROJECTS - *Ivy Fox*

Deadly Love Series *CONTEMPORARY*

Deadly Affair

Deadly Match

Deadly Encounter

CO-AUTHOR PROJECTS - *Kendra Moreno*

STANDALONES

Stolen Trophy *CONTEMPORARY RH*

Fractured Shadows *PNR RH*

Shadowed Heart

Burn Me *PNR*

Cirque Obscurum *PNR RH*

CO-AUTHOR PROJECTS - *Loxley Savage*

THE FORSAKEN SERIES *SCI FI RH*

Capturing Carmen

Stealing Shiloh

Harboring Harlow

STANDALONES

Gangsters and Guns *CONTEMPORARY*, IN DEN OF VIPERS' UNIVERSE

OTHER CO-WRITES

Shipwreck Souls *(with Kendra Moreno & Poppy Woods)*

The Horror Emporium *(with Kendra Moreno & Poppy Woods)*

AUDIOBOOKS

The Wasteland

The Summit

The Cities

The Nations - *coming soon*

Rage

Hate

Den of Vipers *(From Podium Audio)*

Gangsters and Guns *(From Podium Audio)*

Daddy's Angel *(From Podium Audio)*

Stepbrothers' Darling *(From Podium Audio)*

Blade of Iris *(From Podium Audio)*

Deadly Affair *(From Podium Audio)*

Deadly Match *(From Podium Audio)*

Deadly Encounter *(From Podium Audio)*

Stolen Trophy *(From Podium Audio)*

Crown of Stars *(From Podium Audio)*

Monstrous Lies *(From Podium Audio)*

Monstrous Truth *(From Podium Audio)*

Monstrous Ends *(From Podium Audio)*

Court of Nightmares *(From Podium Audio)*

Court of Death *(From Podium Audio)*

Unstoppable *(From Podium Audio)*

Unbreakable *(From Podium Audio)*

Fractured Shadows *(From Podium Audio)*

Shadowed Heart *(From Podium Audio)*

Revolt *(From Podium Audio)*

Rebel *(From Podium Audio) - coming soon*

FIND AN ERROR?

Please email this information to thenuttyformatter1@gmail.com:

- *the author name*
- *title of the book*
- *screenshot of the error*
- *suggested correction*

www.ingramcontent.com/pod-product-compliance
Lightning Source LLC
Chambersburg PA
CBHW051112300726
48981CB00001B/110